W9-CCQ-651

The Iron Tower trilogy introduced readers to the magical realm of Mithgar, and immediately earned Dennis McKiernan a well-deserved place in the pantheon of bestselling fantasy writers. With his *Silver Call* duology, and his most recent novels, *Dragondoom, Eye of the Hunter,* and *Voyage of the Fox Rider,* he drew readers even deeper into his legendary lands, into the wondrous dwelling places of Warrows, Dwarves, and Elves, into the dreaded caverns of Rucks, Hloks, Vulgs, and other Foul Folk. Now *Tales of Mithgar* offers fantasy lovers everywhere an enchanting look at the adventures and adventurers that shaped Mithgar.

"Heroic fantasy on the grandest possible scale."

—Susan Schwartz,
author of *The Grail of Hearts*

"Romance and disaster and plenty of magic: everything that makes up a good, old-fashioned adventure story."

—Kate Elliott, author of *Jaran.*

By Dennis L. McKiernan

Once Upon a Summer Day
Once Upon a Winter's Night

Caverns of Socrates

THE MITHGAR SERIES
The Dragonstone
Voyage of the Fox Rider

HÉL'S CRUCIBLE:
Book I: *Into the Forge*
Book II: *Into the Fire*

Dragondoom

The Iron Tower

The Silver Call

Tales of Mithgar (a story collection)

Tales from the One-Eyed Crow: The Vulgmaster
(the graphic novel)

The Eye of the Hunter

Silver Wolf, Black Falcon

Red Slippers: More Tales of Mithgar (a story collection)

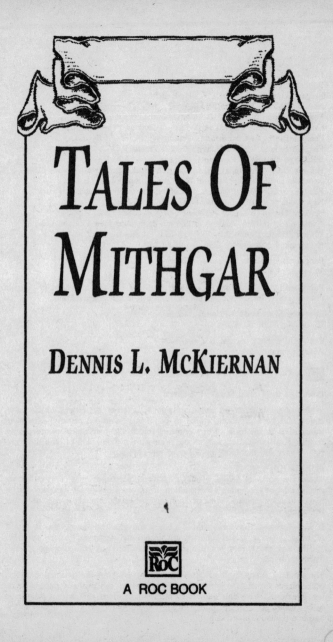

TALES OF MITHGAR

DENNIS L. MCKIERNAN

A ROC BOOK

ROC

Published by New American Library, a division of
Penguin Group (USA) Inc., 375 Hudson Street,
New York, New York 10014, USA
Penguin Group (Canada), 10 Alcorn Avenue, Toronto,
Ontario M4V 3B2, Canada (a division of Pearson Penguin Canada Inc.)
Penguin Books Ltd., 80 Strand, London WC2R 0RL, England
Penguin Ireland, 25 St. Stephen's Green, Dublin 2,
Ireland (a division of Penguin Books Ltd.)
Penguin Group (Australia), 250 Camberwell Road, Camberwell, Victoria 3124,
Australia (a division of Pearson Australia Group Pty. Ltd.)
Penguin Books India Pvt. Ltd., 11 Community Centre, Panchsheel Park,
New Delhi - 110 017, India
Penguin Group (NZ), cnr Airborne and Rosedale Roads, Albany,
Auckland 1310, New Zealand (a division of Pearson New Zealand Ltd.)
Penguin Books (South Africa) (Pty.) Ltd., 24 Sturdee Avenue,
Rosebank, Johannesburg 2196, South Africa

Penguin Books Ltd., Registered Offices:
80 Strand, London WC2R 0RL, England

Published by Roc, an imprint of New American Library, a division of Penguin
Group (USA) Inc. Previously published in a Roc hardcover edition.

First Roc Mass Market Printing, December 1995
10 9 8 7 6 5 4

To my mother, Laura Lorraine

And to Gaffer Tom

in all of his many guises
whoever he or she may be
throughout the wide, wide world

And to all One-Eyed Crows, everywhere

Contents

Foreword IX
Author's Note XIII

The Vulgmaster 17
The Thornwalker and the Wolf 47
The Trout of the Rillmix 63
The Ruffian and the Giant 70
Agron's Army 82
Dreadholt 94
The Hèlborne Drum 126
The Transformation of Beau Darby 149
The Dammsel 161
For Want of a Copper Coin 166
When Iron Bells Ring 194
Epilogues 235

Afterword 241
Final Note 243

Foreword

O, could I but go to Mithgar and see all its many wonders—to see Elves and Dwarves and Warrows and knightly Men and beautiful Women, Utruni and Wizards, Mithgarian Wolves and Draega, and Fire-drakes and Cold-drakes and serpents of the sea, and Krakens, and other fabled creatures; aye, even to see Rūcks and Hlōks and Ogrus, Hèlsteeds and Ghûls, and other Foul Folk and beasts not yet named; to see the Wolfwood and the Skög, the Great Escarpment, Darda Galion, the Quadran, the Great Maelstrom, Dragon's Roost, the Spindlethorn Barrier, Bellon Falls, Kraggen-cor, the Grimwall, Claw Moor, the Iron Tower, Caer Pendwyr, the Greatwood, the Khalian Mire, Dragonslair, Darda Erynian, and more—one of the places that would irresistibly draw me unto it would be the One-Eyed Crow, a tiny inn on the southeast corner of Market Square in the hamlet of Woody Hollow, there in the Boskydells.

It's not that the 'Crow has a magnificent edifice, one that would compete with the glorious wonders of Mithgar, oh no. Instead, this small tavern, with its common room and fine kitchen, with its guest quarters overhead, with its wooden beams and stone fireplace and glass-paned windows and timbers and thatch and clapboards and chimneys, this small tavern is as unprepossessing as an inn can be. Quaint it is, and a step or two out front, out beyond the stoop, there at the edge of the street, hanging by hook and eye from a post arm, a painted signboard swings in the breeze and proclaims *this* to be the One-Eyed Crow. On each side of the placard, a black bird with cocked head and gimlet eye stares out at passersby, as if examining them for shiny objects that birds such as these are said to covet. The crow's other eye is not visible, and given the name it makes me wonder if there is an eye patch on the side we cannot see.

Nay, no towering edifice is this tiny tavern, this tiny inn. Instead, it is a place of *atmosphere*.

Of comfort.

Of companionship.

Cozy in the winter, cool in the summer, and cheery all year 'round.

And could I but go to Mithgar, then *this* is where I would spend some time, soaking up that special atmosphere and listening to Warrow-told tales.

A curious mixture are the stories that Warrows tell, for some are childlike, simple but compelling, and are suitable as bedtime fare for the wee ones in your household; while others seem too intense for the ears of younglings, for they grip you by the throat and rattle your soul.

A curious mixture, aye, but this should not be surprising, for Warrows themselves are a wonderful combination of childlike innocence and grown-up wisdom, of gullibility and skepticism, of folly and discernment, of ignorance and knowledge, of laughter and tears.

And these qualities are reflected in their tales.

Folk and fairy seem some of their tales as well as tales of humor, while others bring a tear to the eye, and yet others might cause your heart to pound and your mouth to go dry. Some are gentle to the soul, some charm the heart, while some are violent beyond reason. Yet in these characteristics—of gentleness, of charm, of violence—are Warrow-told tales any different from the tales of the Brothers Grimm, or those of Aesop, or those of other cultures, other nations, down through the ages?

I say, Nay.

Yet Warrow tales are different in subtle ways from those of our own past. Gentle and charming and violent they are, aye, but they also bear the unmistakable stamp of a different folk, of the Wee Folk, though it is not easily defined.

But I would fill my soul with such tales, had I the chance.

And *that* is why I would spend time in the One-Eyed Crow, watching and listening and drinking deeply from this subtle spring, tasting the pure and gentle waters.

Author's Note

The tales contained herein are a Warrow-told mixture of simple folk tales and personal remembrances, stories of magic, of mystical and mythical and ghostly creatures, of challenges and perils, of valor, of honor, of love. In several instances the reader will be able to guess at the tale's outcome, but that is as it should be, for even in our own folk and fairy tales, often this is true: hearken unto Jack and the Beanstalk, Goldilocks, the Three Pigs, Red Riding Hood, and the like; did we not guess what would happen there? That is not to say that the outcomes of all of these Warrow-told tales can be foretold, for they cannot. But even though the outcome might be anticipated, still the tale should entertain. And I believe that these Warrow-told tales do just that: they entertain, just as if we ourselves were sitting in the One-Eyed Crow listening to Gaffer Tom holding forth.

The tales herein are manifold, and some remind me of old-country folk tales, with their repetitive patterns (things happening in threes or fives, or sevens, or the like), and the lessons embedded within (for example, be good to everyone, and you may be rewarded when you least expect it). Some tell of high magic, Wizards and such in conflict, while some speak only of the cold, cruel iron of War. Some bring a smile to my heart, while others cause it to pound. Even others bring a tear to my cheek, and several cause me to laugh out loud, startling those within hearing. And one or two cause me to grit my teeth and grind them in frustration, and swear vengeance 'gainst all villains.

Yet simple or profound, folk or fairy tale, all are magic, for their glamours hold me spellbound.

Perhaps they'll do the same for you.

Know this, my child,
that when iron bells ring
they can knell in joy or sorrow

The Vulgmaster

It was early afternoon when without warning the blizzard howled down out of the north to whelm upon the Boskydells with ravening fury, the raging wind a wall of impenetrable whiteness, snow hurtling horizontally across the 'scape, making it dangerous, perhaps fatal, for any to venture abroad in its blinding, frigid grasp, trapping folks wherever they happened to be at the time. Even down in Woody Hollow, where the slopes of the vale and the thickset hillside trees ordinarily protected the village from the worst of blows, even there the wind yawled about the buildings and across the spaces in between, only to squall at the eves and shutters and corners and roofs and chimneys of the structures beyond. And in the One-Eyed Crow, the modest inn at the southeast corner of Market Square, buccen Warrows sipped their ale and puffed upon their pipes and watched as Will Brackleburr, proprietor, threw another log upon the crackling fire, while the tavern creaked and groaned and shuddered in the blast raging outside.

"Lor, I can't even see the Commons," said Feeny Proudhand, rubbing a hole through the white frost glazing the inside of one of the 'Crow's east-facing windows and peering out. "I expect I won't be bedding down to home tonight." Feeny, a wheelwright from Budgens, a small hamlet some two miles from Woody Hollow, had brought a repaired waggon to the Hollow just that same morning and had stopped in the 'Crow for a mug and a bite to eat, and now it looked as if he was trapped by the wild elements.

"Don't you worry none, Feeny," said Will, stepping back behind the bar to draw another ale for Teddy Cloverhay, a Willowdell waggoneer. "Your pony's snug in my stables, and I got enough room to put you up, as well as everyone else, should it come to it."

"Wull, be that as it may, Will," volunteered Nob Haywood, storekeeper, "I 'spect that Feeny's dammia and younglings are a might worried over his absence, what with the storm and all."

"Oh, Nob, there was no call for that," protested Bingo Peacher, a hunter of some renown. "Now you'll have Feeny all upset over the worry and fretting that his folks are suffering."

"All I said was what we already know," shot back Nob. "I mean, *all* of our folks will be worried about whether or not we are caught out in this blow."

Silence fell upon the crowd as they all considered Nob's words, and the mood turned glum, and the timbers of the 'Crow groaned and creaked, and the fireplace moaned and whistled, the brutal wind shrieking, howling for entry.

Knowing that nothing shut down the taps quicker than a solemn gathering—"Hoy now, what we need is a tale to last out this blizzard," interjected Will. And all eyes swung toward Gaffer Tom, the eld Warrow unusually quiet, sitting at his customary table in the angle by the corner windows, unfocused viridian eyes staring out into the hurling white. His ale was virtually untouched, and his pipe had gone out, and he absently toyed with a silver bob that he always bore, a bob about the size of a hazel nut, set with a small screw eye and attached with a leather thong to a buttonhole on his vest, as if he didn't want to take a chance on losing the little spheroid.

Gaffer ... Gaffer ...

"Eh?" Suddenly he became aware that someone was talking to him.

"... a story, Gaffer, to while away the day." Will was holding out a flaming taper to light Gaffer's pipe.

The granther buccan clamped the curved stem of his briar between his teeth and took the burning twig in hand, holding the fire to the bowl—the dark wood carved to resemble an owl's head—and as he puffed the pipe into life, his pale emerald eyes looked to see that many of the buccen had already gathered, while others waited for a refill ere joining the circle.

"You seemed lost in the storm, Gaffer," said Teddy, the young buccan's sapphire gaze peering out at the shriek.

"I was remembering, Teddy. Remembering." The Gaffer took a sip on his ale and drew on his pipe, the aroma of Downdell leaf filling the air.

"Remembering what, Gaffer?"

Now all the buccen had gathered 'round, including Will, their jewel-like eyes—emerald, sapphire, amber—glittering in anticipation. And Gaffer Tom pointed the stem of his pipe at the storm outside. "Another blizzard, Teddy. Another storm. That's what I was remembering.

"You see, it was the winter of '51, over by the Grimwall when ..."

Breath coming hard upon the air: rasping, gasping.

Adon! Burden was light when I began. Heavy as a mountain now.

The storm is waning.

Down from the col. Down into the valley. Mountains rearing up all about. Snow still blowing.

Mountain village, clenched in the grasp of a coomb pressing into great stone flanks looming above. Got to be Vulfcwmb.

How can one so little be so heavy?

Village no more than a mile now ...

No more than a quarter mile ...

Tavern, inn, on edge of town ...

The Red Weasel ...

The door ...

Those inside the Red Weasel were startled when the door was kicked open and a hooded, cloaked, bundled stranger staggered in, wearing a pack and bearing an unconscious child, the wind howling inward after.

" 'Ere naow, shut that door!" bellowed the barkeep, a large, burly Man. "This dona be no barn, ye know."

The stranger ignored him and took the wee one to the first table, sweeping the trenchers off onto the floor with a clatter, placing the burden down at last, trembling with fatigue.

"Healer," croaked the stranger, voice no more than a whisper.

"I said, shut the door," growled the barkeep, stepping to the stranger's side and laying a great, meaty hand upon the hooded one's shoulder.

The moment the 'keep's hand came down upon the arm, the stranger spun about, a dark sword seeming to flash from nowhere, point under the bully's chin, the barkeep's eyes wide with fright. "Touch me again and I'll feed thee thine own fingers," gritted the stranger, voice rasping forth from scarf-covered mouth and shadowed hood. "Now get me a healer."

" 'Ere naow, there ain't no cause to get 'ostile." The innkeeper backed away as soon as it seemed safe, turning to his drudge—a thin lad in his late teens—and shoving him toward the door. "Shut the damn door, Bob!"

Ignoring the barkeep, the stranger turned back to the little one on the table. One of the curious onlookers crept close and pulled aside the cloak and peered at the wee one's face. "*Ai-oi!* This ain't no child! 'Tis a *Waldan!*"

What?

Others crowded about, the ones in back craning their necks to see.

Shoving her way through the Men—"One side! Yield back! Give 'im air!"—a large, hefty Woman came to the table. Looking at the stranger—"I be the nearest thing to wot ye might call a 'ealer 'ereabout, so let's give it a look."

Bending over the Warrow—" 'Ow come 'im to be 'urt, naow?"

"Three waggons," whispered the stranger, taking off the backpack, setting it against a wall, returning to the table, the locals giving way to let the stranger pass. "Wrecked. Horses slain. Throats ripped out. Blood still fresh. Overturned wain fell on this Waerling. No one else there."

At the mention of the slaughtered horses, those crowded 'round glanced at one another, nodding. *Stoke*, some muttered, fear in their eyes, *Baron Stoke*.

"Coo, naow, this do be a Wee Un." The Woman had pushed back the small one's hood, and red hair cropped at the shoulder spilled forth, and a pointed ear could be seen; as to stature, the small one would stand some three to three and a half feet tall—it was difficult to judge more accurately with the victim lying down—confirming that indeed this *was* one of the Folk from legend. An ugly welt could be seen upon the small one's forehead.

" 'E be breathing regular"—the Woman carefully ran her hands across limbs—"and nowt dona seem broke nor bleedin'. 'E's tooken a nasty knock, though—

"Bob!" she bellowed. "Bring me somma them salts!"

The lad bolted from the common room, but was back in a trice, bearing a small, tightly corked vial half filled with white crystals. Working his way next to the table—" 'Ere, Molly"—he handed the glass over to the Woman.

Molly uncorked the vial and held it under the Warrow's nose, pungent fumes wafting forth. Hacking and coughing, the Wee One came up struggling, weakly swinging clenched fists, feebly yelling, as if fighting.

"Oo naow, 'old it, Wee Un," soothed Molly, enveloping him with her great arms, hugging the Warrow close to her ample bosom. "There be nowt to be afraid of 'ere. Settle. Settle."

Throughout, the stranger had stood by, face shadowed by cowl, silent yet warding. Bob, bearing a hot mug, made his way next to the stranger's side, giving over the steaming mulled wine to the hooded one. Nodding unspoken thanks, the stranger removed a leather glove, and a slender hand took the mug. Then, casting back hood and unwrapping scarf, golden silky hair tumbled forth, and the stranger was revealed to be a Woman! Incredibly beautiful!— *Nay!* not a Woman! for tilted grey eyes of clear gaze and pointed ears of her own gave lie to that notion.

By gar! it be an *Elfess* what stood before them instead!

Bob fell back in startlement, eyes wide and unbelieving, and those in the Red Weasel gave way before her in awe and wonderment, as she shed her cloak and stepped to an empty table and took a seat, turning the chair sideways to keep the space before her open, her back to a wall. She unbuckled her scabbard and unsheathed her midnight sword and lay both atop the table beside her, lengthwise, the hilt of the blade within easy reach. And her silvery eyes peered over the rim of the mug at Molly and the Waerling, missing nothing, seeing all, as she sipped the bracing spiced drink.

Legends alive! A Waeran and an Elfess, too! She looks to be a warrior at that! Aye, no doubt an enchanted blade! Wonders never cease! What'll the night bring next, I wonder?

"Sharp naow, Bob, brandy!" called Molly, and the drudge scurried behind the bar, past the surly 'keep, and snatched up flagon and cup.

Molly held the liquor to the Wee One's mouth and gently urged him to sip, the brandy staining his lips carmine.

"Vulgs! Rūcks!— Petal!" cried the Warrow, coming fully awake.

Molly still held him and pressed another drink upon him, and as he took the cup to his lips his tilted, jewellike eyes alertly swept 'round the room, swiftly taking in his surroundings.

Sptt! Hkk! Hackk! Clearly he had not been expecting strong spirits, and Molly held him and pounded him on the back as he hacked and coughed, spluttering and gasping.

"There, naow, Wee Un," soothed Molly, "catch y'r wind. I wouldna want ye stranglin' after I done brought ye back to life."

Struggling to get free—"Wh-where am I? Are the others all right? Where's Petal and her dad? Where's my own dam and sire? Where—"

"Hoosh, naow, Wee Un. We dona know nowt 'bout no others," said Molly, releasing him from her grasp. "Ye was brought in by that stranger"—she peered about, looking for the hooded one, her eyes widening at the sight of

an Elfess yet searching onward for a cloaked Man—
"wherever 'e be. Pulled ye from 'neath a waggon, 'e said.
But there be nowt anyone else what came wi' ye."

"Oh my, no," wailed the Warrow in anguish, scooting
to the edge of the table, preparing to get to the floor, gri-
macing in agony, pressing his hand to the bruise upon his
head, then wincing in pain. "I've got to get back. The
Vulgs. The Rūcks. They were attacking!"

He swung his feet over the edge of the table and stood
on the bench, his eyes now not quite level with those
around him. "I need help," he appealed. "Guidance back
to the waggons. Aid in fighting the Rūcks and such. Arrows for the Vulgs." His viridian gaze urgently swept
across the faces about. "Which of you will go with me?"

Faces turned down and aside. Eyes would not meet
those of the Wee One. Men backed away.

"Did you not hear me?" cried the Warrow. "There's
Spawn afoot upon your land! They've got my sire and
dam, my dammia too, and her sire as well! We've got to
do something!"

" 'Tis Baron Stoke," muttered one.

"What?" Green eyes fixed upon the Man. "What did
you say?"

"I said, 'tis Baron Stoke, Wee Un, the Master of the
Vulgs." The Man's voice was filled with fear, falling to a
hiss, his eyes glancing about as if searching for creatures
lurking in shadows. " 'E's come back."

"I don't care who it is," gritted the Warrow. "He's got
my loved ones."

"Then they be as good as dead," came another voice.
"There be nowt you can do to save 'em. They be no one
'ere what will go up against the Baron." Men began to si-
dle away.

"What?" The small one looked about in disbelief.

"Aye, it be true," responded another, backing up.
"The Baron, well, 'e's wicked, 'at's wot 'e be. Wicked.
In'uman. Up in the mountains. In 'is castle, doin' 'oo
knows wot to them wot 'e grabs."

"Won't anybody help me?" appealed the Warrow.

Silence answered the Wee One's plea.

"Right, then, I'll go it alone."

Sliding to the floor, gaining his feet at last—"Where are the waggons? Where am I?" asked the Warrow.

"This be Vulfcwmb," volunteered Bob, looking down at the Waldan. "But as to the whereabouts of your waggons . . ." The youth shrugged his shoulders, looking about.

"Who brought me in? I've got to get back."

All eyes turned to the golden-haired Elfess.

Seeing her for the first time, the Wee One's tilted eyes widened, and he rushed over to her table, blurting out, "My Lady—" and he began to kneel; yet swiftly she leaned forward and stopped him from any obeisance.

"Nay, Waerling"—her voice was soft—"thou shall not kneel to me, as thy Folk have not knelt to any since the Great War."

"Oh, Lady," he pled, "if you brought me in, you must take me back, for I know not the way."

"To return thee to the wrack may not be the swiftest way to reach any who may have survived," responded the Elfess, "for none else were where I found thee. Only slain horses." Her eyes took on a steely glint. "Nay! I deem we must find the holt of this Baron Stoke, yet I know not the way, for I am as new to these parts as thee. Yet mayhap one here will aid us, with knowledge if not with arms."

"Did you say *We*?" The Warrow's gem-like emeraldine gaze looked deep into her silvery grey. "Do you intend to go with me?" A fierce grin spread over his face when she nodded yes.

The Elfess pushed a chair out from the table with her foot, bidding the Warrow to sit. "Give me thy name, and quickly share thy tale. Too, we need food"—here she cast an eye at Bob, who immediately disappeared into the kitchen—"and to sit a moment, for thou took a wicked knock, and I bore thee far, and I would not have us set forth hungry and weary ere we took a single step."

"Tomlin, my name is Tomlin," replied the Warrow, his words tumbling out as folk gathered 'round to listen, though at a respectful distance from the warrior Elfess, "but everybody calls me Tom or Tommy . . . or they call me Pebble because of these slingstones I carry about." Tomlin pulled a pouch filled with river-rounded stones from his belt, as well as a sling, depositing them onto the table before him.

"I am named Riatha, Pebble," said the Lady. "Pray, why were thee and thine out in a blizzard? And say on concerning those who fell upon thee, for the more I know, the greater our chances."

The Warrow took a deep breath and then plunged on: "I know it seems crazy and all, travelling about in the winter, especially in a blizzard, but that's what we were doing, though faring in the storm was unintentional. Dad's a minstrel—lutes, flutes, and harps—and Mom sings. Mister Downtuft, that's Petal's sire, he's a juggler and knife thrower. I play a drum and hunt for game and cook. Petal helps with the cooking, and walks a rope, and stands while her sire flings daggers alongside her, all about. We were travelling 'cross Aven, heading for Dael in Riamon to spend the worst of the winter: Dad, Mom, Mister Downtuft and Petal, me.

"The blizzard came out of nowhere, surprising us, catching us out in the open, and we were trapped in the blowing white, looking for shelter: a stand of trees, the lee of a cliff, anything.

"But darkness fell, and then they jumped us: Vulgs and twenty or so Rūcks, coming out of the hurtling snow like black ghosts. The horses ran wild, Vulgs in pursuit, hauling them down, and the last thing I remember is the waggon tumbling."

Bob rushed in from the kitchen, bearing two trenchers of beef and bread and beans and leeks, plunking one down in front of the Warrow, the other in front of the Elfess, as well as two knives and two spoons. Molly followed, bringing two flagons of ale. With a gesture Riatha stopped Bob and Molly, nodding for them to take seats as well.

Molly sat down quickly enough, but Bob looked over his shoulder at the glaring innkeeper behind the bar, who quickly began polishing the countertop when the Elfess's silver gaze locked with his and she shifted the night-dark sword upon the table. Bob sat next to the Warrow.

"This Baron, tell me what thou know of him." Riatha began to eat, motioning Pebble to do so as well.

"Oo naow," whispered Molly, peering about, " 'e lives in the mountains, 'e does. North into the Grim'alls. Just where . . ." She looked at Bob.

"There be a castle on the side of a high cliff," said the youth. "Up the vale till you comes to the river. Follow it back'ards into the Grim'alls. Twenty, thirty miles or so."

"Well then, Bob"—Riatha spoke softly—"if it's ten leagues or so, Pebble will need a small pack to fit him, a blanket, some rope, a small lanthorn or candles, flint and steel. Whatever else thou deem he might need on this stroll we are to take."

Bob scrambled up from the table and rushed out.

Turning to the healer, Riatha said, "Say on about this Baron Stoke, Molly. Tell all thou know."

"Wellanow, that be nowt o'ermuch, Lady," responded Molly. "But Stoke, 'e wos 'ere long ago, back 'fore I was borned. Then 'e went away for a long time. But naow 'e's back, 'im and 'is Vulgs and Rutcha. Terrorizin' the countryside like wot 'e done in the times past. Somma our own went after 'im last year, but they ain't ever come back.

" 'Tis said 'e made a pact wi' a daemon centuries agone, back when 'e and 'is line ruled these parts 'ereabout. 'Tis said 'e ain't no longer 'uman"—Molly made a warding sign in the air—"that only silver will kill 'im."

Riatha glanced at her sword but said nought, its dark silveron blade winking in the lamplight as if the midnight metal were filled with a scatter of stars.

Bob came scurrying back, a child's knapsack in hand, as well as a blanket roll and a waterskin. "This wos mine when I wos a tad. I 'ad no lanthorn, but candles are within, and crue and flint and steel. Rope, too. I 'spect it'll do." He handed all over to Tomlin, the Warrow nodding his thanks, his tilted emerald eyes lit with gratitude.

Finishing her meal, Riatha pushed the plate away, wiping her mouth upon a silken kerchief taken from her sleeve.

Tomlin, too, was done, his own sleeve serving as kerchief, and he looked expectantly at the Elfess, and she nodded.

Molly, however, reached out and touched the Warrow. "Be ye any good wi' that there sling?" At Tomlin's nod— "Then 'ere, Wee Un, this might 'elp." She unlooped a chain from around her neck, upon which was a spheroidal pendant of silver. Unfastening the chain and slipping it through the eyelet, she gave over the argent bob to the Warrow. "It be silver, and should fit your sling. When ye get a chance, 'it 'im in the 'ead wi' it. Temple or eye should do 'im in."

Tomlin took the ovoid and turned it in the light, and bobbed his head in appreciation for what she had done, for no doubt it represented a great sacrifice on her part.

Riatha scattered a few coppers upon the table for the innkeeper, and gave a gold each to Molly and Bob, their eyes going wide with the wonder of their newfound wealth.

Riatha stood, buckling her scabbard back on, sheathing her sword, stepping to her backpack and shouldering it, her eye contemptuously sweeping the crowd.

Scooping up his sling and pouch, as well as his knapsack, Tomlin, too, stood, yet upon the table rather than the floor. "Again I ask, will any come with us?" his voice loud in the ringing silence.

All refused even to look at the Wee One, turning their faces away in guilt, in shame, too afraid of Baron Stoke to do aught else.

All, that is, but one, one who sat in the shadows, leaning in his chair back against the wall, hearing all, saying nothing. One who also was a stranger to Vulfcwmb.

With his foot this stranger pushed the table away and let his chair back down from two legs to four. And in the shadows he stood up, and up, rising to his feet, stepping forth into the lamplight. He was a huge Man. A broad Man. A giant bear of a Man, easily two hands taller than anyone else in the tavern. He had dark reddish brown hair, lighter at the tips, giving it a silvery grizzled look. His face was covered with a close-cropped full beard of the same grizzled brown. His eyes were a dark amber. He was dressed in deep umber, and wore fleece-lined boots and vest. A morning star depended from his belt, the spiked ball and chain held by slip-knotted thongs to the oaken haft. He took up his great brown cloak and fastened it 'round his neck. "I am Urus, and I will go," he rumbled.

They set forth in the darkness, heading northward up the valley, the storm waning rapidly as they went. Soon the wind died and nought but gentle flakes fell, and then even those stopped.

In the vale, snow lay some six or so inches deep on the ground, the storm having fallen more heavily at the higher altitudes than down on the valley floor. And though he was small, Tomlin took the lead through the shallow white, his quick feet carrying him before the others, bearing Urus's storm lanthorn, its shutter casting a narrow beam, the Warrow's sharp eyes scanning the new-fallen snow for any sign of track yet seeing none.

Next came Riatha, her Elven sight needing no lamp to see by, her eyes watching the dark notches in the vale to left and right.

Bringing up the rear was Urus, his great stride easily maintaining the pace, his senses attuned to the surround.

Every hour or so they would stop for a short rest, to sip water and care for other needs; and in these moments they would speak softly.

"I have told why I am here in this land," Tomlin remarked during one of their rest stops, "yet I know nothing about either of you. Why is it you travel along this marge of Aven? What brings you to these parts?"

Lifting a shaggy eyebrow, Urus glanced at Riatha.

"This Baron Stoke and his curs slew Talar, my brother," said Riatha, her voice gritty, her eyes hot with hatred. "I have been searching for him for nearly two years. Two months past, rumor came to Arden that he now dwelled in his strongholt of old, nigh Vulfcwmb, and so I set forth for vengeance."

Riatha fell silent, her lips drawn thin with painful memory, and it was clear that she had said all she would. Tomlin turned his face to Urus.

"I am a Baeran," rumbled Urus. "Stoke came among the Baeron. With a mission, he said. To rescue his kidnapped wife, he said. From the Rutcha, he claimed. He gathered a small force among my kindred, and set out through the woods. Into the caves they went, there in the Grimwalls south of the Crestan Pass. Stoke managed to drug the Men, and when they awoke, they were in chains, to be used in his experiments.

"One won free of his treachery, escaping. Meanwhile, a band of us, suspicious of Stoke, set out upon his track. And we came across this lone survivor.

"We cleaned out those foul caverns, slaying many Rutcha. But Stoke fled. Where? None knew. Yet I followed every rumor: into Riamon, into Gûnnar, into Jord, and finally into Aven, into the Grimwalls north of Nordlake, then south and east to Vulfcwmb, to here. And now we draw nigh; I can feel it."

"But why do you still pursue?" Tomlin's question hung upon the air for a long while ere Urus answered:

"Honor," he growled at last. "Revenge.

"I was Chieftain when Stoke came to the Baeron. I approved the mission. I sent nine to their death at his hands.

"He flayed them," Urus rumbled. "Alive."

The Baeran glanced at Riatha. Tears glittered in her eyes. She nodded sharply, once, and then Tomlin knew her brother had died that same way, too: like an animal . . . skinned . . . *alive!* Tomlin shuddered in horror, and images rose up in the Warrow's mind of those now within the Baron's grasp.

At another stop, Tomlin examined the silver orb given to him by Molly, feeling its weight, slipping it into the sling pouch and whirling it 'round. Satisfied at last that it would do very well as a sling bullet, he turned to his companions. "Back at Vulfcwmb, they said that the Baron could only be harmed by silver. Molly gave me this bullet, but I only get the one chance, then it's back to rocks for me. What silver do each of you bear?"

Riatha looked long at her comrades. "My sword is not silver, yet it is . . ."—she searched for an appropriate word—". . . *special*. I doubt not that it will slay Baron Stoke."

Both Elfess and Warrow now faced the Baeran. "When the time comes, I have my own way of dealing with

Stoke," growled Urus, fingering his morning star; but as to what that way might be, he would say no more.

They trekked onward in the night, and the skies cleared and a full Moon shone down upon the 'scape, the air crystal and frigid. At last they came to a river, water rushing past 'neath ice, bearing bubbles of air trapped below, dark pools gurging where the surface had not yet frozen.

Easterly they hiked, and then northerly once more, following the wending river upstream, following Bob's directions as to how to reach Baron Stoke's castle, as to how to reach his strongholt of old.

Night fled while they walked, dawn creeping softly across the range. Still they had not seen sign of Foul Folk, and as to the castle, there had been no sign of it either.

"I don't understand it," railed Tomlin. "They could have had no more than six or so hours' lead over us, yet we've seen no tracks. The snow stopped long ago, and if they came this way, surely there would be spoor. Perhaps we follow a false route."

"I, too, think they did not come this way, Pebble," rumbled Urus. "Yet still they could be headed for Stoke's holt." The Man eyed the paling sky to the east. "They would have gone by different route, through the Grimwalls, where there are cracks and crevices to hole up in during the time the Sun is in the sky.

"Forget not, Waldan, Rutcha suffer Adon's Ban. And daylight will destroy them.

"Nay, they did not come this way, yet their goal and ours surely is the same: Stoke's fortress."

And as the Sun rimmed the world, on they tramped through the snow-covered, stony valley, the dark ramparts of the Grimwall Mountains thrusting upward to left and right, marching away beyond seeing to the north, the ice-rimed stream to their left rushing down the vale toward the distant Argon River.

At last Riatha called for rest, called for them to make camp, in spite of Tomlin's protests, for she could see that the Warrow was weary; he was, after all, a Wee One, a bare three feet four inches tall, half of Urus's height. "Ar-

gue not with me, Pebble, for I would have thee arrive at
Baron Stoke's holt with enough strength to whirl thy sling
and hurl thy bullets.

"List, we know not what we may encounter, yet we do
know that speed or stealth or cunning or battle awaits us,
and are we weary, then those things will elude us. So rest
now, and I will watch over thee, and call thee to thine
own watch when it is thy turn."

And so, throughout the day the comrades rested, slept,
and stood ward in turn, though whether the Elfess truly
slept or instead let her mind wander through pleasant
memories is not known.

It was late afternoon when they took up the trek again,
the mountains towering all about them, whiteness spread
o'er the land in airy silence, sheer stone faces starkly con-
trasting, black and grey and dun, dark crags and massifs
bursting upward through the snow. And still the river ran
on their left, dashing 'neath ice down the stony vale
hindward.

Tomlin's bruise had turned in the night: the left side of
his forehead was blotched and purple. Yet in spite of its
look, it was less tender, though still sore. Even so, still the
Warrow took the lead, his eyes scanning for sign of
tracks, and along the valley through stark mountains he
strode, two others following in his wake.

Again full night found them walking northerly, snow
muffling their footsteps. And yet no sign of Rūcks or
Vulgs did they see: no tracks, no dens, no caves.

Vulg's black bite slays at night. The ancient saying kept
ringing through Tomlin's mind.

"What about Vulg bites?" he asked at last. "How do we
treat them?"

Urus's reply came through the moonlight. "First rule is
to avoid getting bitten; take to the trees or high rock when
confronted, anyplace where they can't get at you. Second
rule is to use a gwynthyme poultice if you do get bitten,
to draw the poison away, else you'll fall into foam-
flecked madness; but I have none of the golden mint
leaves with me." Urus looked at Riatha, but she shook her
head *No*. "Looks as if we'll have to rely on rule one,"
growled the Baeran.

* * *

They came within sight of the strongholt just ere mid of night, the full silver Moon shining brightly down into the vale. High on the western wall of the hemming stone flanks, a great black turret hung upon the stone, clutched unto the sheer, dark massif. There was no path, no stairway up, and the tower was hundreds of feet above the floor of the valley.

"A secret tunnel, I ween," said Riatha softly, her Elven eyes scanning the frowning stone yet finding no way up, no way in.

"Maybe they let themselves down from above," suggested Tomlin, "from the top of the cliffs."

"Mayhap, Pebble," growled Urus. "Though to my mind, Vulgs would not submit to a rope nor a lift cage. I deem Lady Riatha likely correct: a secret tunnel."

"Well, we can't spend all night speculating," responded the Warrow. "Let's get on with the search for it."

"Nay, Pebble." Riatha spoke without taking her eyes from the great black bartizan far above. "To find the tunnel would be the sheerest of luck. *Rûpt* hide them too well. And a secret entrance could be before us or behind us, this side or that, miles from here or right at hand. The Rucha are clever with their stonework at need. Nay, I ween we must climb."

"Climb!" Tomlin's eyes flew up the face of the sheer stone. "Up that? At night?"

"Aye." Riatha's voice was grim, yet matter-of-fact.

Tomlin turned to Urus, and he nodded, agreeing with the Elfess. "The Moon will give us enough light, Pebble. And to do aught else will just lose time."

"Then let's get to it"—the Warrow began rummaging through his pack for a rope, preparing to cross the frozen river to tackle the black wall looming upward, preparing for the climb—"though I fear the stone will be icy."

Up the sheer stone face they went, roped together, Riatha in the lead, Urus trailing, Tomlin in the middle. The Warrow had been right: the stone *was* icy, hoarfrost and rime and frozen glaze o'er the rock face. Even so, the Elfess found purchase, though slim at times it was, and she whispered instructions back to her companions, Tomlin relaying them to Urus: "Crack to the left, take grip . . . Stone flakes, take care to seat thy hand deep into the crevice . . . 'Ware thou of the ice here, 'tis smooth and slippery . . ."

And up they went, climbing the sheer face of the massif, creeping ever closer unto the black bartizan, the ebon stone looming above.

And Tomlin's heart pounded with fear, for the stone plunged straight down, sheer, perpendicular, the fall unbroken below. And ice slid beneath his fingers, beneath his toes, threatening to cast him off the high wall. And the Elfess at times could not find a place for his short stature to cope with, and Urus would climb up from below and give him a boost, and though the great Baeran's hand was strong and steady, still Tomlin had nought to grasp as he was lifted upward, and he bit back moans of terror.

And higher they went, and higher still. Now the Warrow could not bring himself to look down. All he could think of was that if Riatha or Urus fell, roped together they would all plunge to their doom. Yet this was the only way to get to Petal, if she yet liv— Tomlin sheered away from that thought. They just *had* to be alive.

Yet Stoke was a madman, if Man he was, for he *flayed* his victims . . . *alive!* What kind of creature would do such?

Tomlin found that when he thought of Stoke, his fear of being on this sheer wall, hundreds of feet high, lessened.

Yet he could *not* think of Stoke, for he *had* to concentrate upon climbing, else *he* would fall, bringing ruin to them all—

—In that very instant he lost his grip upon the ice and fell!

Down he plunged—*Aaaiii!*—banging against the stone, rope trailing; suddenly—*Unhh!*—he came to the end, the line to Riatha snapping taut, the Warrow slamming into the cliff, the Elfess jerked from her hold, her feet dangling free, one hand loose, yet the other still fist-jammed in a crack. Tomlin twisted and turned upside down, for the rope had slipped down 'round his hips; and he struggled to no avail, trying to get hold of the stone, his heart hammering, moans of fear leaking past his lips, the sight of a four-hundred-foot plunge filling his eyes, knowing that if he became frantic, he would surely pull Riatha from her tenuous grip. Below, Urus jammed both hands into a crack and clenched them tight, wedging fists into the stone. Above, Riatha at last got hold of a narrow ledge with her loose hand, then found purchase for her feet, her breath coming in short quick gasps as she strained to hold on against the Waerling's full heft. When he saw that she was again clinging to the wall, bearing the Wee One's weight, Urus opened his fists and clambered up toward the Waldan.

"Hold tight, Pebble," he called, keeping his voice low. Swiftly he reached Tomlin's side, pressing the Waldan against the stone so that he could get a grip, helping to upright the Wee One, the Waldan sobbing with fear and distress and relief at one and the same time.

It took some ten minutes or so for Tomlin to gather enough of his wits and courage to begin climbing again, his inner strength at last coming to his aid. And gasping out Petal's name, once more he took to the stone, and up he went, Urus coming after.

Up over the icy rock they scaled, a sheer drop plummeting below, Riatha gritting her teeth with the effort, for the climb was arduous and far.

Yet finally she came to the overhang of the bartizan, and up beside it she ascended, still upon the mountain wall, the structure to her right, coming at last to a balcony, and onto the stonework she clambered.

Before her gaped an opening, wide doors hanging awry, a room beyond receding into darkness. Here and there snow lay upon the stone floor of the terrace, though for the most part it had been wind-swept clean. Hideous gargoyles leered down from stone cornices.

Tying off her end of the rope to one of the round stone pillars supporting the balcony rail, she took a rappel loop over her torso and shoulder, and taking up slack and continuously slipping the rope about her body, she began aiding those below.

All about her, the dark stone of the Grimwall Mountains thrust upward into the bright moonlight, the ice on the frozen river gleaming, a thin silver thread running through the floor of the valley far, far below.

When Tomlin came to stand upon the stone of the balcony, his legs were weak with fright, and he drew back from the sight of the long fall into the valley below, turning his gaze instead toward the dark interior of the fortress behind.

Ebon shadows met his chary eyes, where the moonlight did not reach. Dark shapes loomed within the clotted blackness: furniture, fabric rotting upon frames. And a feeling of decay pervaded the very air.

Urus came up over the rail, swiftly unhooking the morning star from his belt.

Belatedly, Tomlin took his sling in hand, placing a stone in the pouch, saving the silver bob for whenever they came upon Stoke, if that monster was even here at all.

"I will take the lead," whispered Riatha, "for Elven eyes cope well with gloom."

"But I won't be able to see at all," hissed Tomlin, "not if all is as dark as that within."

"Keep the lantern handy, Pebble," growled Urus. "Light it now, but keep the hood shut tight till needed. Enough will leak out for your eyes."

Tomlin did as told, and tiny slits of light seeped out through the hood, barely illuming the pitch blackness, yet now he could see.

And into the dark environs of Baron Stoke's fortress they crept, Riatha in the lead, her starlight sword in hand; Urus next, bearing his black morning star; Tomlin bringing up the rear, hooded lantern in his left hand, stone-loaded sling in his right.

Through the room they passed, and out a broken doorway and into a hall. Left and right it ran, curving 'round a bend and out of sight to the right, running straight to the left, closed doors standing along the walls upon either side.

Pausing—"Which way?" whispered Riatha, looking at Urus, then Tomlin.

"Left will lead into the mountain," rumbled Urus. "Right into more of the bartizan."

"Either way seems—" Tomlin's words were cut off by a distant tortured scream, coming from the right: a person in agony beyond bearing, but whether male or female could not be told, the hoarse shrieks climbing upward.

"Mom! Dad! Petal!" Tomlin threw the shutter full wide, the light bursting forth, and rightward down the hall he ran, calling out. *"I'm coming! I'm coming!"*

"Pebble!" cried Riatha. "Wait!" to no avail.

And Urus and the Elfess sprang after.

Swiftly they overhauled the shorter Warrow, catching him just as he came to a wide stairwell leading down and inward. And up these steps came the agonized shrieks, raw, hoarse, a throat screaming a sound not meant for ears to hear.

Down the steps they plunged, Baeran and Elfess and Warrow. And at the very moment they reached the bottom, Vulgs came at them out of the darkness: great black Wolflike creatures, standing nearly as tall as a pony, their yellow eyes glowing like hot coals in the lantern light, red tongues lolling over long, wicked fangs set in crushing jaws, poisonous spittle dripping. And behind them came Rūcks. Dark, swarthy, scimitar-bearing Rūcks, goblin-like with their spindly legs and bat-wing ears and pointed, wide-gapped teeth, and wide mouths leering, their yellow viperous eyes glowing in the lantern light as well, the creatures standing some four to five feet tall.

"Back," barked Urus. "Defend the stairs. Make it hard for them to come at us."

Retreating upward, the trio took a stand partway up the stairwell, Urus and Riatha in the fore with morning star and blade, Tomlin on a higher step in the rear, sling whirling. Yet the snarling Vulgs and Rūcks attacked not; it was as if they awaited something or someone.

And still the shrieking echoed through the fortress, until Tomlin could no longer stand it. Yet ere he could do aught, out of the corner of his eye he glimpsed a person, a Man? Wearing a leathern apron slick with blood.

As the Warrow swung the lantern 'round to see, something glittering flew through the air and shattered upon the stairwell wall. Green fumes whooshed forth, and Tomlin felt himself falling down an endless black tunnel.

Tommy. . . . Tommy. . . .

Someone was calling his name. And up out from the ebon pool where his mind had fallen swam the consciousness of Tomlin the Warrow.

When he came to, the first face he saw was that of another Warrow, black hair cascading down 'round her face, tilted golden eyes gazing into his own: *Petal!* It was Petal! And she held him and rocked in distress.

"Oh, Petal," he whispered, "I've found you at last." And he held onto her, and they both wept.

They were on a filthy, straw-strewn floor in a cell in a dungeon. Iron bars surrounded them on three sides, a stone wall on the fourth. The cell was against one wall of a huge chamber, rushlights burning 'round, and a dark opening could be seen leading outward onto another balcony in the night; they were in one of the outer chambers of the bartizan. Hallways radiated into blackness leading back into the fortress, back into the mountain, the openings barred.

Riatha paced to and fro as would a caged leopard, but Urus sat with his back to the stone, his head down, his eyes shadowed.

In the main chamber outside the cell, shackles hung by chains from a bar set in the ceiling, and the floor below was splattered rudden. A table was set against one wall, and thereupon were knives, thin-bladed and long, and bloodstains pooled below. Upon another table were Urus's morning star and Riatha's sword, as well as Tomlin's sling and stones and silver bob. There, too, were Mister Downtuft's throwing knives. Various tools and devices could be seen 'round the remainder of the room, tools used for purposes better left unexplained.

"Oh, my buccaran," sobbed Petal, "we thought you dead. So did the Rūcks. But, oh, Tommy, it's my dad, your sire, and your mom . . . they're the ones who are dead. The Baron, he . . . he . . ." Petal burst into tears, unable to say on.

Tomlin's mind echoed with Petal's words: *They're dead*

... ead ... ead ... The Baron ... aron ... aron ... And through his numbness rage erupted, and he leapt to his feet and rushed to the cell door, grasping the bars, rattling them: *"Yahhhhh!"* a wordless yell howled throughout the dungeon, speeding down halls, leaping out across the balcony and into the valley, echoing, reverberating, resounding within the castle: *Yahhhhh! ... ahhhhh! ... ahhhh ...*

"Stoke! You bastard! Where are you?"

Stoke! ... oke ... oke ... You bastard! ... astard ... ard ... Where are you? ... ere are you ... are you ... you ... ou ...

Petal rushed to his side. "Oh, Tommy, challenge him not, for he will slay you before my eyes, and I could not stand to witness another ... another ..." Her eyes widened in remembered horror, and she buried her face in her hands, trying to expunge the dreadful memory. Tomlin turned and took her in his arms.

"Let *Stoke* come," gritted Urus from the back of the cell. "I would see this monster once more."

Riatha and Tomlin and Petal each looked at the Baeran, for his voice was filled with a hatred so great that it commanded attention.

Baron Stoke came into the chamber in the hour just before dawn, the gears and rachets and chains of a portcullis rattling and clacking and clanking as the bars covering one portal clattered upward, the rust-stained barway screeching into a stone recess above. Pallid he was and tall, with black hair and hands long and slender. His eyes were a pale amber—yellow, some would say. His face was long and narrow, his nose straight and thin, his white cheeks unbearded. Dark humor played with the corners of his mouth, and when he smiled, long teeth gleamed, the canines sharp.

And in he came, accompanied by an escort of a dozen or more dusky Rūcks, bearing cudgels and tulwars, the long curved blades glinting red in the rushlight.

Petal shrank back against Tomlin, her amber eyes filled with fear and hatred. Tomlin put her behind him and stood defiantly, his own eyes glowing with rage.

Riatha stood at the buccan Waerling's side, her silvery grey gaze fixed upon this kinslayer before her.

Urus stood at the back of the cell, his own face in shadow, his eyes lost in darkness.

Long stood the Baron before them, his yellow eyes seeking, his mouth sissing forth bursts of air, and Tomlin came to understand that Stoke was laughing. Then Stoke's gaze settled upon Riatha, and he spoke in a whisper that made Tomlin shudder with the sound of it. "You will contribute greatly to my . . . pleasure, Elf, as will the others, the tiny Wee Ones so dainty next to hulking brutes like the creature in the back, like *Urus*!" The name of the Baeran cracked out like a whiplash.

"Did you think to fool me by standing in the dark, Baeran? Nay, I knew it was you from the first. Come for revenge? Too bad."

Rūcks smiled wickedly at the prisoners, some sniggering at Baron Stoke's remarks, translating them into Slûk for those who did not speak Common.

The Baron stepped to the table bearing the trio's weapons, his gaze running over the collection. "Fools, did you think to slaў me with this morning star?" He picked it up and hefted it. "Pah! It has no hold over me." Stoke dropped it back to the table, his eyes moving on. "And these rock slingstones: Bah! Ah, but the Elven blade, that looks to be a different matter altogether. Yet what's this? A silver sling bullet. How effective." He did not touch bullet or blade, drawing back instead.

The Baron turned to face the cell, stepping before it. "Did you not know what it took to kill me when you set forth? Stones and iron won't do. Neither will steel. Silver, that's what it takes: silver pure . . . or starsilver, as is the Elven blade.

"Why, you ask? Why does this *Man* think that stone and steel cannot harm him?"

His form began to waver—

"Because . . ."

—darkness clustering, shape shifting—

". . . I . . ."

—transforming, dropping to all fours—

". . . am not . . ."

—yellow eyes, black fur, wicked fangs—
". . . a Man!"

Where Baron Stoke had been, a great ebon Vulg stood snarling, virulent spittle dripping to the stone floor. He lifted his muzzle and howled, the horrid sound filling the air; and from distant quarters, Vulgs howled in return, answering their Master's call.

Eyes wide, Tomlin drew back in fear, Riatha with him, the buccan clasping Petal in his arms.

Only Urus had not reacted, standing at the rear of the cell, his arms folded. "Stoke," he rumbled, "it is true that stone and steel will not harm you, just as it is true that pure silver and starsilver will. Yet you forgot that which will also mean your death—"

Darkness gathered at the back of the cell—
"The fangs . . ."
—enveloping Urus, his shape changing—
". . . and claws . . ."
—dropping to all fours, growing huge, brown—
". . . of another one . . ."
—long black claws and ivory fangs—
". . . so cursed!"

And where Urus had been stood a great Bear!

RRRRAAAWWWW! The Bear charged the cell door, smashing it down before him, iron clanging on stone, Rūcks scattering in fear as the great beast hurled outward. And leaping upward, meeting the charge, the huge Vulg sprang upon the Bear, snarling, poisonous fangs slashing.

A Rūck shouted orders, and one began winding the crank of a crossbow. Others took tulwar in hand, dancing about the combatants, ineffectively slashing at the mighty brown beast, seeking to avoid striking the black one.

Riatha shouted, "Come!" rushing forth from the shattered cell, snatching up her darkling sword.

Tomlin, too, caught up his weapon, loading slingstone and hurling, the missile cracking into Rūck skull, felling the Spawn.

And Petal stood beside her buccaran, the damman throwing a knife, the blade flying true, spitting one of the maggot-folk, black blood gushing.

Riatha's blade wove swift death upon the foe, Ruch after Ruch falling before her. Yet they came at her from behind, tulwars raised; and Tomlin shouted warning as he loosed a stone, cracking the head of the skulker.

Petal hurled another of her sire's throwing knives, this blade too flying true, striking where she aimed, the Rūck staggering hindward in astonishment, falling, blood spurting 'round the handle protruding from his throat.

Roaring and snarling, Bear and Vulg slashed at one another, claw and fang, great gaping wounds tearing open along furred bodies, blood splattering. Out onto the balcony they roared, Bear trying to seize the Vulg in a deadly embrace, the agile Vulg leaping back and aside and forward and slashing with poisonous fangs.

And the Vulg lifted his muzzle in a howl that echoed throughout the fortress, and he was answered in kind. And Vulgs hurtled toward the chamber, responding to their Master's call for help, howling as they came.

Above the snarls and roars of battling Vulg and Bear, above the skirling sound of blade on blade, above the screams of dying Rucha, Riatha with her acute Elven hearing heard the Vulgs coming, their howls growing louder as they charged down the halls toward the dungeon.

"Pebble!" she shouted. "The portcullis! Drop it! Vulgs come!"

Tomlin ran to the levers and gears of the portcullis, Petal guarding his back. The barway was wheel driven, a chain wrapped 'round a drum. A ratchetted gear held the wheel in place.

Vulg howls drew closer and closer still, the ravening monsters now leaping down a long stairwell at the end of the hallway.

Tomlin's eye searched frantically. "The tulwar!" he shouted, pointing at one that had fallen from dead Rūck hand. Petal darted back into the chamber, scooping up the weapon, not knowing why Tommy wanted it.

Vulg claws could be heard scrabbling upon stone, they were that close.

Back into the hallway darted Petal, the curved blade in hand. Tomlin strained at the wheel, loosening the ratchet.

"Jam it under, across the gear teeth, it will hold the ratchet open. When you do, run back in, the portcullis will come crashing down."

"But what about you, Tommy?" she cried. "You'll be trapped out here with the Vulgs!"

Howls roared into the hall, claws scrambled down steps, harsh breathing could be heard.

"No I won't, Petal!" cried Tomlin. "Now jam it!"

The buccan took up all the strain from the ratchet, and Petal slid the blade under, to the hilt, holding up the cog.

A Vulg bounded into the hallway, another right behind.

"Run!" cried Tomlin, and Petal darted inward, the buccan holding the wheel a moment longer, the Vulg leaping down the hallway, Tomlin loosing his hold and scrambling for the barway, the portcullis screeching downward, pointed teeth hurtling to meet holes in the stone floor, Tomlin diving for the gap, the Vulg hurling after, the buccan rolling under, the great barway slamming down, points smashing through the Vulg, slaying him instantly.

The second Vulg after crashed into the bars.

Tomlin sprang to his feet, Petal rushing to him.

Riatha grinned, having dispatched the last of the Rucha.

And all turned their eyes toward the wide balcony, where Bear and Vulg yet raged.

Tomlin loaded the silver slingstone into the pouch, and Riatha hefted her starsilver blade, and grimly they strode toward the balustrade, death for Stoke in their eyes.

And at every portcullis Vulgs snarled and howled in frustration, barred by their Master's own devices from aiding him. Yet behind they could hear the iron-shod tread of Rücks marching, coming to let them in.

And on the balcony, Bear and Vulg yet battled under the paling sky, roaring, snarling, claws rending, fangs slashing.

Tomlin whirled his sling overhead, pouch loaded with lethal silver. Yet he was afraid to loose it upon the tumbling combatants for fear of striking the wrong creature, of striking Bear and not Vulg.

Riatha, too, withheld her blade, for it would wound

friend as easily as foe, the starsilver just as deadly to each.

And Petal glanced back at the entrances, for the howls of the barred Vulgs had somehow altered, a triumphant note threading throughout their yawls. And she saw guttering torchlight being borne down the passageway: Rūcks tramping in force. Petal gripped her throwing knives and stepped back into the main chamber—Vulgs snarling and howling to see their next victim once the ways were opened—and the damman saw lights coming down each of the corridors.

"Tommy, it's the maggot-folk!" she cried. "They come to open the gates. And there are too many to stop."

But Tomlin stood, sling whirling, waiting for an opening.

Riatha's blade was ready as well.

Yet at last the great Bear had clasped the Vulg unto him, and he snarled and strained, seeking to crush the black creature. And the Vulg howled in agony as they crashed into the balcony railing.

But poison flowed throughout the Bear's veins, the virulent black bite. And he had not the might left to crush his foe, and he knew he was falling unto death from the venom. Yet with the last of his strength he hurled the black creature outward, over the edge, the monster falling with a yawling howl, plunging toward the valley far, far below, as the Bear collapsed unto the stone.

Tomlin rushed over to the edge, peering downward, watching as the creature fell, the Vulg howl becoming that of a Man as down he plunged, his shape changing.

And then it changed once again, into something dark, something black, something with large leathery wings. And it flapped away, down in the shadows of the valley, heading eastward, toward the mountains opposite, as if fleeing someone ... or something.

And behind, in the hallways, Rūcks came unto the barways and made ready to raise the gates.

Riatha knelt beside the great Bear, its breathing labored, for it was dying, filled with Vulg venom. Yet a shimmering overtook its form, a *changing,* and then Urus lay upon the stone.

"Rule one," he whispered to Tomlin, "never get bitten by a Vulg."

"Petal, have you any gwynthyme?" Tomlin's voice was filled with urgency as he remembered rule two.

But Petal shook her head *No*, and Tomlin's heart fell.

Petal looked out at the Rūcks, starting to raise the gates. She kissed her Tommy good-bye and turned to bravely face death, her throwing knives at the ready.

Tomlin, too, stood to face the enemy, lading his sling with a stone. But Riatha yet knelt by Urus, comforting the Baeran in these last moments.

And Vulgs snarled and raked their claws under the gates, raging to get at these interlopers.

Yet, of a sudden, Rūcks wailed, and abandoned their work and fled in fear, Vulgs howling behind, racing away.

Tomlin turned to Riatha, eyes wide over this remarkable turn of events, his face filled with bewilderment. He said but one word: "Why?"

Riatha pointed to the east, and there peeking over the rim of the mountains rose the *Sun*! The Foul Folk had fled from certain death, from Adon's Ban, for they could not abide the light of day.

Yet Urus lay dying, but Riatha called for help. "Get him up, to that seat!" she cried, her command sounding nought but cruel. Even so, Petal and Tomlin and Riatha, all three, managed to get the huge Baeran up and onto a stone bench, his back to the wall, facing the east. And as the Sun rose up into the sky, Riatha began treating the Baeran's wounds, cleansing them with water from her waterskin, bandaging them with cloth ripped from her jerkin, aided by Petal's gentle hands.

"But my Lady," questioned Tomlin, "why do you do this? It is Vulg poison."

"Rule three, Waerling," responded the Elfess, a great grin spreading over her features. "Black Vulg bite slays *only* at night. The poison is destroyed by the Sun. Urus will die only if we let him bleed to death."

And as the warm rays of Adon's light washed over them, over Tomlin, Petal, Riatha, and Urus, the buccan's thoughts turned to memories of his sire and dam, and of Petal's sire. And he cursed the creature that had slain them, remembering the *thing* he had seen flapping across the valley, fleeing the light of day. And he looked at Riatha and Urus and Petal, and knew that their quest had just begun. . . .

"Lor, Gaffer, that was a spooky tale," whispered Nob.

Full dark had fallen, and the Warrows in the 'Crow clustered in the lamplight 'round the Gaffer. Through the windows they could see snow still hurtling by, for the blizzard yet raged.

"Wull, Gaffer," said Teddy, his voice hushed, "did they get away? I mean, there they were and all, in the lair o' the Vulgs and such. What did they do?"

"They ran, that's what," responded the Gaffer. "As soon as Urus could stand. They found a way to the top of the mountain wall and ran.

"Oh, they didn't get away clean, for the Vulgs caught up with them, but by that time they'd had a chance to find a place that the Vulgs couldn't get up. And Riatha and Petal and Tomlin held off the maggot-folk till the oncoming daylight once again forced 'em to flee, Urus being at that time too wounded to help much, and a great, heavy thing he was, too, getting him up that cliff and all. But the four of them survived, and the Vulgs and Rūcks gave up after that first night, them being leaderless and all, now that the Baron had flapped away, so to speak."

"Ooo, that's the spooky part," whispered Nob. "I mean, shape changing, into an unnatural creature. It sends shivers up my spine."

"Aye, mine too," agreed Bingo, his own voice low. "But say now, Gaffer, did Pebble ever get a chance to use that silver bullet of his? On Stoke?"

The Gaffer's green eyes looked long at Bingo, the granther buccan finally nodding. "He did, but that's another story and I'm weary." Outside the wind howled and raged, the snow flinging past horizontally, a wall of white gone grey in the night. And the 'Crow creaked and groaned and shuddered in the blast.

"Hoy, Will, it looks as if I'll be using one of your rooms, after all," said the Gaffer, haling himself to his feet with the aid of his gnarled cane. "This blizzard is here for the night."

Lit candle in hand, Will rushed over to aid the granther buccan, and toward the stairs and up through the shadows they went, aiming for the second floor, where Will kept his guest rooms, the taper's light glowing yellow about the innkeeper and the granther buccan.

Orbin Theed, the cooper, looked after the retreating pair, speculation in his glittering amber eyes. "Hoo now, ain't the Gaffer's name Tom? Or Tomlin? And ain't his wife named Petal? And that silver gewgaw he carries in his vest pocket—could that be a silver sling bullet?"

All the Warrows in the 'Crow pondered Orbin's words, nodding, for although they didn't know whether or not Gaffer Tom's given name was Tomlin, still they had each on many separate occasions heard his wife, Petal, call him Tommy. And that roundish silver plumb could indeed be a silver bullet. They all looked up the steps where the Gaffer had got to, climbing with Will toward the room he had been offered, seeing the granther Warrow with new eyes, while outside the wind moaned and groaned, and windows rattled, and boards creaked. The gathered buccen shivered, glancing over their shoulders, and some thought they could hear the sound of a far-off howling, wails in the frigid night.

And Orbin threw another log on the fire, driving back the shadows, making the room grow brighter with the blaze, though darkness still lurked in far corners of the One-Eyed Crow.

The
Thornwalker
and the Wolf

All night the wind howled, whelming upon home and hamlet, forest and field, croft and campsite, hurling snow 'cross the 'scape to pile in ever growing drifts. Buildings shuddered in the blast, and trees groaned, their limbs lashing to and fro as if in agony. And still the blizzard yawled as dawn tried and failed to bring any but a dim light into the rage, dark night desperately clutching at the Land, unwilling to loose its black grasp. But at last wan light came groping through the clawing wind, and inexorably the pallid day crept above the unseen horizon, while the storm yet twisted and wrauled in screaming protest.

And in the chill shelter of the One-Eyed Crow, shutters rattled and the chimney moaned, boards creaked and the roof groaned, as one by one the blizzard-trapped Warrows made their way through the dim morning light down from the guest quarters above and into the common room below. Teddy helped Will set the fire in the main hearth, while Feeny and Arla, Will Brackleburr's wife, kindled the stove in the kitchen. Soon the kettle was boiling and bracing hot tea was served all 'round, as other guests came down the stairs, and slowly the 'Crow came awake.

Last to arrive was Gaffer Tom, stumping down the steps, gnarled cane thumping 'gainst the treads, his reedy voice grumbling and complaining, the words lost in the tavern's rattling, the Gaffer's mutterings not understood until he thumped alongside the table: ". . . the wash basin water froze right solid in the night. And if it hadn't been for my blankets, I do believe I'd'a' froze right solid myself, I would."

Still the relentless wind hammered and whelmed upon the 'Crow, as if furious that any could defy its frigid might.

Arla came bustling out from the kitchen, bearing a great platter heaped with steaming pancakes, Will right behind, tin plates and knives and forks ajuggle, an earthenware crock of maple syrup atop the pile. Setting it all upon the common table, serving up the breakfast, soon Warrows were busily stuffing themselves with sweet-dripping hot cakes, gulping down honey-sweetened tea, and talking 'round mouthfuls of food.

"Oi, the blizzard," said Feeny, pointing with his chin in the general direction of the frosted windows, where snow could be seen hurtling past, "she still blows." He popped in another forkful of food. "Wonder when she'll stop."

"Hoo now," mused Nob, "I've seen these things last for days. O' course, that's when I spent the winter up near the Jillians." Nob was referring to the time in his young-buccan days when he'd gone north to the very shores of the Boreal Sea, there where the Jillian Tors ran down to the churning waters, a tale that he wouldn't let any forget, since most Warrows are content to remain near hearth and home and not go gallivanting off on long journeys.

"They say as a blizzard suchlike this will drop you in your tracks, in midstride no less." Feeny's voice held a hushed tone to it, and a murmur of confirmation muttered 'round the table, for others there had heard the same.

"Ar, it's not often that we get squoze in the grip of a storm as this one be," mumbled Billy Cloverhay, Teddy's cousin from north of the Dinglewood. "I mean, it's liable to push the Wolves and all down from the north, down into the Boskydells themselves. Then we'll need the Thornwalkers to set up Wolf Patrols and keep the brutes from the sheep and cattle."

As the fierce wind rattled the shutters on the 'Crow's windows, buccen nodded their agreement with Billy's words, for although the Seven Dells were protected from intruders by a formidable barrier of thorns—Spindle-thorns—growing in the river valleys around the Land, completely be-ringing it, still those who were determined enough or desperate enough could slowly force their way through the Thornwall. In the past, Wolves, driven by winter starvation, had made their way into the Bosky, where their game had also sought refuge from the brutal cold. In these times the Spindlethorn patrols, or Thorn-walkers as they were called, organized themselves into Wolf Patrols to drive the animals away from the sheep and cattle of the Boskydell crofters. Even so, still there were losses, as Wolves raided to survive.

"Hoy, Gaffer," called Teddy, "have you got any tales about the Wolves and all?"

"Eh, Teddy, o' course I have," replied the Gaffer, carving off another forkful of hot cake. "But I won't tell any till I've had my fill o' this breakfast. Anyway, there's some here as what can tell you about the Wolves from firsthand experience." Taking in a mouthful, Gaffer Tom cast a significant eye upon Bingo Peacher, that buccan now standing before the fireplace warming himself, having finished his meal.

"Oi, Bingo, 'at's right," piped up Feeny. "As a hunter, you'd know all about the Wolves. Have you had much doings with 'em, now?"

All waited as Bingo held out his hands to the flames, the buccan finally turning and stepping back to the table. Arla filled his tin cup with more tea, and Bingo took a long pull. Setting the cup down—"Aye, you might call it that, Feeny: *doings.*"

Now all the Warrows gave their full attention over to the hunter, though some still packed away another hot cake or two as he looked through the pale light and out the window at the hurtling snow.

"Aye, doings . . ."

Bingo's eyes scanned the snow, looking for Wolf spoor, for a harsh winter had come down upon the Land, driving the grey hunters south before it. Some had pressed through the Thornring, had gotten into the Bosky, and sheep and cattle were once again at risk. And Thornwalker Wolf Patrols scoured the Land for sign of the raiders, pressing them back from the crofters' fields, away from the herds. Unfortunately, the Wolves' natural game—mice and rabbits, and an occasional deer—tended to seek out the farm fields as well, where the summer grain had grown, and so the hunting Wolves, though they ordinarily shunned civilization, naturally came upon the flocks within the holdings.

Bingo had been posted to guard a number of farmsteads in Eastdell: Huggs', Broxeley's, Sweetberry's, Coldridge's, Hackins', as well as two or three more. And daily Bingo walked the rounds, seeking sign of Wolves, while at night he put up at one or another of the holdings he warded. Oh, it was not that these crofters could not protect their own flocks; rather, it was that if any Wolves *were* spotted, someone was needed who could spend time pursuing them, harrying them from the vicinity, someone who could fly an arrow straight and who could look out for himself in the wilds: a Thornwalker. The task was not without its element of danger, and a Thornwalker would have to be careful not to put a Wolf in a situation where it would feel cornered, for then the beast would become a terrible foe, fighting like fury. Yet it was known that in general Wolves would not raid a guarded flock, and would fade before a Warrow with a bow—almost as if they knew that *this* game was not theirs for the taking, as if they knew that the Warrows simply wanted them away from the flocks.

And so Bingo walked the bounds of his wardship, scanning the snow for Wolf spoor, occasionally glancing at the gathering darkness in the sky, heralding the coming of a late winter storm, perhaps the last ere spring would loose the brumal grip.

He was just turning for Broxeley's, heading across the crofter's fields, when he heard the terrified bleating of a sheep down in a draw, the sound chopped off short. Bingo began running toward the gully, stringing arrow to bow as he went. When he came to the rim, down in the slot he saw a great grey Wolf dragging a lifeless lamb through the snow, blood staining the white earth in a long streak behind.

"Hoy!" shouted Bingo, drawing to the full and loosing the shaft.

At Bingo's cry, the Wolf looked up, leaping aside. Still, the bolt struck home, though not where Bingo had aimed, instead the arrow piercing high along the flank. Yelping in pain and snapping at the shaft, the beast spun on its heels and bounded away, disappearing into the furze at gully bottom.

"Rats!" burst out Bingo, stringing another arrow and scrambling down the steep-sided draw. *Me and my big mouth. If I hadn't yelled ...*

A glance at the lamb showed that nought could be done: it was dead—throat ripped out. *One of Broxeley's strays,* thought Bingo. *Died a quick death.*

Bingo stepped toward where the Wolf had disappeared, his bow at the ready. In the snow among the lupine tracks he could see blood spoor. *Pox and bother! Now I've got a wounded Wolf on my hands.* Glancing at the lowering skies, *Well, bucco, you've done it now. If you've lamed it, it'll turn into a savage killer, picking on the weak and old, on the slow ... not that they don't do that anyway. But, hoy, it might even attack a Warrow. Besides, you know you can't leave an injured beast out on the Land: you can't leave the creature in pain.*

And so, chastising himself for blundering, eyes alert, ears tuned for the tiniest of sounds, bow ready, Bingo cautiously stepped in among the furze on the track of a wounded Wolf.

The day grew darker as Bingo trailed his quarry, the low grey skies filling with churning black. A chill wind sprang up, blowing from the west, driving the dark clouds before it. Still Bingo followed the spoor, ruddy spots among the tracks. An hour passed and then another, and snow began to fall, driven before the blow, ice crystals stinging the eyes. Bingo pulled his cloak hood more tightly about his face and continued to trail the wounded animal, though the snow was beginning to cover the traces of its passage. Even so, Bingo felt that he could not allow the Wolf to suffer, and he did not want it to become a Warrow-killer.

On he pressed as the day waned and the wind grew, more snow hurtling past. And from the east came racing the black shroud of night, while from the west a swirling hoary wall swept across the Land; and in the waning light the great howling storm that whelmed into the Boskydells caught Bingo out in the open among the rolling hills.

The thundering wind tore at him, hurling shrieking whiteness before it, and he could not see beyond a stride or two. Shards of ice blasted against the Warrow, thrashing upon him, clawing at him, lashing as would iron-tipped scourges, slashing crystals hurtling into eyes and face, burning with cold. And the blizzard was as a mighty force hammering at him, causing the buccan to stumble and reel, and bend low to the ground to keep from being swept away, his cloak flapping behind like a torn-loose sail. He turned and struggled downwind, surrounded by the yawling white, caught in the screaming blast, the wounded Wolf now forgotten as he sought refuge. He came to a low-standing rock and attempted to shelter in its lee; but the cruel wind shrieked and spun, whipping him with its harsh eddying.

Lor, what now?

Bingo cast his mind back, trying to remember the lay of the land, trying to remember where he might find safe haven. *Can't stay here. Must press onward. But where? Think, Bingo, think! Let me see, before the storm struck, I recall passing a shallow gorge, nought but a fold in the land, a fold where I might be able to get out of this wind. But that was a long way back, and I might not make it. . . . Hoy! Hold on, bucco: would you rather die struggling or just give up now?*

A grim smile lit his features.

Out from the scant shelter into the yawling howl pressed the Thornwalker. And screaming, blinding, windborne snow swallowed him, snow gone grey in the dimming day, the blast pummeling, hammering, sucking the heat from him and hurtling it to the wind. Yet he toiled onward, bending double in the whelming blow.

Night fell, yet it is moot whether or not he even noted the darkness, for the only thing that mattered was the struggle. And when the shrieking day gradually trans-

formed into dark, howling night, he did nought but fight
onward, yet his energy slipt away with each step.

And as the wind slammed into him, he fell . . . but rose
up to struggle on. But he fell again, the wind pummelling
him. Once more he stood and pressed onward. And as his
strength drained away, he fell more often, yet each time
he got up to go on. Thus he struggled forward, collapsing,
rising, tumbling, getting up, falling in exhaustion, fatigue
mercilessly dragging him down, slipping, failing to catch
himself, his heart hammering with effort, breath coming
in sobbing gasps, struggling up and on, the wind tearing
at him, his warmth fled from him, his strength all but
gone.

Hours fled, and still he struggled through the snow,
seeking the fold seen earlier but now hopelessly lost, no
longer aware of his direction, stumbling, falling, rising
again to go on, each step now a torture, his breath ragged
and burning. And still the white wind crashed upon him,
ice shards coating him from crown to foot, weighing him
down with its burden.

And the yawling, hammering wind shoved and
pounded and mauled him, and ice slashed across his path,
and snow barred his way, yet down the screaming blast he
stumbled, a furlong and then another, fighting for what
seemed like eternity.

For perhaps the hundredth time in a mile he collapsed,
falling in the thigh-deep snow.

And still the icy whiteness hurled into him, while the
wind sucked at his diminishing heat; and the world was
filled with nought but the screamings and yawlings of the
blast.

Slowly, painfully, Bingo stood once again, his vision
blurred, his legs but barely under his control, pressed to
his uttermost, and he pushed onward, his progress measured in yards, in feet, in steps.

And the hurtling ice and raging shriek slammed at him
and tried to hold him back, and hip-deep snow clutched at
his legs and feet like a massive hand barring his way; yet
Bingo Peacher, Thornwalker, Warrow of the Boskydells,
struggled forward, his breath rasping outward in blasts of
white vapor, his cloak hood laden with the crystalline ice

of its freezing, the wounded Wolf no longer even a memory, totally forgotten, as was the fold he sought in the land.

He reeled and staggered before the wind, hammered by its blast, again losing his footing, falling once more in the deep snow.

Yet this time he did not rise again.

And the blizzard hammered down upon his still form, clawing at his unmoving figure, tearing at his winter cloak, trying to rend the scant protection from him.

And Bingo's mind fell down a dark tunnel.

And the raging wind howled across the Bosky, shrieking in power and triumph, mauling all caught in its fury.

Dragging ... pulling ...

For a brief moment Bingo's awareness flickered: *Black. Hear wind. Not in it. Sheltered somehow. Smell of ... smell of ...*

Again darkness enfolded his mind.

When next Bingo came to, it was because something or someone was licking him, and as he lay flat on his back he could feel a weight on his chest. He opened his eyes in the dim light and a small, furred, grinning face peered into his. *Wolf cub!*

Hastily, Bingo sat up, dumping the cub with a grunt onto the earthen floor beside him, the pup tumbling into a pack of cubs about him, the animals scattering with yips at the Warrow's movement, scrambling away in the gloom. Bingo's eyes swiftly took in his surroundings, his head turning this way and that. About him he saw close, shadowy walls: a hollowed-out den. Behind, up a short, shallow slope, grey light seeped in through the mouth of the lair. He could see that a drift of snow had spilled partly down into the den, and the howl of the blizzard could be heard yammering without. In the murk toward the back of the lair he saw the yellow eyes of the gathered pups regarding him warily.

And beyond, in the deepest of shadows, a greater pair of eyes peered at him with amber gaze.

His heart hammering, his breathing rapid and shallow, slowly, carefully, still sitting, Bingo began to back away, up the slope, toward the snow-laden exit. *Easy, bucco. You don't want to scare the big un. Just sneak up and away, and mayhap you'll get free o' this yet.* Cautiously the Warrow edged backwards, toward the way out.

Yet the closer he came to freedom, the greater the shriek of the raging blizzard without.

As Wolf eyes gazed at him, Bingo eased up the drift, the wind's howl drowning out all other sound. Finally the buccan came to the mouth of the den, and risking a quick glance, he could see nought but a shrieking white wall racing past.

Hoy, bucco, you can't go out in that. It's worse now than it was last night. . . . Hiyo, wait a moment. How'd I get in here in the first place? I should be layin' out there dead. Froze. Not in here where it's snug.

Bingo looked back down into the den. Still five pairs of yellow eyes regarded him. And dim memories of being dragged through the snow flitted through the buccan's mind.

A blast of wind lashed into the den mouth, whirling ice and snow before it, whipping it into the Warrow's face, stinging his eyes. Bingo retreated down and away from it, back into the low-ceilinged lair, back toward the wild beasts.

Bingo reached for his bow, still slung across his shoulders. But the moment he did so, a low growl came from the back of the den, yellow eyes flashing hotly, and the cubs scrambled behind the great Wolf, still lying on its side, yet tensed, as if ready to spring up.

Instantly, Bingo stopped, frozen in midmove.

Hoy! It's as if . . .

Long moments passed, Wolf glaring at Warrow, cubs peering from behind. At last: "Hoosh, now," soothed Bingo, and carefully he eased his bow from his back, laying it off to one side, as Wolf eyes warily watched, a faint growl rumbling deep within the animal's chest. Next,

Bingo removed his quiver, placing the arrows beside the bow.

Still the growling went on, but stopped when Bingo moved out of reach of his weaponry.

By this time Bingo's eyes had completely adjusted to the gloom of the den, and he saw that he faced a great she Wolf and her four cubs.

And she was wounded, high on the flank, blood slowly seeping from her side.

Lor! Is this the one that I . . . ?

Her yellow eyes regarded him accusingly.

Guiltily, Bingo looked away, yet his gaze was irresistibly drawn back to hers.

"Coo now, grey Wolf, don't look at me that way."

But the Wolf's eyes never left those of the Warrow.

Quickly, Bingo looked slightly to one side. *They say as if you look a Wolf directly in the eyes, the beast thinks you're going to attack.*

His gaze swept the length of her body. She was gaunt, her ribs showing, as if starving. And still the wound seeped, though no arrow stood forth—*Must have fallen out somewhere.*

Unfastening the snaps, Bingo began rummaging through his knapsack, still slung at his waist by its over-the-shoulder strap. He drew out a biscuit of crue and some venison jerky. The cubs sniffed the air, their muzzles pointing straight up, scenting the food.

"Coosh," he called, holding out the dried meat. "Come on now, me pups."

Slowly, irresistibly drawn by the smell, the cubs crept forward, one pup braver than the others, taking a strip of venison from Bingo and then shying back to hunker down and eat it, but scrambling up, growling at the other cubs who had gathered 'round for their share.

"Ho," barked Bingo, laughing. "Leave 'im alone. I've got some for each o' you." And the buccan enticed them one at a time to take food from his hand, each gingerly taking a piece and darting away.

Bingo tossed several strips to the she Wolf, the bitch snapping them up, bolting them down.

"Hoyo! You *are* fair to starving now, aren't you?"

Bingo took a bite of crue and chewed, watching the pups gnawing on the tough jerky, making short work of it. Quickly it was gone, and they looked up at the Warrow in anticipation.

Rummaging through his pack, he pulled out several more biscuits of crue, the waybread tasteless but nourishing.

This time the pups came eagerly to him, though a rumble could be heard from the she Wolf.

Once more Bingo tossed food to the bitch, and she bolted down the three crue biscuits just as swiftly as she had the venison.

Now the cubs crowded 'round Bingo, tails wagging, and the buccan broke apart his last biscuit, feeding them by hand, making certain that each got a fair share.

He ruffled their soft fur, laughing as they nuzzled him, licking his hands, jumping up to lap at his face, one knocking him over onto his back, the others crawling over him as he rolled and tussled with them, the Warrow laughing and the cubs growling in mock battle, tugging on his clothes with their tiny teeth.

Ha! Some Thornwalker are you, bucco. Some mighty Wolf killer, I would say. And Bingo fended off the assault of another cub.

The morning crept toward noontime, though the wan light never seemed to strengthen, for the blizzard yet howled outside, clawing at the Land.

The cubs were asleep in a pile about the Warrow, and the she Wolf dozed. Bingo, too, had been napping, yet now he came awake. As he did, so too did the bitch, her gaze upon him.

Bingo's glance fell upon the wound, still seeping slowly.

"I didn't mean to hurt you, you know," he murmured.

Oh, didn't you, now? Well then, just what did you hope to do when you loosed that arrow?

"I meant to ... I mean ..."

Spit it out, bucco.

"Well, you had that lamb. Killed it. Was draggin' it off."

The Wolf's eyes regarded him somberly, as if to say, *We are starving. Wouldn't you take a stray lamb if it were you?*

"Wull, perhaps," whispered Bingo. He paused and thought about it. "Yes," he admitted at last. "Yes, I *would* take a stray if I were starving."

The Wolf's gaze fell upon the cubs beside Bingo. Again the Warrow interpreted her look. "Aye, you have the pups and all to look after, and if they was mine, I wouldn't do no different."

The bitch looked again at Bingo, seeming to say, *Then we aren't so unalike, you and I. For I nurture and protect that which is mine, just as I suspect you do for that which is yours.*

The grey Wolf gazed at him a moment more, then turned her head and tried to lick her wound, but it was in a place that she could not reach.

"Wellanow, Lady, *now* I understand why you are still bleeding: you can't reach the wound to treat it. If you'll permit me . . ." Bingo rummaged about in his knapsack once more, drawing out a tiny tin and a strip of cloth.

Slowly, cautiously, so as not to waken the cubs, Bingo disengaged himself from the pups and began easing toward the mother Wolf. Her hackles came up partway, and again she growled, the sound faint, low, deep in her chest. And her fangs gleamed in the dim light. Bingo hesitated a moment, letting her settle, then resumed edging toward her, holding out a hand for her to sniff. Finally as he came close enough for her to get the smell of him, he saw her relax slightly.

"I don't know whether it's me or the pups that you are smellin', Lady"—Bingo's words came whispering—"but whoever it is, I'm going to treat that wound of yours."

Now Bingo eased up next to her, cooing softly under his breath. Opening the tin, he let her smell the herbal salve within. She snorted, as if to clear the scent from her nostrils, and then turned her head away.

Bingo uncorked his canteen and wet the cloth, and carefully, gently, cleansed the blood from the matted fur, all the while the Wolf softly growling yet submitting.

The Warrow's heart cried out to see the wound, and he

became certain that he had caused it; if so, then the arrow
had struck a rib, glancing up and under the fur, causing
little damage until piercing a muscle high in the back.
Even so, when the blood was washed away, Bingo could
see that it would heal, given time, though how she would
hunt, well, that was another matter.

As he applied the unguent, he talked to her: "Soft, soft,
Lady. This won't hurt a bit.

"Hoo now, let me ask you: was it you what dragged me
into your den, or was it instead those pups o' yours? The
pups, I think. I mean, I probably fell right at your door,
and they smelled the food in m' knapsack. That being so,
they came to get it, but the snaps on the sack were just
too much, and so they dragged it into your lair—hauling
me along behind by the strap 'round my chest—so as you
would deal with it wi' those big teeth o' yours. I mean, if
it had been *you* what found me, wellanow, you'd make
short work o' that rucksack o' mine ... probably short
work o' me, too. But I think that when you got here, I
was covered with the scent o' your cubs, and so you
didn't do me in ... either that, or you were just too hurt
to care, what with being injured and all."

Bingo took a critical look at the wound. Satisfied that he
had done all he could, he capped the tin of salve. "There
now. All finished," he said, backing away. The Wolf raised
her head and watched as he moved off; she was no longer
growling.

The howl of the storm lasted all that day and into the
night as well, but by morning of the next day all was
quiet. Bingo crawled up to the opening and peered out
into the day; a light snow gently fell through calm air.
And he turned and came back down into the den, the cubs
frolicking about him.

"Wellanow, pups, don't carry on so, for it's time I was
takin' my leave." The Warrow softly approached the
bitch, the pups gamboling about, falling over one another,
crowding in behind the mother Wolf. And she tolerated
Bingo's presence, neither growling nor baring teeth. Taking a last look at the injury, Bingo applied a bit more

salve to it. "Lady, you won't be hunting immediately, but
I know what needs doing, and I—"

Of a sudden the outside light was blocked, and Bingo
spun about to see a great, dark form coming into the den.
It was a huge male Wolf, dark as night, and it sighted the
Warrow and rushed forward, snarling, fangs bared.

And Bingo knew that he would be rent asunder by
the monster.

Yet, lo! Suddenly the female Wolf stood between the
two, her own fangs bared, hackles upright, barring the way,
protecting *all* her cubs from the male, the buccan included.

The dark Wolf skidded into the grey, and the lair was
filled with terrible snarling, loud beyond bearing. Yet
there was no blood shed, for the male backed away before
the mother, though he did not leave the den. Stiff-legged
he stood, his hackles upright, his eyes hot upon the
Warrow, and once again Bingo turned his gaze aside from
a Wolf.

Long it seemed that the confrontation lasted, yet it
could not have been more than a few moments. And at
last the male turned, trotting up and out.

Limping, the female turned to Bingo, looking at the
buccan, as if saying, *Go now. The storm is ended and he
will let you pass.*

Bingo took up his gear, slinging bow over shoulder and
quiver at hip. He turned and ruffled the pups' fur one last
time. "Take care, little ones. Take care."

Nodding at the mother, Bingo moved upslope and,
bending low, stepped outside, coming out from under the
hillside containing the den. There, off to the right stood
the male, his dark flanks gaunt. The black Wolf watched
as the Warrow trudged through flakes floating gently to
the earth, the buccan moving out upon the fields of white.

Fortune favored Bingo, and as evening drew nigh he
came trudging back toward the Wolves' den, a roebuck
across his shoulders. Upon the hilltop above the lair,
Bingo could see the big male watching. Yet the black
Wolf moved not, as onward came the buccan. The
Warrow dropped the deer before the opening and then
turned and walked southerly, across the field and up a

long hill, heading for the Broxeleys' croft. But ere passing beyond sight, he turned and looked back, and saw the dark male slowly padding down through the snow, with great dignity, approaching the buccan's offering. And from the den came the grey she Wolf, the cubs tumbling after, and they waited until the male came down beside them.

Bingo watched as they sniffed at the deer and then looked up, toward Bingo, their amber eyes gazing in his direction. Then he turned and passed beyond sight.

When Bingo came to the Broxeley farm, he discovered that Marlan and his buccos were out searching for him; they had begun the moment that the storm let up. And when they came home that night, they found the lost buccan stuffing his face with his third piece of Lilly's pie and sipping hot tea.

Bingo resigned from the Thornwalkers within the week, saying that no more could he walk Wolf Patrol. And he returned to his home north of the Dinglewood.

But it was in the winter of the following year that a strange event occurred: In the dead of the night, Bingo was awakened by a noise at his front door. When he got up to see what was afoot, he found a slain deer on his front stoop. And all about were the tracks of Wolves. . . .

As Bingo finished his tale, all in the One-Eyed Crow looked at one another, wonder in their eyes.

"Hoo now," breathed Teddy. "Who'd'a' believed it? Wolves and all, savin' your life. When ud all this happen, Bingo?"

"Twenty-two years back, Teddy. When I was a Thornwalker."

"And that's why you gave it up?" queried Feeny. "Because you believe that a Wolf saved you?"

"Aye, Feeny, I couldn't any longer shoot at them and those what had saved me."

"Hah!" snorted Nob. "I mean, it ain't like Wolves is intelligent and all. I mean, she probably thought you was a pup and all, pulling you into the den like she did, if it was even her what done it."

"Be that as it may, Nob," responded Bingo, "still either she or her pups rescued me from the storm. And, well, like I said before, I just couldn't no longer hunt them what had saved me."

"Wull, that deer what was on your doorstep," persisted Nob, "and the Wolf tracks and all, I mean, it just had to be an accident. I mean, you are saying that the Wolves left it as repayment for what you had done, but I'm here to tell you that it was sheer coincidence, that's all, sheer coincidence."

"Wull then, Nob, that may be as you say," replied Bingo, "but there's something that you don't know: *there's been a deer left on my doorstep every winter for the past twenty-one years.*"

Outside the blizzard whelmed upon the Land, the shrieking storm hammering upon the walls of the 'Crow. With a loud *crack* a fireplace log popped, and all the listeners jumped as if they'd been arrow-shot, and it seemed as if they could hear long wailing howls upon the wild wind.

The Trout of
the Rillmix

Breakfast done, the buccan Warrows gathered in a semicircle before the great stone fireplace in the One-Eyed Crow. For long moments no one said aught, instead fumbling with clay and briar, stuffing pipeweed into the bowls, lighting slender tapers, puffing upon stems and filling the air with the aroma of Downdell leaf. While sounds of the blizzard moaned down the chimney, and the wind without hammered upon the clapboard walls of the inn and shrieked across the rattling thatch above, whelming upon the roof.

As they leaned back and savored their pipes, Dilby looked across the circle at Gaffer Tom, so like Dilby's own granther on his dam's side. And Dilby's mind drifted back to other times, other days, days of summer when the gentle breeze blew, and . . .

"Look! Look! There he is, Granther! There he is!" Dilby excitedly stabbed his finger toward the great swirl in the water while hopping back and forth from one foot to another. "It's the Trout, Granther, the Trout of the Rillmix!" Dilby hastily cast his line in the direction of the whorl.

"You won't catch that un, stripling," said the Gammer, taking his briar pipe from his mouth and tapping the dottle out on a nearby oaken root jutting forth from the rich dark earth of the north bank of the Dingle-Rill.

Now, you might believe that calling Dilby Higgs a

"stripling" was somewhat of a misnomer, for Dilby was in his late forties; yet these kind of liberties were frequently taken by the old Gammer, who could be excused on the grounds that he was considerably past ninety, in fact was bumping up against a hundred. "They's all striplings to me," he'd often proclaim from his favorite chair in the Blue Bull in Budgens as he thumped his gnarled blackwood cane to the floor to emphasize the point. "All striplings."

But though the old Gammer *was* pushing the century mark, he let everyone know that he was just as witty—though occasionally he *did* forget, but only now and again, that is—and as hale—except there *was* a bit of trouble seeing things up close—and as spry—the cane, you see, was mostly for show, though it *seemed* to make walking easier, especially up the grades—and as independent—yet getting up the step and into the Blue Bull was eased a *tiny* jot when a helping hand at his elbow gave him a bit of a boost—as he was at eighty-five; and if you didn't believe it, why then, he'd *tell* you so.

And though it could be said by some that the Gammer was a bit crotchety and querulous, there was no denying that he was a favorite citizen of Budgens. Warrows would come from miles around just to hear one or more of the many tales he held: on warm days he could be found on the banks of the Rillmere speaking with families, or at the Budgens Market talking to the dammen, or at the north knoll where the younglings gathered to romp. But his favorite place of all was the Blue Bull, which frequently would be filled with attentive Warrows, puffing long-stemmed pipes and holding mugs of ale and listening raptly to the thin, reedy voice of this granther buccan spinning forth another Mithgarian tale.

But on this day Dilby had loaded up the Gammer in a pony-drawn cart, and he had driven to the swirl of the Rillmix, there at the junction where the Southrill flowing out of Budgens met the east-running Dingle-Rill a half mile or so north of town. Dilby had then stopped the cart and had helped his granther to his favorite fishing spot under the gnarled oak tree. And they had cast in their lines and watched the bobbers dip now and again as a bluegill or sun perch nipped at the bait.

The day was warm and comfortable and sleepy, and a lazy buzz of insects filled the air. Occasionally, the Gammer would cackle and pull forth another pan fish, as the summer Sun slowly fell toward the horizon and the afternoon shadows lengthened toward evening. And it was late in the day when the Rillmix Trout swirled to the surface of the shaded pool and set Dilby to frantic activity.

"No sir, younger, you won't catch that un," repeated the Gammer.

"There's not a fish that can't be caught," replied Dilby breathlessly as he cast again and again in the area of the ripples.

"That as may be," responded the Gammer, "but bucco, the Rillmix Trout ain't no *ordinary* fish. No sir, it's *special.*"

Dilby, exasperated at getting no results, pulled his line from the water and inspected the bait. "Perhaps a fresh worm . . ." He took one from the tin and rebaited his hook, while the Gammer refilled his pipe and lit it and shook his head as one does when another won't listen to plain reason.

"You ain't listening, tadpole," his thin voice fluted as he leaned back against the oak bole. "I *said*, he ain't no *ordinary* fish."

But Dilby cast his line into the pool once again, and the old Gammer puffed upon his black briar and reflected back. "Seems as if there's always been a Rillmix Trout. There was one when I was a youngling, and my granther and *his* granther said that there was one when each of them was younglings.

"Oh, I ain't saying that it's the *same* trout, though perhaps it *could* be; nobody I know can say as how long a trout lives, how old they get to be. But the Rillmix Trout, well, he's always been and I suppose he'll always be."

With a *ploonk!* Dilby's bobber plunged under. "Aha! Got you!" he cried and set the hook, hauling up and back, the pole bending double. "Drat!" he exclaimed, for a common bluegill had taken the bait and was fluttering and flopping at the end of Dilby's line. The Warrow plucked the hook out, and even though the 'gill was a goodly sized catch, Dilby flung the fish back into the 'Rill and feverishly baited up again.

He cast his line back in and intently watched the float. As long minutes fled and nothing happened, he slowly relaxed his tense stance.

"Nosiree, you won't catch the Rillmix Trout, bucco, no way it'll be done less'n the fish hisself *wants* to be taken."

And as the Gammer spoke on, in spite of the fact that the Trout had shown a flash and a swirl, Dilby found his attention being drawn away from the fruitless fishing and getting caught up in the tale the centenarian was spinning.

"When I was a youngling," said the Gammer, "there was an old, old Warrow living in Budgens: ancient he was, all white-haired. Must've been a hundred fifteen, hundred twenty, if he was a day. And just like a lot of others had swore, he too said he was going to catch the Rillmix Trout. Took an oath on it, he did, right there in the Blue Bull itself, they say. At the time, I hadn't been borned, but they say he weren't no more than about your age, Dilby, when he started trouting. Swore he was going to catch that fish or die trying. Bolley was his name, Gorbediah Bolley, but everybody knew him as the Fisher.

"And he went after it with a passion, he did, fishing every free moment he had. Summer, spring, fall, it didn't seem to matter none to him. Why, in the winter he even cut holes in the ice and went at it. And there was those as said they'd seen the Fisher at times in snowstorms and blizzards, down to the Rillmix, trouting in the water for all he was worth.

"Gorbediah had hisself a family, and you might think it'd be a wonder if his damman and younglings *ever* got to see him. But you know, in all but the worst weather, they'd be right there beside him, fishing away, passing many a pleasant hour dippin' bait in the pool here. Why, I suppose he actually spent more time with his family than any other Warrow I know.

"Well, years passed, and his buccos and dammsels grew up into fine figures of Warrows, and had their own younglings, and he'd fish with them, too. And then they grew up, but then there were his great-grandchildren to fish with. Seems as if there was always a youngling sitting 'side him as his quest for the Rillmix Trout went on.

"The only time he didn't fish was for one complete year after his dammia died. And everyone what knew him thought he would die, too. He seemed to lose interest in living, seemed to actually be *fading*. But one day, nearly a year later, whilst he himself was trudging past the pool, the Rillmix Trout leapt up out from the water and high into the air and fell back with a great splash. And Gorbediah was saved.

"He took to fishing again, renewing his vow.

"That fish, you see, had rescued him, saved him from certain death, for he was *dwindling* till that day. But afterwards, well, he was nearly his old self again, taking younglings to the fishing hole and going after that great Trout.

"And Gorbediah, well, he was the one, in plain and simple fact, as introduced me to fishing, for you see, he was my own great-granther on my dam's dam's side. That'd make him your own great-great-granther, Dilbs, your own great-great-granther.

"Anyway, I used to fish just as hard, I thought, for that Trout as he did. And we spent many a pleasant day right here in this spot, just like you and me, Dilbs, fishing, chatting, and passing the time away.

"About the only thing as was different is that this oak tree was a youngling, too.

"And great-granther told me many stories while we sat on this bank; why, in the three or four short years I knew him, I learned more from him than from any other teacher or book. Simple things, like I've told you, things that make up the stuff of life.

"One day, I reckon I was about eleven or so, we was right here on this very spot, fishing away, when the Trout broke water: leaped so high as I never seen a fish do before or since ... seemed to be trying to fly up into the sky, as if he was chasing after something, straining to catch it. And he rose up to the peak of his great leap and seemed to hang there for a moment, trying to go further.

But then he fell back into the water, for he couldn't follow whatever it was he was after.

"Full to bursting with the wonder of it all, I turned, calling out to my granther: 'Did you see it? Did you see it, Granther?'

"But he didn't answer, for you see, he'd gone on, and only his tired old body was left behind.

"I just stood there and looked at him for a long time, then finally I went to take his pole out of his hands, and *lo!* the Rillmix Trout was hooked on his line.

"But it weren't struggling or nothing: just fanning the shallow clear water with its tail and fins.

"Well, I was crying and couldn't hardly see nothing, and I stepped down to the edge of the Rill and that huge Trout didn't try to flee or thrash; it just quietly stirred the water whilst I gently took the hook out of its mouth and loosed it. And it seemed to pause awhile, then it slowly swam away.

"But even though I was having trouble seeing through my tears, I know one thing for certain: *that Trout had taken an empty line, for there weren't no bait on Granther's hook!*

"You see, not only had that great fish saved my granther from dying of a heartbreak, it had also let him complete his vow.

"But I figured most of that out as I walked home to fetch my dam. And once it came clear as that's what it was all about, I just seemed to feel better. Though the sadness was still and will always be in my heart over that old, old Warrow's death, I stopped crying."

The Gammer paused in quiet reflection, then said after a moment: "So you see, Dilbs, that ain't no ordinary fish, whether or not it's even the same one. 'Cause the Rillmix Trout has always been. And it won't be caught less'n it wants to be."

Dilby slowly drew his hook out of the pool and thoughtfully wrapped the line around the pole, wedging the barb into the cork bobber. And he made a vow he was to keep all his days: "Granther, I don't think I'll fish for the Rillmix Trout ever again."

But his granther didn't answer him. And Dilby looked

around, and the ancient Warrow's chin was down on his chest; his smoldering pipe had nearly dropped from his slack fingers.

Dilby's heart gave a lurch; but then he saw that the old, old buccan's chest was slowly rising and falling as he slept.

Dilby quietly came up the bank and eased the briar from the Gammer's lax grip. And as he took the pipe, Dilby didn't see before him a fragile, beloved, precious old Warrow; rather he looked beyond the nearly transparent flesh and white locks, and saw instead an eleven-year-old youngling trudging forlornly homeward to fetch his dam and tell her that Granther was dead.

And in the One-Eyed Crow, Dilby looked across the circle at Gaffer Tom through eyes blurred with tears and thought of his own granther, then stood and stepped to the window, and stared without seeing out into the hurtling snow.

The
Ruffian and
the Giant

By jing, Delber, 'tis too true!" declared Rolly, slapping his hand down upon the table, causing mugs of beer to jump and foam to slosh down the sides.

" 'Tisn't," responded Delber Wigge obstinately, his jaw jutted out, as he ran his finger up the side of his mug, catching the spilt foam before it got to the tabletop, then licking his wetted digit.

Nettled by Delber's stubbornness, Rolly puffed sharp and fast upon his pipe, wreathing his head with smoke. Then he jabbed the stem toward the other Warrow to emphasize his point and just as obdurately said, "Wull, I says there's Giants in the Land, and no matter what you say, it don't change the facts none."

"Oiyo, would you listen to him, now," Delber appealed to the other Warrows crowded about in the One-Eyed Crow. "Says *I* won't change the facts none. Well, let me tell you, Mister Rolly Biddle, facts is facts, and the *fact* is, there isn't no such thing as Giants, no matter what old dammen's tales you've been led to believe."

At that, both Warrows jumped up with their fists clenched, and it would have come to a couple of blows being thrown, and perhaps even a black eye or two, except Will Brackleburr, proprietor, stepped between the two.

"Hold on now, you fighting cocks. Sheathe your spurs!

"You, Delber, get your outthrust chin back into your

face. And you, Rolly, with that pout you're liable to step on your own lower lip."

Will put a hand on each of their shoulders and gently but firmly pressed them back into their seats. "Hoy, now, you've been friends since you both were wee buccos"— Delber huffed in disgust and turned his face sideways, and Rolly sniffed and scootched his chair about till his back was completely to the table—"and it'd be a shame to come to blows over such a thing as to whether or not there are great Giants hulking in the woods or mountains."

" 'Tis," snapped Rolly.

" 'Tisn't," snorted Delber.

"But I'll tell you this"—Will Brackleburr's voice cut through the renewed argument—"if anyone in the 'Dells knows the which of it, it's Gaffer Tom."

Will's pronouncement brought nods from the small crowd of Warrows in the 'Crow, and a few voices called out, *Hear! Hear!* and *The old Gaffer'd know, right enough!* And so Will's bucco, Alban, was sent running to fetch the Gaffer from his room, where he'd got to midmorn after breakfast, if he'd come, to settle this most important question.

The 'Crow was abuzz with speculation as to which way the Gaffer would come down on this vital issue. And through all the waiting, Delber glared sideways at the wall, while Rolly grumpily sat with his back to the table, a bit to his discomfort, for he couldn't reach his beer without turning around, and he certainly *wasn't* going to do *that.*

And outside the blizzard continued to rattle the roof and shake the walls and moan down the chimney of the fireplace, snow hurtling across the Land.

Finally, after what seemed an eternity, Alban came walking slowly with the old Gaffer as that venerable Warrow hobbled down the steps, supported by his gnarled blackwood cane. Silence reigned among the blizzard-trapped Warrows as the Gaffer was helped down the last step and into the common room, but many called out greetings as he thumped his way to his favorite chair by the window, where Will had waiting for him a mug of his favorite black ale.

Slowly he sat down, and while he filled his briar with Downdell leaf, he peered about the room to see just who was there. Finally, lighting up and taking a puff or two, he swallowed a slurp of ale, thumped his cane on the floor, and asked in his thin, reedy voice, "Now what's all this question about Giants?"

Well every Warrow there began talking all at once, including Rolly and Delber, and of course no sense at all could be made of it, especially when the original two arguers began yelling and shouting to be heard above one another, and again it would have come to blows, except with amazing energy the old Gaffer whacked the flat of his cane down on the tabletop, and the earsplitting *CRACK!* cut off the roar and babble of the unruly mob.

In the silence that followed, the Gaffer jabbed a forefinger at one in the crowd and snapped, "You! Speak for all these yammering ninnyhammers. Answer my question . . . and all you others, button your lips! Now, what's all this about Giants?"

Hob Alder, the singled-out Warrow, painfully aware that the tilted, glittering eyes of all the other Warrows were upon him, flushed and stammered and finally blurted out: "W-w-well, *harrumph,* well, Rolly here says that there *are* Giants"—Rolly rapidly nodded his head *Yes* while Delber shook his *No*—"and Delber here says there *aren't*"—Delber now bobbed his head up and down while Rolly indicated *Nay*—"and you, sir, well, uh, we all thought as you could settle it once and for good." And as Hob spluttered to a stop, *all* heads joggled up and down.

With excruciating deliberateness the old Gaffer puffed on his pipe and looked at the snow racing past the inn windows, his eyes following the hurtling stream, as if attempting to track the route of the howling blow down the coombe from Hollow End past the Commons and across the bridge above the Dingle-Rill and out over the fields and beyond the High Hill to Brackenboro and Thimble and through the Thornring at distant Tine Ford, perhaps even raging across Trellinath and Gûnar and Jugo and unto the very Avagon Sea itself a thousand miles away, the old Warrow seeming to speculate upon the blizzard's full shrieking path, though clearly he couldn't see beyond a foot or so through the whiteness. And while the Gaffer sat thus, not a word was said by any, and nary a soul moved.

"Wull," he finally said, "let me tell you a true story. It's the tale of the Ruffian and the Giant."

A murmur washed throughout the listeners, and Rolly puffed up and cast a meaningful look at Delber. "See! I told you!" crowed Rolly. "This is a *true* story about a *Giant*!" Delber's face went glum, and they all fell silent as the Gaffer began:

"Bring to mind Mid-Year's Day, the time of the festivals and the fairs, especially the one at Rood. Recall, leading up to that grand finalé, each village and hamlet holds a town fair, and nearby Warrows come bringing a prize chicken or lamb or pie or piece of stitchery or hundreds of other polished, groomed, or otherwise 'specially set-out or fixed-up kind of cookery, creature, or doodad. O' course, all the prize winners go on to the big Fair in the fields at Rood, there in Centerdell, where they are judged all over again. And the winners there are the top dogs of the Seven Dells for an entire year, till the next Mid-Year Day.

"Well, not too many years past, in the little Northdell town of Needle, there along Two Fords Road, up near Spindle Ford, they was holdin' the preliminary judgings for the nearby farmers and their dammen, and for the townsfolk, too. They had a parade, and the cows, chickens, sheep, ponies, dogs, and other creatures was marched down the main street, which was the only street, headin' for the judging field. Behind came all the pretty dammsels, blushing and twittering, vying to be Maid of the Fair. Behind them came the big paper and cloth figures, held up on poles: figures of a huge chicken, whose wings actually flapped; of a big, ugly Giant; and a great snake whose tail had somehow fallen off, so as it looked like an unfortunate reptile what had been run over by a pony cart. And behind came the younglings, got up as Elves and Dwarves and other *Outsiders*. And in back of the entire procession came Aberdy's beer waggon, what with the wheels papered all in rainbow colors. It seems as if they wasn't nobody standin' on the street *watchin'* this parade 'cause everybody was *in* it! But that didn't stop them none, though, and it went off as scheduled.

"As you can imagine, it took all day to pick out the prize winners; but after they was named and the fair declared officially over, there was some disappointed losers, though everybody had fun.

"This year, three temporary Thornwalkers was the most disappointed: Hanlo, Harlo, and Hadlo Higgs—they was the ones what had entered the great paper snake in the parade and contest, but, due to its tail falling off, they had lost ... the flapping-winged chicken was the winner and was going on to the Centerdell Fair at Rood.

"Now, the reason as that trio was most disappointed was, being as how the Higgs brothers was temporary Thornwalkers, losing meant that they would have to return to their task of patrolling the Boskydell boundaries up there in Northdell, instead of getting to go to the big Fair like everybody else. You see, had they won, they could have got special permission from the Northdell Captain to take the snake to the big Fair, and substitutes would have come to walk the Thorns in their steads. But the tail fell off and they lost, and so it didn't come to that.

"So, disappointed, they went back to Thornwalking, checking for unsavory *Outsiders* coming into the Dells, it being twenty-two years back in those unsettled times when bothersome *Big Men*, up to no good, occasionally came into the Bosky. Oh, not that all *Outsiders* are unsavory: just like apples and crackers and every other thing, they's good uns and bad uns in every barrel.

"Anyhow, times being what they were, the Thornwalkers had taken on some temporary help, those as was to walk the Thorns till they could get some training in how to shoot arrows from a bow. And the Higgs buccos was three what had signed on to do Thornwalker duty in those unsettled days, and although they wouldn't get their training till late summer, still they was put to duty patrolling in an out-of-the-way place.

"A week after the local fair, 'most everybody in the Dell went down to Rood so as not to miss the opening of the big one, but the three Higgses was patrolling and bemoaning the fact that they hadn't got to go. The Sun had just set when they espied a campfire in the woods and they went to investigate.

"Well, they came upon the camp of a regular Ruffian. Big he was, and a Man, and mean. He'd built a great lean-to, and it looked as if he was thinking on moving in permanent-like. And they found that he was skinning one of the Ferrises' missing lambs, they knowed it was so 'cause Will Ferris was the only one what raised pure black sheep in the surrounding area, and some had been disappearing.

"When they confronted the Ruffian with the fact, he just sneered something about them as was the strongest, got, and them as was the weakest, git! And with that, quick as a bear, he buffeted them each a hard thump, and then threw Hanlo Higgs through the air out of the camp. He would have thrown Harlo and Hadlo, too, but they was already gone by the time he whirled back toward where they had been.

"The Higgses ran hard till they got far away from the Ruffian, then stopped to examine their wounds. Amazingly, Hanlo, who was throwed, was no worse for the wear, but it looked as if Harlo would have a black eye, and Hadlo's nose was bleeding.

" 'That big bully,' said Hanlo, 'I'd like to throw *him* into the woods so's *he* can see how it feels.'

" 'But . . . *sniff* . . . you aren't even . . . *sniff* . . . hurt'— Hadlo sniffed to stop the flow of blood, and dabbed with his kerchief, too—'whereas I'm near to mortally . . . *sniff* . . . wounded: blood all over . . . *sniff.*'

" 'What're we going to do?' asked Harlo, gingerly probing his eye with a forefinger. 'I mean, everybody's gone to the Rood Fair, so's we've not got no help we can call on. And them what can use a bow and arrow are patrolling near Spindle Ford. And if that Ruffian isn't routed out soon, well, the Ferrises aren't going to have no sheep left in their flock!'

" 'If . . . *sniff* . . . we'd only won that contest . . . *sniff* . . . we'd've been down at the Fair with our snake, and . . . *sniff* . . . someone else would have had to deal with this . . . *sniff* . . . Ruffian.' Hadlo tried to look at his own nose, but only succeeded in crossing his eyes.

" 'Hey!' exclaimed Hanlo. 'That's a good idea!'

" 'What? What?' quacked Harlo, forgetting his tender eye. 'What's a good idea?'

" 'Why, what Hadlo said is a good idea,' replied Hanlo.

" '*Sniff?*' questioned Hadlo, not knowing what it was that he'd said as was so brilliant.

" 'About the snake!' snapped Hanlo, exasperated by the blank looks upon the faces of his brothers. 'We'll just go get the snake, and in the night and by the light of his campfire we'll come upon him unawares, and the snake will scare him off, what with its fierce looks.'

" 'But . . . *sniff* . . . the snake is all tattered . . . *sniff* . . . totally unconvincing: it's not got no tail!' sniffed and bemoaned Hadlo. 'How about the great chicken . . . *sniff* . . . with the flapping wings?'

" 'Arrg! Who'd be afraid of a big chicken?' snorted Hanlo, frustrated because neither of his brothers seemed to be aware of the subtleties of what was needed here. " 'Sides, it's off to the big Fair.

" 'But you're right about the snake, Hadlo: without its tail, it's totally unconvincing.'

"Hanlo fell into deep thought, and Harlo and Hadlo stood by silently, one sniffing, the other probing his eye, letting their elder brother think. After all, Hanlo had always been the brains of the three.

"After a moment: 'Hoy! If the snake's out, and the chicken is out, then we'll just have to use that great Giant what Teddy Umber made,' declared Hanlo. 'Here's what we'll do: You, Hadlo'—*sniff?*—'take your knife and make a tall pair of stilts out of saplings, say, ten or twelve feet high—that ought to do quite well—while me and Harlo run and get the big paper head and the Giant's cloak. We'll meet you right here as quick as we can get to Teddy's cote and back with the things.' Then Hanlo paused and said, 'Oh, won't that bully boy Ruffian be in for a big surprise, though?' "

The Gaffer stopped long enough to take a swill of black ale to wet his throat, and to look around at his rapt audience. Then he continued:

* * *

"Now, there's some as said afterwards that it were a tom-fool plan, and some as said it weren't, but that ain't the point. The *point* is, the Higgs brothers was fulfilling their oaths as Thornwalkers, temporary though they might be, doing their level best to rid the Boskydells of unsavory folk; how they was trying to do it might have been less than brilliant, but at least they was a-trying. You see, you got to remember, at this time they hadn't got no training in the use of arms, so they just couldn't quill that Ruffian with arrows. So they was left to using what wits they had, to get the job done and all.

" 'Tweren't no more than an hour or so before Hanlo and Harlo came lugging that great ugly paper head and the Giant's cloak, but Hadlo wasn't to be found nowhere with the stilts. And so they waited and wondered, hissing out his name in the dark—'Hadlo! Hadlo!'—quietlike, not wanting the Ruffian to hear them and come to investigate.

"And a thin sliver of a Moon, no more'n a fingernail's width, was still up over the trees, lighting the 'scape with feeble rays, just barely enough to see by.

"Finally, after a bit, Hadlo comes dragging not only the stilts, but also a tremendous large, knobby club with a spike driven through one end.

"Before the others could berate him for being late, Hadlo said, 'Sorry I wasn'd here, bud I'b habig trouble breeding. You see, da bleedig has stobbed, bud dow, by doze is all stubbed ub.'

" 'What? What'd he say?' asked Harlo, squinting out of only one eye, the other now puffed shut from the thump the Ruffian had given him.

" 'Does having a bashed-closed eye shut off your hearing, too?' snapped Hanlo, his voice querulous, irritated. 'He said he's having trouble breathing 'cause his nose is stuffed up.'

" 'Oh.' Harlo peered out of his one good eye at Hadlo's nose. Then he looked at the stilts and the big Giant's club and said, 'Well, nose or not, it looks as if you've done something right. These stilts look useable, and the club is just the kind of weapon a Giant would use.'

" 'Thags, Harlo,' answered Hadlo, 'bud I odlee back the sdilds; da club I fowd id da woods.'

" 'What? What'd he say?' asked Harlo, squinting toward Hanlo for a translation.

" 'Never mind!' snapped Hanlo impatiently, champing at the bit. 'We've got to get the Ruffian! Let's go!'

"So, they crept up to the Ruffian's campsite, carrying the Giant's outfit and stilts and club, and you all know that when a Warrow is trying to creep silently, there ain't nothing as can move quieter, not even an Elf.

"In the wan moonlight they slipped through the trees and night shadows, only to find the Ruffian asleep by his low-burning fire.

"Then it at last came time to choose which one would get on the stilts and put on the Giant's outfit ... something none of them had thought of until then, but now one of 'em would have to be it.

" 'Dod bee,' whispered Hadlo. 'By doze woad led bee be da Giad. Wid diz doze, whad coud I say dad wood frided hib?'

" 'What? What did he say?' breathed Harlo, again squinting with his one good eye at Hanlo for a translation.

" 'He said,' hissed Hanlo, ' "Dod bee," er, I mean, "Not me. My nose won't let me be the Giant. With this nose, what could I say that would frighten him?" And he's right, Harlo. It's got to be you or me.'

" 'Well it can't be me,' whispered Harlo. 'With this eye, how could I see what to say?'

"And so, as if that made sense, by default Hanlo was picked to be the Giant, and perhaps that's justice, 'cause it was really his idea in the first place to dress up and scare the Ruffian.

"Thus it was that right there, only a pace or two from the sleeping Ruffian's fire, they leant the great spiked club against a tree, which Hanlo then climbed. They passed up to him the big, ugly paper head, which he put on, and the Giant's cloak, which he draped over his shoulders and it hung to the ground.

"And with Hadlo and Harlo each hiding under the skirt of the cloak, standing and bracing the stilts, Hanlo mounted up. He teetered a bit, but his brothers each held a stilt steady, and then all was ready.

" 'Hoom, ha!' Hanlo roared, his voice sounding all hollow in the big, ugly paper head as he made a noise to waken the Ruffian so as to produce the effect of scaring him off. And after a couple more *Hoom-ha*'s, the Ruffian wakes up and rolls over and sees in the flickering shadows this thirteen- or fourteen-foot-high ugly being standing there with a big spiked club leaning at hand against a tree.

"When Hanlo saw that the Ruffian was awake, he then cried out the only Giantish thing he could think of to frighten the big Man in that moment of stress, for you see, once again the brothers' planning hadn't been all that complete, and no one had figured beforehand just what they should say to scare the Ruffian. So, Hanlo was on his own, and what he said, well, unfortunately, it wasn't very bright, yet it was the only thing he knew of what a Giant was supposed to say to its intended victims. And so it was that from a child's hearthtale he took his text and said, or rather, he screamed at the Ruffian:

> *'Fee! Fum! Fie!*
> *I'll grind your bones to make a pie!'*

"And again Hanlo's shouting voice was all hollow, and he couldn't hardly hear nothing 'cause being got up like he was and yelling as loud as he could was just like sticking a bucket over your head and screaming at the top of your lungs; about the only thing you'll hear for the next three or four days is a steady ringing.

"Well, the Ruffian wasn't quite convinced that he was seeing a real Giant there in the wavering light of his campfire, though he wasn't quite sure just what this tall, ugly, narrow-shouldered, shrill-voiced thing was. But since its weapon, the big spiked club, was not actually in its hand, instead leaning 'gainst the tree as it was, well, the big Man made a grab for his own bow and quiver.

"Hanlo saw this and turned to flee, forgetting that he was on top of twelve-foot-high stilts.

"At the same time, Hadlo couldn't stifle a sneeze what

had been working on his stuffed-up nose ever since he had got under the Giant's linen cloak, and he let fly with a brain-jarring blast, jolting the right-leg stilt forward, wrenching it out from under fleeing Hanlo above.

"Harlo lost his own grip on the twisting left-leg stilt, and since Hanlo's weight was now all upon the left leg alone, the foot peg over there broke off, and Hanlo, ugly paper head and all, fell forward with a shriek.

"The big Man looked up from his fumbling with the arrow to see this shrieking apparition falling forward over the fire and down upon him, a monster rushing down at him to squash him. The Ruffian thought that he was being attacked for grabbing at his bow, and he jumped up screaming out that he didn't want to be no pie and ran off toward Spindle Ford and the road out of the Bosky.

"And the three Higgs brothers? Well, they got Hanlo out of the twisted-up cloth and the paper head fairly quickly so he was only a bit scorched by the fire, but they couldn't save Teddy Umber's Giant from burning all up.

"Nothing else was damaged, except Harlo, whose other eye got whacked by the stilt in the crash.

"So there they was, after it was all over, sittin' 'round the now gone Ruffian's fire: one with his nose stopped up, one with both eyes swelled shut, and one with his ears ringing loudly.

"And in their capacity as temporary Thornwalkers, the three Higgs brothers confiscated the goods what the Man had left behind in his rush to get away from the Giant. And as they sifted through the abandoned backpack, seein' what they could give to Will Ferris as payment for his killed sheep, they found thumb screws and a blood-stained iron-tipped scourge and a stranglin' cord and other tools of villainy. And the one with the broken nose *tch, tch*ed over these foul implements, commenting at great length concernin' the evil of such things; but he talked so poorly as he couldn't be understood by the one as couldn't see; and the one as couldn't hear wasn't able to translate for him 'cause he didn't know what was bein' said.

"It was what might be called a case of 'speak no evil, see no evil, hear no evil!' "

* * *

Gaffer Tom leaned back in his chair and cackled with laughter, and he was joined by all the other Warrows in the 'Crow, mirth ringing forth. Long they laughed and loud, each pointing at one another and bursting out afresh. Yet at last the babble died away, Warrows wiping tears of glee from their eyes.

When quiet returned, Delber asked, "Gaffer, when you started this tale you said that it was a true story. Well, are you certain that it's a fact?"

"Oh, bucco, it's true as can be," averred the old Gaffer. "You see, the three Higgs brothers was my twice-removed nephews on my dammia's side, and all of 'em, to this day, swear that it really happened. And knowin' them tomfools as well as I do, well, I for one believe them."

"Ha then!" crowed Delber, turning in triumph toward Rolly. "There you have it, Rolly Giant-believer. I mean, *this* is the way that Giant stories get started. That Ruffian, no doubt, ran off to the Big Folk, *Outside,* and he told his cronies, who then told their cronies, and so on, about this ferocious Giant what attacked him in the night."

Rolly looked crestfallen, the wind taken out of his sails, for it seemed as if the old Gaffer had put the lie to Giant tales, and Rolly felt the fool for ever having believed them in the first place.

But then the Gaffer leaned back again in his chair and fixed a gimlet eye upon the beaming, victorious Delber. "Hold on there, whippersnapper," Gaffer Tom called. "Just what makes you think there ain't Giants about in the Land?"

"Wha-what?" stammered Delber, feeling as if he'd been struck in the stomach, shooting a glance at Rolly, who had perked up. "Why, whatever do you mean, Gaffer?"

"Just this, bucco," answered the old Gaffer. "If there ain't no Giants about, *just who or what do you think owned that big spiked club Hadlo found in the woods?*"

The silence in the One-Eyed Crow was deafening.

And no one heard a thing in the roaring, yelling arguments that followed.

Agron's Army

"Hoy now, Will," called out Teddy, "wot be y'r favorite story?"

Will Brackleburr, proprietor of the One-Eyed Crow, stopped polishing the pewter mug he held and stood a moment in thought, while outside the frigid wind continued to hammer the clapboards. "Ar, Teddy, I reckon it'd be the glorious tale of Agron's Army, and how they met the Rūcks and such in the grim grasp of the Gwasp."

"Ooo now," responded Teddy, turning to his visiting cousin, "that do be a grand and glorious tale. Have you ever heard it, Billy?"

"Long agone, Teddy," answered Billy Cloverhay, placing his empty mug down on the bar, motioning for a refill. "Aye. Long agone: back when I was a youngling. But I wouldn't mind hearing it again, though."

Other Warrows crowded about, watching as Will drew another ale for Billy, some also placing their empty mugs before Will, each buccan there anticipating the telling of that familiar story.

As soon as Will saw to it that all mugs were filled to the brim, the buccan set aside his towel and drew a schooner of ale for himself. Taking a sip of the golden-brown liquid, as if to wet his throat, Will began; and silence fell upon the Warrows within, though without, the blizzard raged and hammered at the Dell.

* * *

"Back in the elden times, back in the days of the Ban War some four thousand years past, far to the north in the Angle of Gron, that vile Land trapped 'tween the Gronfangs and the Rigga, there in a cold iron tower standing on the far edge of Claw Moor yet dwelled a most foul Wizard named Modru." A stir shivered through the Warrows at this naming of the Evil One, but quickly died as Will spoke on:

"And into this wicked Realm rode a mighty band of warriors, set to throw Modru down: 'twas King Agron and his army, champions all, mounted upon mighty steeds, clad in shiny armor and bearing bright shields, sharp sabers at their sides and lances bristling into the air, the spears tied with splendid pennons crackling in the wind.

"And Modru and his minions quaked before this Host come to conquer them. . . ."

Gnasha hobbled down the stone hallway, the scales of his armor chanking one upon the other, heading for his Master's quarters. The Hlōk did not wish to speak to Lord Modru, especially bearing news that would send the Master into a frenzy of rage, yet he had little choice in the matter.

And so, onward hobbled the tall goblin, limping toward a dark door warded by two others of his kind—Hlōks: Man-sized, bat-wing-eared, sharp pointed teeth set in a wide-gapped mouth, yellow snake-like eyes, dark-skinned; the two guards armored in leather sewn with brass scales, armed with tulwars.

As Gnasha neared, the Hlōk warders drew themselves up into a semblance of alertness, their shifty eyes glancing at the oncoming commander, as if readying for attack or flight. At his snarl they cowed to one side, and Gnasha raised the iron knocker and let it fall against the metal doorplate, once—*Tok!*—the sound muffled, as if swallowed by the pools of gloom clustered in the angles of the stone hallway.

Long Gnasha stood waiting, in vain it seemed, yet at last the door swung open, revealing a shadowy chamber within, and a mute Rūck, one whose tongue had been torn out, slavishly bobbed and weaved and scraped, the four-foot-tall goblin-like being cringing back, motioning the commander inward.

Gnasha stepped into the room. Behind, the door thudded to, the mute Rūck scuttling somewhere out of sight, and fear coursed through the Hlōk, for now he was trapped in the lair of his Master.

Within, a great stone fireplace stood at one end, and rudden flames consumed a dark wood, casting writhing shadows throughout the chamber. Yet though the fire burned, it created no warmth and little light, and a chill silence filled the very air.

To one side stood a massive black stone throne, draped in ebon velvet, and a great darkness clotted thereupon. And Gnasha hobbled past a huge table set with an iron service for thirteen, and he fell to his face before the vile shadow upon the throne.

How long he lay thus he could not say, yet at last a sibilant whisper came hissing through the darkness: "Ah, good Gnasha, what brings my moor commander before me?"

"Lord Modru"—Gnasha raised his head just enough to speak clearly—"the outrunners report that a great army has marched forth from the Gronfangs, just south of Claw Gap, an army of Men and Elves." Gnasha swallowed, his throat dry with terror, for he feared to say his next words, yet he knew the penalty to do otherwise. "Master, they bear the standards of . . . of Agron."

"*What!*" Modru's voice lashed out, blackness rushing forth, and Gnasha cringed against the stone, hiding his eyes, expecting death or worse for bearing this news to his Master. Words hissed forth from the shadows: "You imbecile, that cannot be! I *destroyed* Agron and all the fools that came with him!"

Now the vileness clotted upon the throne once more. "Meddling Agron and his host marched into *my* domain, in *my* season, and the blizzard *I* sent slew them, there among the frozen peaks of the Gronfangs . . ." —The darkness began to expand, until it filled the room entire— ". . . Their agony was exquisite."

A long silence filled the chamber, yet trembling

Gnasha did not look up. At last he said, "Aye, Master, your magnificent victory was total." Here Gnasha paused, trying but failing to swallow past a throat choked with fear, for he did not dare contradict his Master. *The scouts. Blame it on the scouts.* "Yet, my Lord Modru, the outrunners report that it *is* the banner of Agron, and they march forth from the Gronfangs, from nigh the place of their slaying, yet why they would wait till summer to do so—"

"Pah! A trick!" hissed Modru. "They were winter killed!"

Gnasha said nought, for he knew that his life hung by a slender twisting thread.

"Take the Moor Swarm and run down this false Agron's Army," came the command at last. "Slay them all! . . .

"And kill the messenger who brought this news."

Gnasha felt the wings of Death pass above him, and he scrabbled backwards without raising his face, his voice still distorted by terror. "Yes, my Lord Modru. At once. Slay them all."

As he rose up and turned to flee, one more command issued forth from the darkness behind him: "And take my eyes with you!"

Gnasha shuddered, his very guts roiling with the fear of doing so, yet he would obey this last command as well.

In moments the stone walls of the dark bastion were ringing with the brazen tolling of the alarm gong and the raucous blatting of Spawnish assembly horns . . . and within an hour a great clattering Rūcken Horde jogtrotted out across the iron drawbridge above the deep be-ringing chasm and onto the flats of Claw Moor, drums beating out a forced-march pace, squad leaders lashing out with whips, striking any who appeared to be lagging, the Swarm boiling southward through the bleak Land. . . .

Will's voice held them all spellbound: "Down into the wicked Realm they went, Agron and his glittering Host, riding their mighty steeds north toward Claw Moor, toward Modru's cold iron tower."

Again at the naming of Modru, Warrows glanced at one

another, some looking over their shoulders. And still the blizzard hammered upon the walls of the One-Eyed Crow.

"League upon league they rode across that foul countryside," continued the innkeeper, "through long days and short nights, for it was midsummer, and the Sun rode high in the sky. And as they neared the Gwasp, that dreadful swamp of Gron, they espied one of Modru's Swarms and took up the chase. For the Horde was sore afraid of Agron's might, and fled before him and his Host.

"A day and a night and another day they ran—"

"Hoy now, Will," protested Nob, thunking his mug to the bar, interrupting the story, "how could the Rūcks and such run through the daylight; I mean, what with the Ban and all—"

"Hold up there, Nob," interjected Will, raising a hand, palm out, stopping Nob's words, stopping as well a mutter of agreement rumbling up from other Warrows. "What you are forgetting, buccos, is that this was back in the time of the Great War, back before there *was* a Ban, back before Adon set His restriction upon the Foul Folk. You see, in those days the Rūcks and such could walk about in the daylight just as freely as you or I, though it is told that even then they preferred the black of night for doing their foul deeds."

Warrows nodded to one another, and Nob, satisfied, motioned for Will to continue his tale.

"*Harrumph.* Now, where was I? Oh, yes. . . . Agron and his mighty Host chased them up against the Gwasp, and still the cowardly Horde ran. Even though they had the Free Folk outnumbered ten to one, they ran. Into that mire. Into the very clutches of the morass. . . ."

Gnasha had the vacant-eyed, slack-jawed idiot brought to him. Spittle drooled from the corner of the Man's mouth, and he had soiled his breeks, the stench of excrement floating in a miasma about him. Even so, the aides treated the Human with great respect, gently easing him down from his horse.

"Clean him," snarled the moor commander impatiently; and Rūcks scrambled to do Gnasha's bidding, stripping the imbecile's clothing from him, bringing scented soap and water and washcloths and towels unto him and carefully washing his legs and buttocks and privates.

When they had cleansed the idiot and toweled him dry, and had dressed him in fresh stockings and breeks and boots, Gnasha had them lead the mindless fool unto an observation point along a ridge located several leagues south of Claw Gap. To the east could be seen the peaks of the Gronfang Mountains; to the west in the far distance loomed the curving spine of Claw Spur, while closer in, the turgid waters of the Gap River moved sluggishly southward; and in the distant south, partially hidden by a grasping haze, lay the green clutch of the Gwasp, the far borders of the mighty swamp beyond seeing.

Yet it was not these things that captured Gnasha's eye. Instead, southerly, far off, moving across the Land like a vast, silent ghost, noiseless in the distance marched a glittering Host: Agron's Army.

Turning to the vacant-eyed idiot, *"Gulgok!"* spake Gnasha, and watched in horror as the mindless fool's eyes *filled* with an evil presence.

Long moments passed as the vile being glared at the distant foe, watching the sparkling array march southwesterly.

"So, it is true," came the voice of darkness. "Somehow, Fool Agron and his ragtag Legion avoided dying in my Hèl-sent blizzard." Gnasha could hear destruction in the *thing's* voice, and he stood very still, hoping to avoid all notice. "What report the outrunners?"

"My Dread Lord, they say that the course of the army varies not," responded Gnasha. "They make for the Gwasp. Too, there is something strange: Agron's Host leaves no tracks!"

"That they run toward the Gwasp surprises me not" came the vile voice. "They seek to evade my wrath, and hope to escape me in the swamp. But fear not, my dear Gnasha, for *my* Horde shall seek them out wherever they flee; *you* will attend to that.

"But this *tracklessness* of theirs . . . —Take me closer that I may see for myself."

And suddenly the vile intelligence *emptied* from the

Man's face, and once more a drooling imbecile stood beside the shuddering Hlōk.

"Fools! Blind fools!" raged the hideous voice in the dawn. "Of course there are no tracks!" The Man raised his hand and pointed. "Look, fool, and learn."

Gnasha's eyes followed the outstretched arm, and there in the dim morning light, trailing Agron's Host, strode someone who wore no armor and bore no arms, one who carried nought but a walking staff. A Man he seemed, or perhaps an Elf, and he was dressed in grey robes and grey cloak. His hair was long and silver, and his skin fair. Nothing else could be told of this strider, for the distance was still too great, though Gnasha and the Man beside him were now within easy sight of the Legion, Agron's Army no more than an arrow-cast below. In silence the grey one marched behind the glittering array, pausing every now and again to make arcane gestures at the earth and at the Host going noiselessly before him.

"Master," whispered the Hlōk, his voice choked with fear of retribution, "I do not understand."

"Pah! Fool! It is Dalavar!" The words lashed out from the surrogate. "And somewhere nearby will slink his curs: the Draega, the Silver Wolves."

"But my Lord Modru," asked Gnasha, needing to know despite his fear of directing his Master's ire at himself, "what is it that this grey one does?"

"That which I would do were I in his place," hissed the response. "The fool thinks to escape me by using his art to conceal the passage of this Host: he erases the tracks; he strangles the sound of their march. Unheard, they pass across the Land, their steps eradicated even as they are made.

"Yet he is weak in his power, for were it *mine* to do, then I would make mine Swarm unseen as well.

"Hah! But Dalavar has not my power to deceive the eye, and so he does only that which his simple art can manage.

"But I will *not* cast invisibility upon my Moor Horde, for I want Dalavar and Agron to see their death rushing at their heels, running them to earth, even if they *do* flee into the Gwasp."

At mention of the great swamp, Gnasha glanced up to see it, the near edge of the vast mire no more than two leagues distant. The Hlōk shuddered, for he did not wish to go therein, for it was said that the Gwasp contained ancient evils beyond the power of *anyone* to control, even beyond the power of his own Lord and Master.

"It is time, Gnasha, to show my Horde to these interlopers, to put the fear into them, to rout them in panic, to run them down and crush them," hissed the 'surrogate. "Sound the horns. Beat the drums. Let them know that we pursue, and that they are soon to be slaughtered."

Gnasha turned down the slope to give the signal to the waiting Swarm behind, but ere he could do so, one more command hissed forth from the mouth of the surrogate ere the face emptied, ere the vile malignancy was gone: "The outrunners, those who scouted these interlopers, see that they are put to slow, agonizing death, for they did not report to me that Fool Dalavar was within the foe's ranks."

Will Brackleburr paused long enough to refill the mugs of the Warrows gathered about, their eyes wide with the wonder of a great shining army chasing foul Rūcks, Hlōks, Ogrus, Ghûls, and who knows what else into a great steaming swamp, the heroic Men and Elves with glittering swords and sparkling shields and burnished armor mounted upon racing chargers thundering down upon a cowardly fleeing Swarm ten times their size, the frightened Horde scrambling to get away.

"Well now," said Will, taking a pull from his own mug, setting it down upon the bar, "when they ran the Foul Folk into the swamp, Agron and his Men, and the Elves what were with him, they took their swords in hand and dismounted and led their horses and such through the sucking mire, giving chase, vapor rising up all about them, it being the middle of summer and all, the air thick and hot . . ."

Sweat runnelled down Gnasha's face, stinging his eyes, dripping from his nose, leaking down his neck and under his armor, joining the seep ebbing beneath the sodden underpadding galling his body. A buzzing cloud of gnats and mosquitos, biting flies, and other blood-mad insects swirled about his face and swarmed upon any exposed flesh, crawling into eye and mouth and ear, biting, puncturing, stinging, sucking. Muttering and cursing, swiping and swatting and slapping, Gnasha sloshed onward through the mire. All about, grey moss dangled from gnarled trees twisting up out of the muck, the long tendrils reaching down, clutching, as if to strangle any who fell victim to their grasp, and a vaporous steam rose up from the morass, and foul-smelling gases bubbled forth from the slimy quag sucking at his boots. Leeches clung unto him, bloating themselves with his dark blood, their swollen bodies dropping off as they became sated. To each side and behind, the Horde struggled through the suck, arms and armor clattering and clacking, the drums and horns now silent, for Gnasha did not wish to drive the ones they pursued any deeper into these foul environs. Yet deeper they went, and Gnasha followed, for to do aught else would lead to disaster.

They had obeyed their Master's orders, sounding drum and horn, clattering up and over the hill and onto the track of the Legion before them. And they had pursued in the early daylight, seeking to close the gap between themselves and the Men and Elves; and they had gained some ground, though precious little, yet by midmorn Agron's Army had reached the marges of the Gwasp and had disappeared therein.

And now Gnasha and the Swarm gave chase into that dire swamp, pursuing the elusive foe, following the faint belling of an Elven horn, or perhaps the ringing of one of the black-oxen horns of the Men, sounding just above the clack and slosh and splash of the Horde.

The day had fled, the Sun riding up and over the morass, bringing its blazing heat to bear down upon the vast mire, causing it to bubble and belch and heave, filling the air with suffocating stench.

More hours had passed, the Horde slogging through the muck, and now the eventide drew near, and Gnasha's worst fear seemed inevitable: they would be trapped in the Gwasp when night fell. Yet he dared not violate his Master's command, and so continued to pursue.

And at last they caught up with the enemy, at swamp's core, the Host of Agron standing in silence in the midst of a vast black watery slough.

A great shout of victory rose up from the Horde, for although it seemed that Agron had finally turned to fight, the Swarm outnumbered the Legion ten to one.

At Gnasha's exultant shout, drums thundered and horns blatted—though no response came from the Men and Elves, standing in their eerie silence—and the command to attack was given.

The Swarm charged forward, splashing through the knee-deep ebon waters, a wordless howl yawling forth from ten thousand Rūcken throats, tulwars and cudgels and scimitars and war hammers raised to strike, barbed spears set to hurl, black-shafted arrows hissing forth, dhals and sipars held to deflect return arrows, though there were none.

And closer and closer the Horde came, and the Men and Elves shifted not, but stood in silence and waited.

And Gnasha grew frightened and blew his horn, but the Horde was beyond recall.

And just as the first ranks reached the phalanx of the Men and Elves ...

... Agron's Army vanished!

And there was a great heaving and sucking below Gnasha's feet, and the waters roiled and belched, an unspeakable odor rising up, and *something* grasped the Hlōk's ankles.

Shrieking and beating at the water, Gnasha did not see the Horde jerked under, for at that same moment a hideous strength wrenched the Hlōk commander deeply down into the foul muck far, far below, his mouth and throat and lungs filling with water and silt and slime as he screamed and screamed and screamed and ...

"Well, buccos," said Will, "it was deep in the swamp that the Rūcks and such were finally cornered. Hoy, there was a big battle, swords reaving, spears slashing, cudgels crushing, arrows piercing, tulwars cutting ... it was slaughter, bloody slaughter. And when it was done, nobody came out. No Men, no Elves, no Rūcks, no Hlōks, no one! They all died in there, slain by one another's hand.

"But let me tell you this: Agron's Army, they was heroes all. Outnumbered ten to one, still they fought. And they destroyed the Horde, to the last o' the Spawn.

"And that's the legend, buccos. That's the story. Just as it's been passed down through the long ages, as my dam would say."

His tale told, Will downed the last of his ale and returned to his polishing of mugs. And it was long ere any said aught, thinking as they were about what they had just heard.

"Lor, but they were brave," opined Feeny at last, shaking his head in wondering admiration. "I mean, sacrificing themselves like that and all. None coming out at the end."

"Oi now, I wonders just who was the last to survive there in the Gwasp?" asked Teddy. "Myself, now, I'd put a copper on old Agron himself. I'll wager he was a great warrior."

"Yar, Teddy," responded Nob, "but listen: one of the Foul Folk had to be among the last to survive as well, 'cause someone had to be there to take up arms against whoever it was that was last among the Men or Elves. I mean, them last two had to kill each other, else someone would have come out o' the swamp with the true tale as to just exactly what happened . . . and we know that nobody came out!"

A babble rose up at Nob's words, each buccan shouting out just what his own opinion was; but in the end, all had to agree with Nob, for if anyone had survived, surely they would have told of those valiant last hours of Agron's glorious army.

Dalavar finally emerged from the grasp of the Gwasp on the morning after the destruction of the Horde. Joining him there at the edge of the swamp came the Draega, the Silver Wolves, and they stood and waited as the Wolfmage turned his gaze northward, toward Claw Moor, toward the cold iron tower at its far edge. And Dalavar cast forth his senses, but nought did he detect of Modru's spoor. Modru was his foe, and certainly more powerful than this Magus of the Silver Wolves, yet Dalavar was not afraid.

Twice now Dalavar had defeated Modru: the first time by sheer fortune; this time by cunning. He had sensed the foul presence of the Evil One dogging his heels as he had marched his phantom army out from the Gronfangs and toward the Gwasp. Even so, the foul one had been deceived, and one of his Hordes destroyed because of it, slain by the monstrous *thing* that dwelled below the Gwasp, a *thing* called up from the bottom by Dalavar, though the cost had been high.

Dalavar's eyes turned toward the mountains in the east, toward an icy slot where Agron's Host had perished in a blizzard dire, a Hèl-spawned storm summoned by Modru in the depths of winter. *Farewell, my friends. Perhaps now you will rest more easily.*

Dalavar then turned unto his companions: six Silver Wolves. Reaching out, the Wolfmage ruffled the fur of the large male Wolf standing at hand. "Come, Greylight, let us be gone."

And *seven* Silver Wolves raced across the Land toward the rising Sun.

In the One-Eyed Crow, Warrows sat about the warm fire, puffing upon their pipes, sipping from their mugs.

"Say, Gaffer," asked Feeny after a long silence, "do you think that we'll ever know the truth of what happened to Agron's Army?"

And the silence of the 'Crow was filled with the sound of wind-hammered windows rattling in the blast, as if someone or something sought sanctuary from the deadly cold outside.

Dreadholt

I say, Gaffer," asked Nob Haywood suddenly, shifting his weight forward, *thunk!* the legs of his chair thumping onto the wooden floor from its tilted-back-against-the-wall position, "what about this Baron Stoke? I mean, it just doesn't seem right, him getting clear and all. Besides, you as good as promised that Pebble got another go at him. . . ."

The Gaffer stopped twiddling with his extinguished pipe and looked up blinking, as if the question from Nob had somehow caught him off guard.

"Yar, Gaffer," piped up Dilby Higgs, "you did say as how Pebble met up with Stoke again."

Bingo set aside his whittling knife and the tiny wooden Wolf's head he was carving and glanced up at the eld Warrow. "And them Rūcks and such as was left behind at Stoke's holt—whatever happened to them?"

A chorus of voices joined those of Nob and Dilby and Bingo, each Warrow there calling out for the granther buccan to share the tale, entreating him to continue the story from where he had left off last time.

A sudden shiver shook the old buccan's frame, but whether from cold or from memory . . .

Will Brackleburr quickly filled a mug with steaming hot tea and stepped to the side of the Gaffer. "Here, Tom," said the innkeeper, his voice uncommonly gentle, placing the drink before the granther, "something to take the chill away."

As the other Warrows got their own tea and pulled up chairs nearby, or hastened to the bar for a refill, the Gaffer sipped the bracing drink, the aroma of mint steaming upward from the heavy earthenware cup. There was a low murmur of conversation among the buccen that fell to silence when the Gaffer cleared his throat.

In the ensuing quiet, the granther buccan leaned over toward the fireplace and tapped the spent dottle out from his pipe against the stone of the hearth, then straightened up. Stuffing the owl-carved briar into his vest pocket, Gaffer Tom's pale green eyes swept across the eager faces before him, and outside the 'Crow the blizzard moaned. . . .

Leaving Vulfcwmb behind, they went to the Dwarven Mineholt of Kachar next, Tomlin, Petal, Riatha, and Urus: two Warrows, an Elfess, and a Man—a Baeran. And there the Châkka received them in that stiff, formal way the Dwarves have about them.

And Riatha made arrangements with a Dwarven silver-smith, paying him with a jewel no less, to fashion a brace of silver throwing knives for Petal, as well as a set of silver sling bullets for Tomlin—ten in all, it seems. For Baron Stoke yet lived, and to their knowledge only silver could do him harm—that and starsilver rare.

The Dwarven smith crafted what was asked of him, fashioning the two argent knives as directed by Petal, shaping blade and handle to give the heft and balance the damman sought.

The sling bullets were an easier task, for they were patterned after the silver bob given over to the smith by Tomlin, a bob he had received from Molly in Vulfcwmb to slay Baron Stoke—"It be silver, and should fit your sling. When ye get a chance, 'it 'im in the 'ead wi' it. Temple or eye should do 'im in."

As for Riatha, she already had her marvelous dark silveron blade, the metal glittering as if filled with stars; and Urus yet insisted he needed no weapon to deal with

Stoke on his own, even though when last they met, Stoke had nearly slain the Baeran, by poison bite, black and dire.

And while the silver weapons were being forged under the guidance of Tomlin and Petal, Riatha and Urus closeted themselves with DelfLord Bork, speaking of Stoke's holt eastward in the Grimwalls, telling of the Foul Folk dwelling therein; for the Lian Elfess and the Baeran knew of the great enmity the Châkka held toward the Grg, the name the Dwarves gave to those interlopers from the underworld of Neddra.

Bork welcomed this news, for he sought every opportunity to continue the unending War with the Squam.

The DelfLord marshalled a great Warband, and this Dwarven army marched unto the dark bartizan there high upon the sheer stone rampart north of Vulfcwmb, Riatha and Urus accompanying them along with Tomlin and Petal, the buccan and damman now bearing their new-forged silver weaponry.

Yet they found the strongholt deserted, though exploration of the interior caverns revealed a long tunnel to a secret entrance on the opposite side of the vale. Perhaps here it was that Stoke had fled from the Sun, though that was by no means a certainty; but now there was no trace of him.

Too, here it was in the caverns behind the bartizan that Riatha discovered the vile purpose of Stoke's hideous pastime, what he did with his flayed victims, with her brother, with the Baeron Men, with Tomlin's sire, his dam, with Petal's sire and others. And when Urus and the Warrows saw, they stood white-lipped and grim-faced, and rage filled their hearts.

Riatha, Urus, Petal, and Tomlin all took an oath that day, there in the holt of that monster: to aid one another 'gainst Baron Stoke until Death claimed him or them.

And Bork's army took Dwarven mattocks and chisels and drills and hammers and utterly destroyed the place, collapsing the tunnels, bringing the dark bartizan crashing down and asunder at the base of the cliff.

And two years passed. . . .

Thwak! The sling bullet struck home. Tomlin's left hand darted into the open-mouthed pouch at his belt; within a heartbeat another swift missile hurtled through the air hard upon the flight of the first, and one more bullet hammered into the target *thack!* Again *whack!* and again *thwack!* the sling shots punched into the silhouette, that of a Vulg, virtually all bullets striking the head, though now and again one would hammer into the neck at the base of the skull.

Out of shot, the buccan strode to the target and surveyed the damage done, then stooped and began gathering up the rounded stones. He had been at his daily practice for nearly an hour—

"Tommy . . ." It was Petal's voice, calling from the far edge of the glade. "Oh, Tommy . . ."

"Hiyo," he called back, standing, stuffing the bullets into the shot bag. "Over here, love. By the Vulg."

"We've a visitor, Tommy. *From Riatha!*"

Riatha! It's been more than two and a half years since Stoke— Tomlin began jogging across the forest clearing, heading for the pathway through the oaks to his and Petal's cote, the small cottage located on the fringes of the Weiunwood. Petal waited for him at the far side of the glade, and together they hurried to the tiny thatch-roofed home.

Outside the wooden dwelling stood a saddled horse, wet with the sweat of hard riding; and nearby, at the well, a Man drew up a bucket of water. It was apparent that the stranger had journeyed far, for his cloak and clothing were travel-stained, and he looked gaunt, weary, his face drawn. Slim he was, nought more than a youth; he could be no older than seventeen, eighteen, or thereabouts.

As he drank, his grey eyes peered over the rim of the hollowed-out gourd at the oncoming Waldana, his gaze widening slightly at the sight of these tiny folk, no bigger than children, the female perhaps but three foot in height, the male a hand or so taller. But no children were these, with their pointed Elven ears and strange, large, tilted, jewel-like eyes, hers of gold, his of emerald; nay! these were *Waldfolc,* a remarkable people straight out of legend, straight out of folklore, and as such, they were a novelty to him. Even so, these were not the first Waldana the young Man had seen, for he had come through Stonehill, a league or so to the south, and there he had first glimpsed

the Wee Folk, there high up on the hill above the rock
dwellings which gave that walled village its name—a
Waldan in fact had given him directions to Tomlin's cote.
And now a red-haired buccan and a black-haired damman
came toward him as he lowered the gourd and swirled and
cast the remainder of the water to the green earth, hanging
the vessel by its string on the dipper peg jutting from a
wall stanchion.

"I am Tomlin, sir," said the buccan, bowing to the Man,
"and this is my dammia, Petal."

"I be named Arnor," responded the youth, canting his
head first to Petal, then to Tomlin.

"I am told you bear a message for us from one we hold
dear." Tomlin looked expectantly at the Man.

"Aye," answered Arnor, "that I do . . . if you be the
Tomlin I seek . . . and the Petal, too. You must forgive me,
but I be pledged to make certain that you be the ones I was
sent to find, and for that I have a test: tell me, what be the
name o' the bear?"

Tomlin's eyes widened in surprise, and he glanced at
Petal.

"I was told by her that you would know the answer to
that riddle, if you be the right ones, that is," added the
messenger, noting the hesitance of either Waldan to reply.

"You say this word comes from Riatha?" asked Tomlin
in his turn. As the young Man nodded, "Then the answer
is Urus," responded the buccan.

"Aye, that be the answer I was given," smiled the youth,
"though I do not ken its meaning myself."

The courier stepped to his horse and began loosening
his saddlebags, tied by thongs to rear cantle, talking all the
while: "I must also tell you this, Wee Uns: this message be
over three weeks late getting to you. I set out from Arden
more than a month past, but fell ill along the way—some
might say it was the plague, though myself, I think it was
poison—drank from a stream in Drearwood, I did, and that
foul place was my undoing, even though 'tis said that evil
no longer dwells within, ever since The Purging some nine
years past.

"Regardless, I stumbled to a crofter's door in the
night—a small steading in the Wilderland to the east.

"Ill I was, and suffering a deal, or so they say, the crofter and his wife. I wouldn't know, for most of the time I was raving with a fever they could not break. But they stayed by my side, even though they did not know whether it was the plague raging through my veins or something else, something less deadly to them.

"There were herbs and such that they could give me, and they bathed me in cool water to help take the heat away, and wrapped me in warm blankets when the shakes came upon me. They made me drink mint in water, and fed me soup now and again. Two weeks or so I shivered and sweated, but at last came free of the grip of whatever vileness had hold of me.

"But I was too weak to ride, and so rested another five days, knowing all the while that the messages I bore were urgent, one to you two, the other to High King Galvane."

"You carry a message to the High King?" Wonder filled Petal's voice, finding herself alongside a person going to see the High King.

"Wait a moment, now," questioned Tomlin, "isn't Briand the High King?"

"No, Master Tomlin," answered the Man, pulling loose the saddlebags at last, setting them to the ground. "Briand was struck down during battle with the Kistania. Galvane now rules.

"That's why I was in Arden to begin with, bearing to them the news.

"That's when Lady Riatha gave me her message to you"—the youth rummaged in one bag and took out a ribbon-tied packet and a wax-sealed letter, giving the first to the damman and the second to the buccan—"but again I say that her message is perhaps a month late coming to you, though 'twas the best that could be done under the circumstances."

His heart thudding, Tomlin watched as Petal opened the small packet; in it was pressed golden mint leaves giving off a clean, crisp odor. *Gwynthyme! —Vulg's black bite slays at night. . . .* The eld saying sprang to Tomlin's mind, while visions of slavering jaws leapt up behind his eyes, images from a night fraught with terror, a night filled with Stoke's curs coming to slaughter him and Petal and Riatha and Urus, a night when Stoke himself had *changed*, had *transformed*, had become one of the great, ebon Wolf-like beasts, vile and poisonous. And it was said that gwynthyme would counteract the venom, would neutralize the poison of the Vulg's black bite.

"Stoke," Petal gritted, looking up at her buccaran. "Riatha has located Stoke."

As the damman carefully rewrapped the packet containing the precious golden leaves, Tomlin broke the seal on the letter. In fine-flowing script a short message verified what they already knew:

> *Pebble, Petal,*
>   *Stoke is found: near Sagra, in Vancha, at the end of the Grimwall. If ye would join us, Urus and I will await ye in the ruins of Luren. Make haste, for we shall no longer be there come the Moon of Harvest.*
>   *Riatha*

Without speaking, Tomlin handed the note to his dammia.

"The Moon of Harvest?" blurted out Petal, looking up from Riatha's dispatch, her voice filled with dismay. "But that's upon us now, this night or the next, and Luren lies some eighty, eighty-five leagues south."

"Aye," agreed Tomlin. "We've two hundred fifty miles to go—ten days by pony. But Riatha and Urus, they'll be gone when we get there."

" 'Tis only five days by horse, if we press," interjected the young Man.

"Horse?" questioned Tomlin. "Sir, we know not how to ride such great beasts, much less know how to push them at such a pace as you suggest."

"Vanadurin long-ride," responded the youth, as if that explained all. Then seeing the blank looks upon the faces of the Waldana: "In my Land, Valon, we learn how to vary the gait of a horse such that many days of long rides—seventeen, eighteen leagues each day—can be borne by the steeds. And so you see, five days would suffice to get us the two hundred fifty miles to Luren."

"You forget, Arnor," spoke up Petal, "we are Wee

Folk, and horses are too large for us to handle day in, day out, ponies being more suited to our statures as well as our tastes. Besides, we know not the way of a Vanadurin long-ride."

"Aye, and we have not the time to learn," added Tomlin.

"Hah!" burst out the courier. "As to the riding of horses, nothing could be simpler, e'en for one your size. But I see that you be right: learning would take some few days, days of which you have none to spend learning nor I teaching, for I've got to get back to Caer Pendwyr, bearing Lord Talarin's message to High King Galvane. Yet this will I do: can we get the horses, I will pace you behind me, your steeds upon long tethers, and I will get you to Luren in the five days; this I swear."

"That will still place us some three or four days behind Riatha and Urus," Petal calculated.

"Mayhap they themselves will be delayed," responded Tomlin. "I say that we give it a go."

At Petal's nod, the buccan turned toward the youth. "Horses are to be found, Arnor, and this I charge you with, for 'tis you who must judge what will keep up this 'long-ride' pace of yours. There is a stable in Stonehill." Glancing up, Tomlin judged that the hour stood at noon. "Go there now, and we'll meet you ere the Sun passes across a quarter of the sky."

Springing to the back of his steed, Arnor saluted the Waldana and then hammered off toward Stonehill. As the two Warrows rushed into the cottage and began packing, Petal asked, "But, Tommy, what'll we use for money? Horses aren't free, especially ones that'll run all day long, as Arnor seems bent upon them doing. And we've only a few coppers and a silver or two."

"Banlo and his dad run the stable," replied Tomlin. "And you know that they've wanted this place for their own."

Misgiving filled Petal's face, and her gaze swept across the well-kept interior of the cottage. Though her golden eyes filled with tears, her jaw set with resolve. "Aye, Tommy."

* * *

Long shadows streamed easterly as Tomlin, Petal, and
Arnor came into the ruins of Luren at sunset, the Man riding in the lead, the Warrows astride two horses on long
tethers trailing behind. All about them in the eventide,
partially concealed by the growth of underbrush and trees
creeping in from the surrounding Riverwood, lay the skel-
etal remains of the once proud city that had perished by
fire, a fire, said some, set by agents of the Evil One, a fire
that had finally accomplished what the Evil One's plague
could not.

Dusk washed across them as the trio rode the final mile
down the Post Road to come to the River Isleborne,
named Fainen by the Elves. There, near the roadside
along the shore, they found stones set in a ring holding
charred wood where a campblaze once burned. Arnor dismounted and took up a burnt chip, sniffing the char,
thumbing black burn from the wood and smelling again.
"Four, five days old, I ween. Mayhap six," he announced, casting the piece from him.

A look of anguish crossed Tomlin's face as well as that
of Petal.

The trio set up camp there along the Post Road near the
shallows of the ford, the last along this great river as it
ran down toward the Ryngar Arm of the Weston Ocean
beyond the setting Sun. Tomlin kindled a new campfire,
while Petal gathered wood. Arnor unsaddled the horses
and used handfuls of grasses to rub them down, feeding
them some grain after currying them. While they did this,
the waning Moon rose, five nights past fullness, five
nights past the appointed time of the rendezvous. And of
Riatha and Urus there was no sign—except perhaps for
the char in the stone fire ring. Only silent trees and long-
abandoned ruins stood in the argent light, mute witness to
what may have passed when the Moon was silver from
brim to brim.

All their hearts were heavy, for until this moment they
had hoped against reason that the ones they sought might
still be here.

Tomlin heated water above the flames, preparing a len-
til stew, and when it was ready, the trio took their supper
in silence.

Afterwards, they washed their utensils in the clear water of the gurging Isleborne.

"Arnor," queried the damman when they had returned to the fire, "you know about the lay of the land, the routes across it; whither, by what route would they go, Riatha and Urus? How would they reach Vancha?"

"As to what be their course," replied the youth, "they could have gone down the Isleborne by raft or boat, all the way to the Ryngar Arm of the Weston Ocean, then booked passage on a Gothonian ship, circling 'round Gothon and Basq to Vancha; or mayhap they took an overland route, southeasterly through Gûnar to Valon, then westerly along the Grimwall through Jugo and Hoven and Tugal and into Vancha. Ach, there be a hundred ways to go, but as to the which of the way they went, I cannot say."

"Tomorrow," said Tomlin, "in the daylight we shall seek sign of their direction. Perhaps they left a message we've not yet seen."

"But if we find none, Tommy," asked Petal, "then what?"

"They need us, my dammia," answered Tomlin. "If we can't follow them, then we'll just have to make our own way to the end of the Grimwall, to this place called Sagra, and hope to find them there."

The buccan turned to the young Man. "Tell me, Arnor, what is the swiftest way for us to get to the end of the Grimwall in Vancha?"

Arnor fell into long thought. " 'Tis a gamble," he said at last, "but I'd advise riding south to Arbalin, and thence by swift sailing ship west o'er the crystal waters of the Avagon Sea to the very shores of Vancha; for 'tis said that none be faster than the flying craft of the Arbalinia, except perhaps the Dragonboats of the northern Fjordsmen, or so it be said.

"Even so, you'll need luck to find an Arbalina ship in port, one that'll be willing to bear you to Vancha."

"Not only luck, Arnor," responded Tomlin, "but it will require considerable payment, too, and we have nought but a few coppers ... no gold, no silver—" Tomlin's voice jerked to a halt, and his hand strayed to the pouch

of silver bullets at his side, his viridian eyes drawn by the
sheen of the silver throwing knives strapped in their scabbards 'cross Petal's chest, alongside the ones of steel.

The damman saw where her buccaran's thoughts had
taken him, and reluctantly she nodded in agreement.
"There's nothing else for it, Tommy. You said so yourself:
Riatha and Urus need us. We've got to overtake them, silver bullets, silver knives, or no."

"But Stoke—"

"Hush, Tommy. We'll find a way. We'll find a
way. . . ." But the timbre of Petal's voice was at odds with
her words.

As in mornings past, they broke their fast upon cured
venison and crue, and afterwards they searched in vain
for sign as to which way Urus and Riatha had gone. Finding none, they gathered up their things and mounted upon
the horses, Arnor leading the way, the Warrows' steeds
upon long tethers trailing after.

The Harlingar youth set out southerly, heading for
Gûnar and Valon and Jugo beyond, heading for the shores
of the Avagon Sea, heading down to where the ferry rode
across to the Isle of Arbalin, the horses running at a
canter, the first of the many varying paces of a Vanadurin
long-ride.

Ten days later at the ferry, Arnor bade them farewell, the
young Man turning east to ride for Pellar to bear Lord
Talarin's message to High King Galvane, a message long
delayed by fever and by the urgent needs of the *Waldfolc*.
He took with him the two horses ridden by the Waldana,
horses to be used as remounts to hasten his journey to
Caer Pendwyr.

He had given over nearly all of his funds to the Wee
Ones—a few silvers—and had promised to return the
horses to Stonehill to redeem the Weiunwood steading of
Tomlin and Petal. "Take care" were his last words, and
the youth had galloped away, the unburdened mounts
trailing after.

Tomlin and Petal watched until they could no longer
see Arnor, and then they turned and made their way up

the gangplank and onto the ferry, the shuttle boat Captain's dark eyes wide with wonder at sight of these tiny Folk from legend.

"Forty gold it'll be," declared the olive-skinned Man, white teeth smiling, "and I'll put to sea on the eventide. Of course, would you wait three weeks when I'm set to lade for the Vancha port of Cardoña, then silver will be my fare, and not much at that."

"No, Captain Solini," replied Tomlin, "we can't wait. But forty gold! Surely you can't mean it."

"Ai, but I do, Wee One," responded the Captain. "The *Fairwind* is fleet, yet still 'tis a trading vessel. Why, you were fortunate to find me in port at all and not on some voyage across the deep. And to hale all the way to Vancha, to Castilla, to a city where I don't ordinarily trade, with nought but two Waerlinga as cargo, well ... forty gold is a cheap price, considering what I'd make with a load to barter, needing to pay my crew and all. Too, I'll be gambling that I'll find a shipment to bear back from there; of course, I take that gamble in any event.

"Besides, the Rovers of Kistan are stirring along those routes, and the sou'western waters be dangerous. Have you not heard about Briand? They killed him. Nay, with the Rovers abroad and no cargo, forty gold—"

"But we don't *have* forty gold!" Tomlin broke in.

"But we *do* have these," interjected Petal, placing the two silver throwing knives before the Arbalinian. "They are silver pure, and Dwarven made."

"But, Petal, without these, you have no weapon against—" began Tomlin, anguish in his eyes.

"Hush now, Tommy"—Petal stopped his words, reaching out and placing a hand on his arm, her amber eyes gazing into his of emerald—"we'll make do."

Captain Solini took up the blades, hefting them, testing their edges, their balance, gauging their Dwarven crafting, their worth.

"Done!" he exclaimed, standing, slipping the knives into his belt. "Make ready, for the tide runs seaward ere the twilight falls."

* * *

Sshsssssh . . . sissed the water past the hull, the ocean splitting in twain, hissing alongside larboard and starboard, and churning into a foaming wake swiftly left behind, the mark of their passage diminishing in the distance, disappearing, the agitated brine smoothing once more into unbroken swells rolling under the Sun, under the Moon. Canvas cracked in the brisk wind, ropes creaking and timbers groaning with the strain.

Day and night the ship sped o'er the azure waters, Captain Solini a master of wind and wave, tacking now and again to make the best of the prevailing air, more or less nor'easterly this season of the year. And when they were not asleep, Tomlin and Petal paced the deck or stood in the bow and scanned the distant horizon, as if somehow their very will could cause the ship to move faster. Yet nought the Warrows did made the craft run one whit more swiftly, though the crew and the Captain got the most out of canvas and cord and mast and hull and heading that the following winds would allow. And so, across the blue waters flew the *Fairwind,* though the pace was not up to what the Warrows would will.

Days passed, and nights, until a week had fled. And always the *Fairwind* bore southwesterly, running before the breeze, running toward Vancha, toward danger, toward Destiny.

And now they were come upon the Straits of Kistan, waters plied by the Rovers, vile raiders of the seas.

Two more days they sailed thusly, and nought did they see of the pirates.

It was on the third day that a scarlet sail was espied low on the horizon, some three points off the starboard bow.

" 'Tis crimson, Captain," called down the lookout. "A lateen. A Rover."

Larboard tacked Solini, bringing the *Fairwind* to a southerly course, and all hands were called to alert, including Tomlin and Petal, as sabers were distributed, and archers broke out bows and arrows, or crossbows and quarrels, and the catapult was readied, its pitch and sulphur missiles set out for ignition and hurling should it come to a firefight at sea.

The two Warrows each readied their own weapons, though there was little to do but ascertain that they were at hand: Tomlin his sling and stone bullets; Petal her steel throwing knives, the ones inherited from her sire.

At a gesture from Solini, the buccan and damman joined the Captain up on the stern castle, a place of advantage should they be boarded.

Yet the *Fairwind* had run no more than a half hour or so, the sinister red canvas low to the starboard beam, when another lateen-shaped vermilion sail hove into view, this one bearing but a point larboard of the bow.

"Ar," growled Solini, "like a pack of sharks, they cleave these waters." The Captain turned to his steersman. "Split between them, Nio, and hope we remain invisible."

Tomlin turned to the ship's master. "*Invisible?* What do you mean, 'invisible'?"

"Our sails," replied the Captain, gesturing at the canvas. "Unlike the Kistani—who revel in terrorizing their prey, hence run with blood-red sails—those of us who trade for our living seek to glide unseen o'er the deeps in troubled times. Thus, our sails are dyed blue-grey, as are painted our masts: hard to see 'gainst an ocean sky.

"Aye, could I have real invisibility, then would I take it. Till then I can hope to do nought but fool the eye."

Nio brought the ship starboard, bearing dead center between the two Kistani, each low on the horizon. Yet the angular lateen sails were but seven points apart, some eighty degrees or so, and to pass between them meant to draw closer to each, risking discovery. Too, the Kistani ships were beating into the wind and would perhaps change course, and who knew whither they would then head?

Into the slot between sailed the *Fairwind*, the crimson-laden dark masts of the Rovers drawing up and over the horizon as the Arbalina ship closed the distance ... until the Kistani hulls themselves could be seen, the raider ships now abeam, off to the right, off to the left, still small in the distance. Even so—"They come about, Captain!" called down the lookout. "They've spotted us and turn to give chase!"

"Steady as she goes, Nio," commanded the Captain. "Let us see what these Rovers have got." And southwesterly fled the ships, running before the wind: the Arbalina trader; the Rovers of Kistan.

And even though Tomlin and Petal were unaccustomed to gauging hull speeds and distances at sea, still they could see that the raiders drew closer, slowly, steadily, following an intercept course, the corsairs trimming sails, making the most of the wind.

Solini eyed his own sails, calling out orders to the crew, making minor adjustments to the canvas.

Still the raiders came on, overhauling the *Fairwind*, for she was a trading vessel, and though swift—e'en swifter running unladen as she was—she was not a warship built for speed as were the Kistani corsairs.

"They seem to be gaining, Captain," called out Tomlin, checking his sling stones once more, glancing at Petal. "It looks like a fight for certain."

"Hèl's depths!" growled Solini. "They are too swift. We shall have to use our advantage."

"But, Captain," protested the helmsman, "the Rovers will see."

"We've no choice, Nio," responded the ship's master, "they overhaul us. Besides, in these troubled times, I intend to show it to the Fleetmaster; the other ships of Arbalin need such, and it will be a secret no more."

The Captain cupped his hands 'round his mouth and called out to the forward crew: "Let's show these thieves our heels! Break out the new sail!"

As the crew sprang to do his bidding, Solini turned to the Warrows. "What you are about to look upon must not pass your lips, for it is a trade secret known but to me and my crew. And though the Kistania will see it, perhaps they are yet too far to fathom its import. Aye, the *Fairwind* is the fastest trader in these waters, mayhap in all the oceans, when the wind is right, and *this* is why. . . ."

The forward crew clambered into the fo'c'sle and, haling on ropes, furled the spritsail, the *Fairwind* slowing a bit as they did so. Tomlin and Petal looked first at one another and then at the Captain, for slowing down wasn't a tactic that either had expected. But then the crew raised a great billow of silken cloth, triangular in shape but rounded in the belly, like the curve of a great three-cornered bag set to catch the air, the apex attached to a line threaded through a pulley affixed to the top of the foremast, the base corners attached by ropes to the bowsprit crossbeam.

And as they haled the apex upward, the wind filled this strange headsail, this great clew, belling it outward o'er the bow waters in a wide bend, the blue-grey cloth swelling to the full as it gathered in the air and held it.

And the *Fairwind* leapt forward, fleeing before the wind, wing on wing, the great spinnaker—unknown upon Mithgar until envisioned but three years past by Captain Solini—filled and straining, the ship steadily pulling ahead, leaving the Rovers in its wake, the Arbalina crew cheering their Captain and jeering their enemy, Tomlin and Petal laughing and holding hands and dancing in a circle, the Kistania cursing and raging as the prey slipped away from their certain grasp.

Another five days passed, and on the tide, in the middle of still night, in the fog below the moonlight, a becalmed ship was haled into a harbor by crewmen plying the oars of dories and towing the vessel behind. Thus it was that the *Fairwind* dropped anchor in the port of Castilla on the southern coast of Vancha.

And two tiny passengers were rowed to shore.

"I don't like this at all, my dammia," complained Tomlin, "first it was your knives, and now my silver sling bullets."

"Hush now, Tommy," replied Petal. "We needed these ponies. The supplies, too. And yes, the map as well, for how else will we get to Sagra?"

"I know," sighed Tomlin, guiding his steed past a rock outcropping, "but your silver knives are gone, and I've only got two silver sling bullets left: one made by the Dwarven smith and the one given to me by Molly in

Vulfcwmb. If this keeps up, we'll have nothing left, *nothing*! for slaying that fiend."

Petal made no reply, and they continued riding northward, dust puffing up from plodding hooves, having crossed the encrusted, parched, heat-laden plains of Vancha, coming into the yellow foothills of the far range ahead, aiming for Sagra, there at the end of the Grimwall.

They had bargained in Castilla for ponies and supplies, but if it had not been for Captain Solini, they would not have succeeded in obtaining what they needed for the journey. Yet the Arbalinian had come to their aid, haggling with great skill, bargaining perhaps as well as would an inhabitant of the Karoo, the desert south of the Avagon Sea, where it is said that the native merchants could and would deal even with daemons if there were profit to be made. In any case, Solini had sealed their bargains for them, including obtaining a map, though the chartmaker had shuddered and made signs of warding when he heard they journeyed to Sagra.

And they had inquired about Riatha and Urus, on the offhand chance that those two had come this way, yet of the twain none knew aught.

But that was four days and nearly a hundred miles agone, and now as they came up through the arid foothills, the Grimwall hove into sight, some fifty or so miles ahead.

When they made camp that night, Tomlin studied the map and reckoned that another forty miles would bring them unto Sagra. Yet they knew not what they would find there, whether Riatha and Urus, or Baron Stoke, or nothing at all.

A day and a half later, the ponies stepped through fields of yellowed grass and toward a high stone wall be-ringing a drear town clinging to the edge of a dark wood, there at the foot of the mountains. Through the wall and past the village gate they went, the portal partially torn from its hinges, hanging awry. Among twisting dirt streets Tomlin and Petal found themselves; and as they rode inward, passing amid the dwellings, they could feel eyes peering through shutters, and no one moved on the streets in the midday Sun.

The buildings were close-set, the wood weathered, worn, not maintained, as if no one cared ... as if it did not matter. Clearly some structures were abandoned, yet others seemed occupied.

Once this might have been a beautiful town, bright and sparkling. But a great doom seemed to have overtaken it, the village now drab, grey, somehow oppressed.

They came to the central square, and there they found a well. Someone was drawing water, yet fled as the twain hailed her.

Tomlin and Petal dismounted and drew water for themselves and their steeds. An eerie quiet lay upon the streets as they drank, their emerald and amber eyes peering about as they quenched their thirst.

"Tommy, there's an inn on the corner," murmured Petal. "Perhaps we can ..."

A Man stepped out upon the porch of the hostel, shading his eyes, looking toward these diminutive strangers.

Warily the barkeep looked over his shoulder and into the shadows, as if checking for listeners in the murk. Then his whispered reply came, the accent of Vancha heavily coloring his use of the Common Tongue. "Ai, on the mountain een the old ruins ees somewan heedeous, een Dradholt. Two years back eet came, the black whoolbs with eet."

"Whoolbs?" Tomlin looked at Petal.

"Wolves, Tommy," she replied. "Black Wolves, he said. Vulgs."

"Ai, Bulgs, leetle wan," agreed the Man, Juaren by name. "And tereeble they are, most tereeble. But the wan who ees their master ..." The innkeeper shuddered, his eyes lost in some horrible memory. "Eet ees as the old legends wance again; een the night the Master of the Bulgs breengs terror.

"Many fled, those reech enough to do so. The rest of us, ai, we lock our dorse and weendows. But eet no matter; he take who he want."

The 'keep fell silent, and no one said aught for a while.

At last Petal spoke: "And you say that no strangers have come through here in the past few weeks, the past few days?"

"Nad," replied Juaren, moving his hand horizontally, palm down, a gesture of negation. "Een seex, sebben weeks, ju are the forst."

The next morning, over the protests of the innkeeper, Tomlin and Petal set out for Dreadholt, the ruins just visible in the morning light. Yet no one else saw them off, except perhaps from behind closed shutters, for although they had met with more members of the closemouthed community, the townsfolk were afraid, and would not tempt Fate by speaking of the evil that lived on the mountain, much less invoke its name. And as the Sun had set, those brave enough or curious enough to come and see the strangers had scuttled off to their dwellings and had shot home the bolts and slammed the bars to, locking themselves in for the night.

But it was clear enough from what they had said and what they had not said that two years past, Stoke had moved into the hulk of the old mansion, barely discernible to the naked eye, clutched there among the crags and pinnacles above the forest, bringing terror to the countryside.

And now, in the dawn, Tomlin and Petal set forth for those very same ruins, some twenty or so miles distant as the pony trots, perhaps only fifteen as the raven flies, the Warrows armed with but two silver sling-bullets capable of doing harm to one of Stoke's kind.

Their plan was simple: "Tommy, when we get there, in sight of Stoke, I'll keep the Rūcks and such at bay using these"—Petal gestured toward the half-dozen steel knives cross-strapped to her torso, her dead sire's old throwing knives—"and you deal with him."

Two bullets.

Six knives.

But Tomlin was a crack shot, unlikely to miss . . .

. . . if he got the chance.

All day they rode, wending up the mountain, aiming for the remains of the mansion. They hoped to reach the ruins ere nightfall, ere Stoke and his foul minions could move about, while the Sun yet ruled the sky, bringing with it Adon's Ban, the Withering Death, a bane that would turn Foul Folk into ashes should any come into the clean light of day. But the way was through dense forest, and the going slow, for close-set trees and fallen logs and underbrush and thickets and thorns barred the way; and at times they had to backtrack to pass around a ravine or to find a route up the face of a bluff; and ever the way forward was upslope, and the ponies needed frequent rest.

And as the two rode upward, the Sun rode through the sky as well, rising up in the east and across the blue vault above and falling to the west, the golden orb now slipping down toward the horizon.

Tomlin took a swig from his canteen. "We're not going to make it, Petal. The Sun will set while we are yet in the woods."

"I know, Tommy," replied the damman. "But still we must press on, for at night the Vulgs will come, and it is no safer here than elsewhere; for if they find us, and they will, they'll bring the Rūcks, and we won't even get a chance at Stoke.

"Nay. We've got to get to the mansion, perhaps to hide from the Vulgs among the smells of Stoke's prisoners, of Stoke's victims, till daylight comes again."

And so they pressed onward, through the deepening gloom as the Sun slipped behind the mountains to the west, casting long shadows over the forest.

Night fell, pitch black; the waning half Moon would not rise until nigh midnight, and ebony cloaked the deep pines. As Tomlin lit a hooded lantern, cracking the shutter so that a wan slit of light faintly illuminated the way before them, long juddering howls came through the darkness.

"Vulgs!" hissed Petal, and onward they crept, now afoot, leading their ponies, the small steeds skitting, shying, unsettled by the howl of the Vulgs, the Warrows moving toward a dim glimmer afar: a light from the distant mansion.

How long they crept thusly, Tomlin could not say, yet

suddenly—"*Ssstt!*" sissed Petal, and the buccan shuttered the lantern, squelching all light.

They stood in the darkness, holding their ponies' muzzles to prevent a whicker from betraying them, feeble light from the stars above filtering down among the trees, faintly reaching the forest floor.

And they could hear something in the night, in the forest, moving, toward them, something large, something ponderous, pressing through the underbrush, slowly, deliberately.

Of a sudden the ponies snorted and reared up, squealing, frantic, jerking loose from buccan and damman, the steeds bolting in fear, crashing off into the dark and away, their panic-stricken flight shattering the night with noise.

Each of Petal's hands filled with a knife, readied for throwing, and Tomlin loaded a bullet, then whirled his sling overhead, both Warrows ready to loose death upon whatever it was thrusting through the brush toward them, though neither could see aught but black on black in the darkness, in the feeble starlight.

And just as *something* dark and massive loomed out from the underbrush ahead, hindward came a quiet voice: "Hold! It is Urus!"

Tomlin spun about, unshuttering his lamp, and there behind, dressed in leathers and with sword in hand, stood a golden-haired Elfess with silver eyes.

"*Riatha!*"

"Shield thy light, Pebble!" hissed the lithe Elfess, flinging up a hand to shadow her face. "Else we'll have all of Stoke's lackeys at our throats."

Tomlin closed down the lantern, leaving but a narrow crack so that he and Petal could see.

Petal! Tomlin whirled about, and found his dammia hugging the neck of a great brown bear.

And a dark shimmering came upon the beast, Petal stepping back, and swiftly it *changed,* altering, losing bulk, gaining form, and suddenly there before them stood a giant of a Man, a Baeron: Urus.

"When thou didst not come to Luren at the Moon of Harvest—"

Tomlin interrupted Riatha: "The messenger fell ill, and we got there five days late."

"—we continued by Elven boat down the Fainen, the Isleborne, until we reached Gothon—"

"Garn! We went the other way."

"—and waited ten days for a ship to bear us to Vancha."

"Lumme! We could have caught you still in port had we had a boat to follow the river after you, had we known that was the way you had gone."

"We booked passage on a craft that was bound first to Basq, then on to Portho in Vancha, there on the border between."

"We came the other way, on the Avagon Sea."

"But the Rovers of Kistan ply those waters, Tomlin; hast thou not heard of Briand's death at their hands?"

"Aye, we did hear. But as to the Kistani, we saw two of their ships, but Captain Solini and the *Fairwind* outran their crimson sails."

"There's a tale here for the telling," remarked Riatha, curiosity in her grey eyes, "but now is not the time.

"Into Vancha we came, ahorse, toward Daemon's Crag, toward Dreadholt, toward Stoke.

"We passed through Sagra late this morn—"

Tomlin blurted, "Then we were ahead of you!"

"Aye, though none said aught in that downtrodden village.

"Up through the woods we came, slow going until at last we tethered our horses and left them, for 'tis swifter on foot in this thickness.

"Yon lay our goal"—the Elfess pointed upslope through the dark branches toward the light glimmering in the mansion—"and we made for it.

"But then we heard thy ponies, saw a glint, and came to investigate," explained Riatha, "Urus from one direction, I from the other."

"Our ponies!" exclaimed Petal. "They've bolted. Our goods."

"Long gone, little one," rumbled Urus, "and for that I'm sorry. 'Tis not often that ponies, or horses for that matter, can abide the scent of a bear. Mayhap tomorrow . . ."

"It is of no moment, Petal," added Riatha, "for we must go afoot unto the vile one's den. And swift, for his curs roam the black, and I would not have them find us ere we come unto the master's abode."

And so, in the ebon night, Urus, Riatha, Tomlin, and Petal—a Baeron, an Elfess, and two Warrows—slipped among the pines and up the slopes and toward a strongholt of evil, named Daemon's Crag by some, called Dreadholt by others.

And yet they had not gone more than a furlong, when from behind, deep in the woods aback, there came the screams of steeds, sounding like cries of terrified Women, mingled with a savage, hideous snarling.

Of a sudden the woods rang with a deadly silence . . . soon filled with the yawling howls of Vulgs upon a kill.

They pressed on through the blackness, striking toward the glimmer ahead, Riatha leading, Urus trailing, Tomlin and Petal between. Guided by the Elfess, they at last came to the apex of a small stone ridge; and lying on their stomachs and peering over the crest of the rib, they looked down into a torchlit swale. Opposite, towering and dark loomed the mansion, crafted from the timber of tall black trees of a former time, the fell wood gone grey with age, the entire structure reeking of ruin, of decay. Dark spires twisted upward into the ebon night, limned by cold stars glinting. Gabled roofs pitched steeply, and cornices were capped with hideous gargoyles leering down, stuttering torchlight writhing 'cross carven visages obscene in their stone japing. Here and there balconies jutted outward from gaping black holes, and darkness oozed forth from within. And below, flanking a great ironbound door 'neath a pillared portico, slouched Rūcken sentries bearing tulwars.

And even as Elfess, Baeran, and Warrows watched, a jostling band of Rūcks, bearing goods and great bloody gobbets of hacked meat, tramped forth from the woods and across the swale and toward the mansion. Yet as they passed into the torchlight—"Look, Urus!" hissed Riatha. "Our saddles, bedrolls. 'Twas *our* steeds the Vulgs slew, not the ponies of the Waerlinga."

Urus merely grunted acknowledgment, saying nought as the Rūcks disappeared inside.

Long moments passed.

Suddenly a shouting could be heard coming from within, and the hammer of running footsteps. Too, there came the growls of Vulgs. Moments later a force of Rūcks and Hlōks scrambled outward, Vulgs atrot in their midst, the Spawn assembling in the cusp of land before the ramshackle mansion.

And evil stepped forth upon a balcony.

Stoke.

Baron Stoke.

Tall he was, with raven hair and pale skin and yellow eyes and long, slender, grasping hands. His pallid face held a thin, straight nose and white unbearded cheeks, and the ivory glint of long teeth and sharp canines gleamed in the red gash of his mouth.

And he sissed orders to the assembled maggot-folk in a guttural, slobbering speech—Slûk. In his right hand he grasped a long cloak, and growling, he held it up and inhaled its scent, then cast it down unto the Vulgs below, who leapt upon it, snarling and snuffling, taking in its smell even as they rent it to shreds. And Stoke raised his face to the darkling sky and wrauled, and his howl was answered from near and far by like howls—the bone-chilling ululations of Vulgs on the hunt.

Stoke leaned forward, his hands braced upon the balcony railing, his yellow eyes glittering down upon the force below, and with a final yawl he gestured toward the woods.

Haphazardly wheeling, the undisciplined aggregation jog-trotted across the clearing and into the woods, Vulgs leading with noses to the earth, Hlōks lashing whips at any who lagged behind.

When they had gone, Stoke spun on his heel and disappeared into the blackness behind the balcony.

"The cloak," murmured Tomlin.

"Mine," grunted Urus. "Taken from the goods lashed to my horse. We must hurry, for the Vulgs will not be long in running us to earth."

* * *

The four Free Folk crept down from the ridge and toward the looming hulk, keeping well to the shadows, slipping alongside the structure, looking for another entry. Yet the back of the mansion was clutched 'gainst the dark stone of the mountain behind, and no alternate way inward was found.

"We can climb the stone aft and come at Stoke from above, or we can attempt to scale up to a balcony," whispered Urus, "yet I deem we have not the time for either of those choices, given that Vulgs are on our track."

"Then there's nothing for it but to go through the front door," breathed Tomlin. "And we've got to take out two Rūcks ere they sound the alarm."

"Then that's ours to do, Tommy," whispered Petal, a steel throwing knife in her hand, "for we've the means."

And so the two Warrows crept through the shadows and toward the front entryway, their progress all but silent, moving nigh soundlessly, as only the Wee Folk can do. And undetected, when they were within but a few yards of the maggot-folk, Tomlin glanced at Petal and she at him, and as they had practiced numberless times over the past two years, on a silent count of three each hurled their perilous missiles, deadly knife and lethal bullet flashing into throat and smashing into temple, the Rūcks crashing hindward against the wall and falling slack to the porch, dead ere striking the planking.

Swiftly the Warrows stepped within the portico and unto the ironbound door, where Petal retrieved her steel and wiped it clean of dark Rūck grume, Riatha and Urus slipping out from the shadows to join them in the torchlight.

Urus grasped the iron ring upon the door and glanced at the Elfess and the Waldana, and at a quick nod from each he twisted it. With a *clack!* the handle pivoted, drawing the bolt. And pushing the great door inward, armed with morning star and sword and knife and sling, they stepped into a wide, musty hall lit yellow by oil lanterns upon tables and by torches burning in cressets along the walls.

All about them were signs of decay and ruin: half-rotted tapestries clung to the wood-panelled walls; litter and waste lay scattered in the passage; splintered furniture sat awry; and the wood of the walls and ceilings and floors, of the stairs and bannisters, was ancient and split, and tinder dry, and where there had been paint or varnish, nought was left but crazed crackings and flakes. And great, dark wooden beams crisscrossed the high vaulted ceiling above, matching the splintered dry timber of the black panelled walls below.

Ahead, the broad hallway ran some forty feet ere fetching up at the foot of a stairway against the right wall. To the left of the steps, a narrow corridor ran onward, disappearing into the gloom beyond. The staircase itself curved up and leftward some thirty, forty steps to a landing high above, and there yawned a shadowy opening, an archway, while a balustraded passageway ran rightward. In the immediate hall at hand, to left and right were doorways, some closed, others gaping and dark.

And into this blighted ruin stepped four Free Folk, seeking a monster.

Ancient floorboards creaked 'neath their feet as inward they crept. Yet ere they had taken more than a pace or two, one of the rightward doors opened and forth stepped a Hlōk. With a shriek of alarm the Man-sized goblin sprang aback, his hand clutching at the hilts of the scimitar at his side. But before he could draw it, *Crnch!* Urus's black morning star smashed into the Wrg's chest, dashing him hindwards, the Hlōk crashing into a small wooden table and overturning it, the oil lamp hurtling to the floor and shattering, yellow flames running along the boards and to the wall, licking upward, desiccated tapestries catching afire.

Urus sprang forward, yet what he would have done is moot, for at that moment four more Hlōks stepped into the hallway, scimitars in hand, and violence exploded as with shouts of alarm and rage the maggot-folk attacked.

Krnch! Chnk! The morning star of Urus whelmed into two Wrg ere they could react.

Shhkk! Riatha's midnight sword took another through the heart.

Thkk! Down fell the fourth Hlōk, a thrown dagger in his throat.

But the alarm brought more maggot-folk: Rūcks and Hlōks, armed with tulwars and scimitars, dirks and cudgels, chains and flails.

And fire roared up the walls and overhead, the dry, splintery wood exploding into flames, tapestries flaring, furniture ablaze, litter enkindled, fire racing up the stairs and onto the landing above, the ancient hulk of a mansion nought but a tinderbox whose long wait for a spark had come to an end. And amid this incandescent Hèl, Free Folk and Foul hammered at one another, blade and bullet, dirk and dagger, tulwar and morning star, sword and cudgel, steel and stone; wounds given and taken; red blood seeping, dark grume runnelling into the fire.

Whoom! A great overhead timber gave way and crashed flaming to the floor, smashing down upon the combatants, crushing two Rūcks beneath, their screams lost in the thunder of its fall.

And still Urus whelmed Wrg left and right; and Riatha slashed the Yrm; and Tomlin and Petal, not armed for mêlée, dodged and darted to and fro, remaining aback, hurling slingstone and steel when opportunity afforded.

Overhead another great beam gave way at one end, swinging down, thundering into the wall, *Boom!*

The Foul Folk looked up, and turned and ran, fleeing through the burning doorways, leaving the four invaders behind to claim victory in this raging conflagration.

Yet the entire hall was now ablaze, the heat nearly beyond enduring, the burning air choked with writhing smoke, and Tomlin knew that they had to escape, else they would perish in the flames.

Just as he called out for a retreat, turning to catch Petal by the hand and run from this pyre, from the hallway beyond the burning stairs came Stoke . . .

. . . Baron Stoke. . . .

Snarling he came. . . .

Raging he came. . . .

. . . And he bore a long, curved, serrated knife in his right fist, and his hands and arms were slathered with dripping, red, glistening blood—blood not his own.

Foam flecked his lips, and he screamed in fury, for he had been interrupted.

And amid the churning smoke and roaring fire and beams ablaze crashing down, "He's mine!" shrieked Riatha, leaping over a burning timber, the stars in her dark blade glittering red in the flames.

Shang! Sword met knife as Tomlin's hand stabbed into his pocket, seeking bullets of silver.

Stoke's eyes darted desperately about, for a starsilver blade slashed at him, a blade that would slay him; and he sought escape and saw none, for Urus blocked the way.

Chang! Again Stoke parried, yet he knew that he was no match for this avenger, and he turned and sprang up the blazing stairs, running before the pursuing Elfess.

Upward he ran, up the burning steps, racing to escape. And his heel caught upon a tread and he stumbled slightly, pitching forward just as *Spakk!* a silver bullet smacked into the wall not a jot from his head, grazing his hair, it was so close, hurled by a Warrow below. Yet Stoke managed to keep his footing and ran on, fleeing upward through smoke and flame, oblivious to this argent danger from a Wee One, seeking only to escape the pursuing starsilver blade he knew he could not defeat.

"Get him, Tommy! Get him!" shrieked Petal above the bellow of the fire, as Tomlin's hand darted into his pocket once more, withdrawing another silver bullet, this one his last, this one the silver bob given to him by Molly. Yet as he loaded it and glanced upward through flame and fume, Stoke disappeared at the top of the steps, running through the blazing archway, Riatha just behind.

Tomlin sprang toward the burning stairs in pursuit, following hard upon the heels of Urus, with Petal running after, while about them conflagration roared in triumph, racing to destroy all within.

Through the leaping flames and roiling smoke ran the Warrow, the heat searing his face and hands, the very air he breathed torrid and filled with choking black reek swirling up from the blazing timber. Ahead, the bulk of the Baeran led the way; behind came a damman, unwilling to leave her buccaran's side. Below the flaming archway they ran and into a greatroom. Through the raging fire before them, through the churning smoke, they could see Riatha and Stoke nigh the far end, battling, sword against longknife, and it was clear that Riatha had the upper hand.

'Round and 'round they whirled, smoke and flame spinning likewise. *Shing! Chang!* skirled steel on steel, and suddenly—

Ching! Stoke's knife was sent spinning—

And as Riatha's star-filled sword flashed up and back and slashed downward in a deathblow—

Whoom! An overhead beam thundered down to smash the Elfess to the floor.

Stoke, his back to the archway, jerked up a great burning timber brace and raised it high overhead to smash down onto Riatha's unmoving form.

Sszz! A silver streak sissed through the whirling air and *Thakk!* struck Stoke between the shoulder blades.

"*Yyyaaaagh . . .*" a wordless shriek yawled forth from Stoke, and he crashed forward into the mantel stones of a great fireplace, clutching at his back, unable to reach the argent bullet, the vile shapeshifter falling sideways into the flames, the fire whooshing up.

Whoom! Another great blazing timber fell from the overhead, and the entire ceiling began to sag, raging with ravening incandescence.

"To me! To me!" cried Urus.

And through the roiling smoke and roaring flames, Tomlin and Petal stumbled to Urus's side, while around them Dreadholt burned. And Riatha lay at his feet, the Elfess trapped 'neath a great burning beam.

The huge Baeran bent down and took one end of the fiery timber in his grasp, ignoring the flames raving up his arms. With a grunt he lifted, his legs straining to remove the weight, his face distorted with the attempt. Slowly the massive beam rose, hoisted by an effort beyond reckoning.

"Now!" groaned Urus, and Tomlin and Petal dragged Riatha out from under, the small Warrows getting her clear.

Whump! Urus dropped the timber just as *Whoom!* another great beam crashed to the floor, and the entire ceiling began to collapse.

"Out!" cried Petal above the roar of the fire. "We've got to get out!"

Urus scooped Riatha up in his massive arms, and he and the Warrows bolted for the archway, Petal snatching up the silveron sword as she darted outward.

Just ahead of the collapsing ceiling they stumbled, out and down the flaming stairs, also beginning to sag, smoke whirling and fire thundering all about as they ran for the fiery doorway to the outside.

Coughing and hacking, onto the burning portico they stumbled, and down the steps . . .

. . . only to see standing before them a host of Hlōks and Rūcks and Vulgs, returned from the hunt.

And they stood there swaying, spent, gasping for air, the four of them, a Baeran carrying an Elfess, with two small Warrows at his side.

They didn't stand a chance, battle-weary as they were, whelmed by the heat, nigh overcome by the smoke, the Elfess totally unconscious with a broken arm and leg, the Baeran burnt and bleeding, there being nought but two Warrows to defend them, with only one knife and eight slingstones between the twain if you counted not Riatha's starlit sword, for no one there knew the wielding of it but the Elfess, and she was in no state to use it.

Even so, Tomlin and Petal gritted their teeth and prepared for battle, a lone throwing knife in the damman's hand, a stone in the sling of the buccan.

The Spawn looked at these helpless victims, at this feeble prey; and they looked at the burning mansion beyond, now totally engulfed in flame, fire roaring upward into the night, lighting the countryside for miles, ruddy luminescence painting the stony crags above.

And with yawling howls, the maggot-folk turned tail and ran! Fleeing. Scrambling *across* the mountain and *away.* Ignoring the four comrades.

The fire finally burned itself out sometime during the next day. Riatha was by then conscious though in pain, her ribs bound, her left arm and left leg in splints, the cuts she had taken in battle bandaged, Urus having seen to her needs. He, too, was treated, there where the fire had burned his arms, a soothing mint poultice applied and held in place by cloth wrappings, the Warrows having done so; and they bound his bleeding cuts as well. Except for scalded skin and singed hair, Tomlin and Petal were unharmed, and after rendering aid to the Baeran, the two had taken turns standing watch through the night.

But now it was the next day, and when they could, the Warrows picked their way into the still smoldering ruins, Petal managing to retrieve her steel knives from the char of the destroyed foyer. Tomlin found a way to clamber up through blackened timbers and to the stone hearth where Stoke had fallen, the fireplace backed up there against the crags, Petal climbing up after.

They found no trace of the Baron—no bones, nothing. They did, however, find a hidden stone door next to the fireplace, slightly ajar, burned timbers blocking it. And beyond the door a passageway receded into the wall of the mountain behind.

And as they stood there wondering, a gleam of argent caught Petal's eye; it was Tommy's silver bullet lying amid the ashes, the very same bullet that had hammered into Stoke.

As the granther buccan's voice fell silent and the wind whistled 'round the inn, Warrows sat without speaking, their large, tilted, jewel-like eyes wide in wonderment. Finally Teddy cleared his throat. "Lor! What a tale. But tell me, Gaffer, why did the Rūcks and such run? I mean, they had Pebble and Petal and Riatha and Urus cornered, at their mercy, and everybody knows that the maggot-folk ain't got no mercy. So why did they run?"

All eyes swung toward the Gaffer as he took a sip of his tea. Wiping his mouth on his sleeve, he set the mug down. "Well, Teddy, I don't know for certain, but Riatha thought it might have been because they were running to save their hides again. I mean, running from the Sun, from Adon's Ban. Look here, even though it wasn't yet midnight, and they had plenty of nighttime left, the mansion was on fire. So as they couldn't get underground through there, through Dreadholt and into the secret passageways 'neath Daemon's Crag. And who knows how far it was to the nearest bolt hole? Why, I mean, it could have been leagues to a place where they could get underground before the Sun came up—"

"Argh!" interrupted Nob. "That ain't what's important here. Why the Rūcks and such ran, where they got to— it's all beside the point! The important thing is Stoke! Was he dead? Did they get him? Did Tomlin's silver bullet do him in? Was he burnt up? What, Gaffer, what?"

Again all eyes turned to the Gaffer.

Slowly he filled his black pipe carved in the shape of an owl's head, none saying aught in the silence, Neddy quietly getting a burning taper to light Gaffer Tom's briar. After a couple of puffs, the granther buccan's eyes swept across the expectant faces of the waiting Warrows.

"Well, Nob, let me say this about that . . ."

Outside, the blizzard shrieked and yawled, and darkness descended upon the hammered land as icy day slipped into frigid night, though no one in the 'Crow took note of it.

The
Hèlborne Drum

Still the wind howled about the One-Eyed Crow as the blizzard raged on into the night. Windows rattled. Clapboards clattered. And a moaning groaned down the chimney. A wall of white hurled by, gone black with the coming of the darktide, and nought could be seen beyond the overhang of the porch, vaguely illuminated by the pale yellow lantern light shining out through the 'Crow's ice-laden windows.

Nob Haywood turned from the bar, bearing a steaming cup of hot tea toward the table where fresh, hot bread was being sliced and slathered with butter and shared out to the waiting Warrows by Arla Brackleburr. "Ho, Feeny," called Nob, "be there any tales told down there in Budgens what we haven't heard?"

Chewing, Feeny Proudhand looked up from his half-eaten slice. *"Ngh dmp 't,"* he replied, his words lost within his full mouth. He chewed a bit more, then swallowed. "I doubt it," he repeated, this time his speech clear. "Budgens is only two miles from here," he continued, explaining all.

No one said aught for a while, concentrating upon consuming the fresh-baked loaves. Will Brackleburr came bustling out from the kitchen, a honey crock in his grasp. "I found it, Arla," he said, handing the stone vessel over to her. Warrows crowded about as she ladled dripping sweet over the buttered slices.

As Will saw to it that the Gaffer got a goodly share of the food, the eld granther cocked a jewel-like eye toward Feeny. "Y'r own granther used to tell a tale of Beacontor. You know, the story about what happened there nigh the beginning of the Great War."

Feeny paused, honey oozing over the edge of the buttered slice he held. "Ar, now as you mention it, Gaffer, m' granther did tell such." The buccan paused long enough to lick the creeping honey ere any could drop from the bread to the table.

"Beacontor?" queried Hob. "Over there beyond Stone hill?"

"Aye," responded Feeny. "Part of the Signal Mountains, m' granther alluz said. Told that Challerain Keep itself stood on the northernmost mount, up there in Rian, and down there at the southernmost end stood Beacontor."

"Down there by the Crossland Road, in the Wilderland," chimed in Neddy.

"Hush, now," grumbled the Gaffer. "There ain't no need for interruptions. Let Feeny tell his tale."

All the Warrows gazed expectantly at Feeny. Even Arla and Will pulled up chairs.

Feeny looked about in self-consciousness and for a moment considered refusing, for he didn't consider himself a storyteller and did not wish to show up as a complete fool. But the Gaffer gave him a smile of encouragement, and so the Budgens' wheelwright swallowed the last of his bread and took a swill of hot tea, and then began:

"It was back in the days just before the start of the Great War—the Ban War—when rumors of Adon and Gyphon and Modru and what all were whispered in every tavern, inn, village, household, and steading across the land. Remember, too, that this was in the time before there was a Ban, and so the Rūcks and such could get about in the day as well as night, though as has been said here before, they liked the dark of night to do their skulkin' in.

"And the Foul Folk, it seems, were mustering for War, and so the Free Folk, too, prepared.

"Part of this preparation was to set balefires in readiness atop towers and hills and mountains throughout all the Realms, the pyres to be lit should War come, their flames and smoke to call out to one and all that the struggle had begun, and to rally folks to the banner of the High King.

"And one chain of these watch fires was set along the Signal Mountains, them tall hills standing there like sentinels in a great long arc from Challerain out to the east and south till they came to the other end there at Beacontor.

"Now, I don't know about the others, but granther alluz told that the fire at Beacontor was tended by Men, by Wilderans, he said. . . ."

Jörn watched as the tall, rawboned, ginger-haired youth came chuffing up the slope through the snow, haling hard on the reins of a flop-eared jack laden with deadwood, the beast of burden reluctantly and stiff-leggedly lagging behind, balking, their breath blowing white in the bleak winter cold, the lad swearing at the mule, his voice drifting up through the icy air and to the top of the tor. "Come on now, you misbegotten son of an ass, stop being so cursed stubborn."

Jörn smiled unto himself at this contest of wills, and after a quick glance through the window slits to north and south, east and west, he turned to the inside of the room atop the stone watchtower and set aside his lute and took up his winter cloak. Stepping to the trapdoor and opening it, he pulled on his winter gloves and clambered down the ladder, swiftly reaching the base and stepping through the door and out upon the crest of Beacontor.

In the open, the winter air was crisp, a slight breeze blowing chill from the east, and a shiver shook Jörn's frame as he strode among the squat stone buildings and toward a great mound of wood stacked under a simple pole shelter to protect it from the weather. In that same moment, the youth and the mule came through the low rock-and-mortar wall be-ringing the hilltop—not a defensive wall, but one instead that merely marked the traditional boundary of the hilltop where quartered the sentinels—and headed toward the pile as well.

"Ho, Aulf," called out Jörn, "is old Ironhead giving you trouble?"

Aulf, a lad of sixteen summers, looked up at his uncle and shook his head in rue. "Had to drag this pigheaded jackass all the way back," he declared, still haling hard on the reins.

As if he understood, Ironhead decided then and there that he would not take another step, and he stopped cold in his tracks. And by neither strength nor threats nor promises could Aulf get the mule to move.

"His feelings are hurt," said Jörn, grinning, moving downslope to come to his sister's son. "What this needs, my young nephew, is the sure hand of age and experience. Here, let me. . . ."

Aulf turned the reins over to his uncle, a common Man of average height, a Man in his middle years, some forty winters old, yet hale, his dark brown hair showing but a few strands of silver.

"Coo now, Ironhead," soothed Jörn, mimicking the accents of those who dwell in the Jillian Tors along the shores of the Boreal Sea, where Jörn had campaigned in his youth, for Ironhead had come from that far north Land. "Wouldna ye like t' ha'e a wee taste o' th' oats?"

As if utterly disgusted, Ironhead sat down, the bundles of firewood lurching back, individual branches and small logs sliding loose from their lax rope bindings, clattering onto the ground, some to roll a bit down the grade, both Aulf and Jörn exploding into laughter at the sight of the thoroughly offended mule sitting in the snow.

"So much for age and experience, Uncle," gasped Aulf between guffaws, his eyes filled with tears.

"When are they coming?" Aulf's words betrayed the impatience of youth as the two sat in the watchtower in the night, a candle casting dim, wavering light within the small room.

Using a last small bit of crue biscuit, Jörn sopped up the remainder of his stew. "I know not, son of my sister. . . . Soon. . . . Soon."

"But it's been nearly two weeks."

"Aye, that it has," replied Jörn, his mind hearkening

back to that night when came a horse galloping unto his cottage followed by a pounding upon his farmstead door.

"All right. All right. I'm coming." By the light of the coals in the fireplace, Jörn stepped to the foot of his bed and opened the chest and withdrew a soldier's sword, cold steel from his younger days.

Jörn slipped into his boots. *Weapon first, boots next,* his mind echoed the words of Llwyn, the Wilderland armsmaster who had trained him. *Y'never know when y'll need t'run.*

Taking taper to lantern, Jörn signaled Aulf to pull on his boots as well, the lad rising from his cot.

As if in response to the striking of a light within, again there came a pounding upon the door, and a voice called out, "Open in the name of the King!"

Aulf sprang up and headed toward the door, but Jörn reached out and stopped him, whispering, "Could be anyone out there, boy, invoking the name of the King— Brigands. Bandits. Rūck or Hlōk. Could even be a Kingsman as claimed. Here, take this."

Handing an oaken club to Aulf, Jörn quietly moved to the door and set the lantern upon the floor, freeing his off hand to take up his cloak from the door peg and wrap it 'round his left forearm.

Looking at Aulf and receiving a nod, Jörn lifted the latch and jerked open the door just as whoever was without began pounding upon it again.

Startled, a Man dressed in a red and gold tabard stepped backward, away from the shortsword and the cudgel behind, shielding his eyes from the light of the lantern. "What the—"

"Hoy," interrupted Jörn, lowering his weapon. "Down club, Aulf, it really *is* a Kingsman."

That had been nearly two weeks back, some twelve days agone when the herald had come with the news that the Foul Folk were stirring, large bands moving through the mountains—the Gronfang, the Rigga, the Grimwall— gathering in the Angle of Gron, the Land where stood Modru's iron tower. Too, they were moving in nearby

Drearwood, a dire place of ill repute—peopled by monsters most foul, it was said—on the eastern edge of the Wilderland. Like as not, War was brewing. And the High King had commanded that the beacon fires be laid, that the watchtowers and mountains and hills be manned, and that the sentinels stand ready to call the Realm to arms should events so dictate.

Ere he had ridden onward into the night, the Kingsman had levied Jörn and Aulf to lay the balefire and set guard at Beacontor, until a warding force could be mustered and sent to man that southernmost knoll of the Signal Mountains.

And so, heeding the High King's command, uncle and nephew had gathered together those things needed and had laden Ironhead and then made their way unto that stand, coming to its slopes on the eve of the following night. They had gathered wood and laid the signal fire atop the crest, a fire that if lighted would call out to all in the Wilderland that War had begun, sending its baleful message far and wide: to the Wilderness Hills in the east and to the Weiunwood and Stonehill in the west, to the Dellin Downs in Harth to the south, and upchain along the Signal Mountains toward Rian in the north.

But most likely, the signal would come downchain, *from* the north, *from* Rian: from Challerain Keep itself, passing southerly from mount to mount unto Beacontor and thence beyond.

Yet for now Jörn and Aulf sat watch atop a cold stone tower upon this sentinel stand, dividing the night and day into shifts, taking turns sleeping, gathering more wood, preparing meals, and standing guard, waiting to relay the flare of War onward if need be, waiting, too, for their replacements to come. And they were weary, for such unremitting duty is meant for more than just two, a squad or perhaps a platoon being called for instead. But until the replacements came, the two of them would be on their own.

It was only at meals that they could find the time to sit and talk, or occasionally at the change of shift. And always they speculated upon when the relief would come, as well as mulling over the state that things had gotten to.

Yet though Aulf was weary, still his talk turned ever and again to the prospect of battle, and the chance for *adventure*, his eyes shining. Jörn would listen to the eagerness in his nephew's voice and shake his head in gentle regret, deploring the folly of youth, deploring that which once he himself had been.

On this night, as they sat in the cold stone tower and wondered when the warders would arrive, again Aulf spoke of the glory of War and how he longed to fight. "Lor, Uncle, wouldn't it be a marvel should we get to join in the battle? I mean, think of it: knights in armor on great warhorses tall as a Man and a half, with swords flashing in the Sun, silken pavilions pitched upon the sward, red and green and purple and blue pennons cracking in the breeze, pennons of every color, like rainbows trapped in the cloth. And shields and spears, bows and arrows, footmen, pikemen, marching and warding. . . .

"—Garn! I'll never be in it, trapped like I am here in the wilderness, sitting atop a cold mountain where *nothing* ever happens."

Jörn set aside his tin plate and took up his lute once more, strumming softly upon the strings, saying nought, waiting for this mood to pass from Aulf. But that was not to be; not yet.

"Uncle, you were in battle in the Jillians. What was it like?"

"Mostly waiting," replied Jörn.

"No. I mean the fighting itself."

"Confusion. Above all, confusion . . . and fear." Jörn stopped strumming the lute. "When it rained and we fought, it was a struggle just to stay afoot, the ground churned into a quag as it were. —Hèl, boy, you could get killed by your own, for no one could make out your colors, nor could you tell the colors of those of your own.

"Death there was, and little glory. And that was not a great War at all, up there in the Tors, up there along the Boreal. Instead we fought to suppress the clan battles. Did it, too, for a while. But only because they united against us, a common foe as we were.

"I hear tell that after we left, they took it up again: clan against clan. This time the High King let 'em fight it out;

no longer did we act as constabulary to that pack of highland Wolves.

"But we lost many a good Man in battle ere then. And to no end. And that is what War is all about: fear and death, death and fear. Most of it futile."

Aulf was not to be deterred. "Be that as it may, Uncle, still would I like to take up the sword and join in battle 'gainst the foe. Still would I like to march to War. For surely could I make my presence felt, could I win renown, could I be *someone*."

Jörn looked hard at Aulf. "If you would be *someone*, sister's son, then do it otherwise than in War. Have you not hearkened to a word I've said?"

Seeing the disbelief upon Aulf's face, Jörn turned his lute topside down in his lap. "Here. There is an eld chant that speaks to this point, one I think that came from the Elves, or perhaps the Dwarves, I know not which. Yet wherever it came from, still it speaks the truth of War more eloquently than can I."

Jörn began striking out a rhythm upon the body of his lute, using the instrument as a timbrel, as a muffled drum. And he chanted:

> *Follow not the Hèlborne drum,*
> *The savage, glory beat.*
> *Seek ye not the Roads of War*
> *To march with Death's Elite.*
>
> *That Legion treads upon a red*
> *Path of deep despair,*
> *Of shattered dreams, of agony,*
> *No matter where they fare.*
>
> *The glory road, a gory road,*
> *Is not where heroes run,*
> *For heroes are but common Men*
> *Just doing what must be done.*
>
> *So follow not the Hèlborne drum,*
> *The savage glory beat.*

Seek ye not the Roads of War
To join with Death's Elite.

Wield not the strike of hard, cruel iron,
Slake not its brutal lust.
Seek not a heartbeat to make still;
Smite only if ye must.

For fame and glory cannot salve
Wounds taken by y'r soul
When slaying on a slaughterground ...
Pay not this dreadful toll.

Follow not the Hèlborne drum,
The savage, glory beat.
Seek ye not the Roads of War
To join with Death's Elite.

Follow not the Hèlborne drum.
Follow not the Hèlborne drum.
Follow not the Hèlborne drum.
Follow not!—

Jörn's voice fell silent, the drumbeat ending. Neither said aught for a moment, Aulf looking at his uncle's worn armor, his uncle's soldier's sword, visions of splendor thundering behind the youth's solemn mask. Yet at last:

"But, Uncle," protested Aulf, "I don't think that the words of that chant are true. *Your* soul wasn't damaged. Why, you've *always* been the best friend—the best Man—any could ask for, as long as I can remember. And *you* went to War. . . ."

Again knights on horseback whelmed down upon the foe, and armies marched past cheering crowds through cobbled streets of vast cities. Aulf sighed. "Aye, you got to *do* something, to *see* something, to *be* somebody, to be a *fighter.* And I'm stuck here atop a hill, leagues and leagues away from where the action is going to be, stuck up here with no chance for glory."

Aulf leapt to his feet and stepped to the limits of the tower and peered out at the black night, northward, toward Challerain Keep lying far beyond the horizon. Striking his clenched fist down upon the sill: "I'll *never* get to have a day in the Sun, like you did. And I would give *anything* for just one moment of glory."

Jörn set aside his lute and looked up at the lad. Candlelight fluttered, shadows flickering across faces. "Boy, these grand dreams of youth are but flights of fancy." Jörn held up a hand, palm out, forestalling the protests springing to Aulf's lips. "Listen to me, lad. I *know*. I've *been* there.

"Aye, I did my time. Most of it standing about and waiting for something to happen. And when it did, what was it? Skirmishes, mostly. Over water rights. Over land rights. Over petty squabbles not worth a brass penny.

"But in the Jillians, it was War. And I'll tell you here and now that War is a Hèllish experience that has little or no *glory* to it.

"Heed me, sister's son: there are no good reasons to go to War, only bad ones. Aye, sometimes War is thrust upon us, and then we have little choice. But of all the things I can think of, glory is the *last* reason, the worst reason of all. . . . Aye, glory be the worst reason of all to go to War."

Unconvinced, the muscles in Aulf's jaw clenched and unclenched, as if he would say something, yet he could not meet his uncle's gaze. And at last, after long moments of tense silence, the youth took up the utensils and clambered down from the tower, leaving Jörn to sit watch in the night.

Over the next two days, working with Ironhead, Jörn and Aulf managed to finish the gathering of wood. Now there was enough to set fires for weeks on end, or so Aulf claimed. And still the replacements had not come.

The talk of the two Men did not broach again upon the glory or Hèl of War, though it was plain to see that the words lurked just behind the lips of uncle and nephew alike, each merely waiting for the other to say aught ere loosing arguments pent up. But neither trod into this quagmire, and so the contentions continued to marshal in silence, points and counterpoints, rebuttals and rejoinders, assertions and refutations, all readied for battle.

And still they waited, uncle and nephew.

* * *

Jörn was awakened in the night by Aulf's hand on his mouth, cautioning him to silence, a shielded candle dimly illuminating the interior of the small cote they had taken as their own. "They're coming up the hill," hissed the youth.

"Who, boy?" Jörn reached for his soldier's sword. *Weapon first, boots next.*

"I don't know. Mayhap the replacements. I could hear them coming. But it doesn't *feel* right."

Setting his blade at hand, Jörn rose up from his pallet and pulled on his breeks and slipped into his boots. "What is the hour, Aulf?"

"Halfway 'tween mid of night and dawn," replied the youth.

Stuffing jerkin into belt, Jörn quickly donned his underpadding, then took up his armor and slid it over his head, the patched chain jingling as it settled into place. "You're right, lad, there *is* something wrong about this. Replacements shouldn't be on the march at this dark hour. They'd wait till after dawn.

"Whence their direction?"

"They come up the northeast slope, Jörn," responded Aulf, his face grim. "And they bear no lights, not even a torch. That's why I slipped down to wake you. They seem to come in stealth, yet I heard one cursing, cursing in a tongue I know not."

"No lights?" Jörn snatched up his soldier's sword and glanced at Aulf to see that the lad had his stave in hand. "That's bad. And they come not by the west road upward, but through the eastern trees instead, where runs no path.

"Drearwood lies easterly."

Snatching up his winter cloak and thrusting a bit of bread and cheese into a sack—*'N if y' do run, it might be for days, so as try to have some food laid by*—Jörn stepped to the door, motioning Aulf to follow, whispering, "Douse that candle."

With his back to the wall Jörn eased the portal open and peered outward into the quarter-Moon night, standing still for what seemed an endless time. At last, tugging

Aulf's sleeve and crouching low, he moved quickly downslope and westerly, the youth hard upon his heels, following Jörn's lead. Slipping over the low stone wall and squatting, the two stopped and listened, hearing nought but the winter night silence. Cautiously, Jörn peered over the rock and back toward the open crest of the tor, Aulf at his side doing likewise. Even as they watched, two dark figures—no! three! four! more!—came creeping through the moonlit snow and onto the hilltop, pale moonbeams glinting off wicked curved blades.

"Rūcks!" hissed Aulf.

"Hlōks, too," breathed Jörn.

"Let's get 'em," growled Aulf, beginning to rise. But Jörn roughly jerked the youth back down, the lad thudding hard to the ground.

"Don't be a fool, boy!" hissed the elder. "We don't know their strength nor their goal. We *do* know that we are outnumbered, and that they bear weaponry superior to ours."

"But—"

"No buts," interrupted Jörn. "We'll stay right here and see what they are up to ... till dawn comes nigh, then we'll hie to a better hiding place to do our spying from."

Sensing Aulf's frustration, Jörn's voice took on a conciliatory tone. "Look, boy, 'tis better that we watch. After all, they just might move onward ... though I misdoubt it. Like as not they're here for some purpose, and we'd better see just what that purpose is."

Jörn felt his nephew give back slightly, though still the lad was tense and filled with rage as he watched the Spawn upon the hill.

Up through the pale moonlight came scuttling some forty of the dark, goblin-like creatures—bat-wing ears, viperous eyes, pointed teeth, the Rūcks short and bandy-armed and -legged, the Hlōks Man-sized with straighter limbs, all the Foul Folk dressed in leather armor sewn with iron rings—and with weapons ready they went from cote to cote looking for warders, kicking doors open, rushing inward, only to find each of the stone cottages empty.

At one point there was a great shout of victory, then a

loud thudding, and Aulf thought he heard Ironhead scream, and once again Jörn had to restrain the youth.

"Come on, lad, we've got to move now!" sissed Jörn. "I'd forgotten. The mule is a dead giveaway. They'll *know* that we were here."

Aulf could not believe his ears. "Run? Run from Spawn?"

"Yes!"

Aulf glared at his uncle. "Are we rabbits to run before these hounds? There is no honor in fleeing a foul foe. No glory."

Jörn ground his teeth in ire. "There is no honor in stupidity either, Nephew. No glory in being an utter fool. And to cast our lives away upon a tack-witted notion of honor, of glory, that would be fool's folly, indeed.

"Heed! None but we can carry word of these invaders to those who should know. Yet first we must spy out their purpose, their reason for being here. And for that, we must survive and observe. And to do so, we must go to ground."

Aulf looked at his uncle in disbelief. "Hide? Like cowards? Are we to creep about like frightened mice, afraid of our own shadows?"

"Yes! And now!" shot back Jörn, yanking up a scrub by the roots and thrusting it at his nephew. "And cover our tracks."

No sooner had they begun moving downslope, Jörn leading, Aulf reluctantly following and brushing the snow behind, than the Rückish force fanned out wide and began searching among the buildings, a ring of maggot-folk expanding outward from the crest as it moved slowly downgrade toward the perimeter wall.

Jörn and Aulf made their way down through the pines west and north till they came unto the Crossland Road below, where they crossed over to Northtor, a sister knoll just beyond the margin of the road. They climbed up the slopes till they came to the crown, taking up station where they could watch the Rücks and such from the concealment of thick pines. Their ruse had worked, for none of the Foul Folk had found a trace of them, giving up the search after coming down to the wall and slightly beyond. Too, one of the Hlōks was commander of this band, and he had other things for the maggot-folk to accomplish, and a blatting horn sounded recall ere the seekers wandered too far. And Jörn and Aulf watched with dismay as the Spawn took sledge hammers and wedges to the tower, whelming nigh the base with heavy blows, driving the angled irons deep into the mortar between the stones. And near midmorn, with a thunderous *Whoom!* that echoed throughout the hills, the watchstand was felled, stones shattering asunder, and the sentinel tower of Beacontor was no more.

Jörn shared out the meager supply of cheese and bread, knowing that this might be their last meal for several days. Yet food-weak warriors were not wanted, especially in these first hours when strength and endurance would be needed should they be discovered and have to fight or flee. And so the elder Man shared it all out, and the food was soon gone.

As the Sun rode up the sky and down again, the two took turns watching and resting, catching what slumber they could, knowing that weary warriors were as dangerous as weak ones. Aulf was asleep when the Rūcks began tearing down the cotes: the thatched roofs were ripped from the stone, and walls were felled, the shelters made uninhabitable.

When the lad awoke, once again Jörn had to restrain him, for Aulf would fight these wreckers regardless the odds, regardless the need to bear word back to Stonehill and thence unto Challerain Keep.

And when his uncle commanded him to lie quietly and merely observe, to stay down—"Voles!" snorted Aulf. "Hiding in the leaves."

"By damn, sister's son," declared Jörn, "one would think you lack-witted did he not know better. We are not voles, rabbits, frightened mice. Turn your thoughts away from those paths. Think instead that we are foxes, wise and wily. Better yet, think that we are Wolves, espying our prey, knowing that we must signal the pack when it comes time to bring down the quarry, knowing that numbers are needed for a successful hunt."

Aulf turned to his uncle. "Rather would I be the Eagle, swooping down upon the victim."

"But, lad," rejoined the elder Man, "the Eagle is a lone hunter, and crafty, and singles out but one well-chosen target at a time, isolated and apart. An Eagle will not swoop in among a nest of vipers to slaughter but one; yet let that viper become separated from the mass, and then . . ."

And as the twilight shadows swept across the land, Jörn's eyes turned toward the crest of Beacontor. "Yet we are neither Eagles nor Wolves, but Men instead. And we have before us a nest of vipers. . . .

"Come, Aulf. We've seen enough. Darkness falls and we can make good our escape under cover of black night ere the Moon rises."

And so they began their descent, stealthily working their way down and 'round the lesser hill from which they had spied, moving northerly, intending to swing westerly out of sight and down and make their way to Stonehill, some twenty leagues hence—sixty or so miles by foot along the Crossland Road—forcing march to come there within a twoday.

Yet they had moved but some quarter way around the hillside when Aulf tugged at his uncle's arm and pointed through the pines toward the north. Far off could be seen a glister, as if a tiny fire burned in the remote hills.

Quietly Jörn led them back upslope, higher, moving to a place of advantage. And both could see that indeed it was a fire burning, atop a distant mountain in the remote fastness far beyond the next station in the chain, a dim glimmer at this range. Yet both knew that what they looked upon was a balefire shrieking out its dire message.

"Garn," groaned the elder. "My sister's son, *this* is why the Foul Folk have come to Beacontor. The War has begun, yet they stop the call to arms."

Aulf looked blankly at his uncle. "I don't—"

"Beacontor is the highest of them all, Aulf," explained Jörn, "but the crest we stand on, Northtor, is next. That's why we can yet see two stations north. And the blaze we see in the distance is that second station—there the balefire burns brightly. But none to the south, east, or west of here can see yon flames, for no other station in our region has the height to do so, and Beacontor itself blocks the view from the Dellin Downs.

"Ah, me," sighed Jörn, "I think that not only has Beacontor fallen into Rückish hands, but so too has the Wilderhill station next north, for no fire burns there . . . or here, for that matter. Hence, the chain is broken."

"But that means none in the Wilderland nor in Harth nor any to the south will get the warning." Aulf's voice fell grim in the night. "The muster will be delayed."

"Just so, lad. Just so. The muster will eventually come—but late—perhaps too late to prevent some machination of Modru."

"Then, Uncle, we *must* take steps. But what?"

"There's nought for it, Aulf, but that we must somehow light the fire atop Beacontor. Yet first we must deal with the Rücks and such atop, else they will quench the signal."

Jörn fell into long thought. At last he spoke. "A ruse to lead them astray, I deem, would fail, for even should we draw them off and light the balefire, still would they return to quench it. And we cannot take them all on, boy, no matter your inclination. And who can say whether the balefire would burn sufficient time to spread the alarm south and east and west.

"At first I thought to gather deadwood and set a fire atop *this* hill—oh, not as a beacon, for we have not the height, but instead to draw them off from Beacontor. Yet they would surely leave a ward behind, fully alert, in goodly numbers, and we would have to defeat them first. Too, it would take long to gather up enough branches and kindle a lasting blaze, for as you know fallen wood is scarce, and we have no tinderbox, no flint or steel, though mayhap we can find a stone that when struck against my sword would cause some sparks to fly.

"Nay, a ruse will not suffice. But list, night falls, and they have been at hard labor all this daytide, destroying stone buildings, and they will be weary and sleeping the sleep of the dead. Hence, I deem that we must act as did Durgan of old, and creep among the exhausted foe in the night and slit their throats, and pray to Adon that we waken them not."

"But," growled Aulf, "slitting throats in the night smacks of cowardice, Uncle. I deem such an act bears no honor, no glory."

"Prate not to me about glory, Aulf," rasped Jörn, "for this is War and not some courtly game we play.

"Now listen well, for I will tell you how to cut the throat of one who sleeps—it is not simple, for no sound must escape. . . ."

Within the hour and without further argument, they crept down from the hill and toward Beacontor, Aulf accepting the necessity of what must be done, even though he did not relish it.

Long they watched from the edge of the crest, did Jörn and Aulf, crouching down behind the stone wall, noting the disposition of the Rūcks and Hlōks, noting that they made brief trips to the stable, coming forth after a short while.

By torchlight they were yet hammering at the remains of two cotes, though it appeared that they had not touched the three closest to the stables there on the far side. At last it seemed as if their labor was done, and amid what sounded as threats and a lashing of whips, four guards were posted, while the others relieved themselves and then went inside the standing cottages, twelve or so to a cote.

Jörn turned to Aulf and whispered, "Let us give them time to fall asleep. Mayhap a guard or two will slip into slumber as well, though we cannot count upon it."

And so they waited, and another hour slipped into the past. Yet the sentries continued to make frequent trips to the stables, entering for a brief while, emerging with their mouths full, chewing.

By this time the Moon was rising, and the cover of night was fading before pale rays aglance upon the snow, though atop Beacontor the snow had been churned into black muck by trampling feet.

Motioning his nephew to silence, Jörn began leading the way around the perimeter, staying low behind the wall, making for the stables, Aulf creeping after. At last they came to where they would cross over, and waited until no Rūcks were within the mews. Slipping over the wall, they ran silently to the simple byre and ducked into the deep shadows within, their eyes scanning the dark stalls, ready to slay lurking Spawn. Yet all was silent, but for their own harsh breathing.

A dread odor filled the air, one of Death. And in the pale moonlight seeping inward Aulf discovered its source: Ironhead was slaughtered, blood soaking the straw, his mangled remains scattered, haunches rent from his carcass, gaping holes showing where the Foul Folk had feasted.

The youth felt his gorge rise, and he came near to retching at this bloody sight, yet Jörn's whispered words focused him upon the task at hand, and he mastered his nausea. "Here we'll wait, slaying the sentries as they come to take food, for I deem that is why they enter the byre, to taste the flesh of mule. Yet heed me, it must be done without making a sound, for three dozen maggot-folk are but little more than an arm's length away.

"This is how we will do it . . ."

When the first sentry came, he nearly took them by surprise, for his foot was soft upon the Land; yet he bore a burning brand, and the wavering light gave Jörn and Aulf warning. Wedging his torch in a wall cresset, the guard entered the stall. And as the Rūck bent over the half-consumed mule, Jörn stepped quietly out from the shadows behind him and clapped his hand across the sentry's mouth, roughly jerking the small foe to him, running his shortsword through the Rūck's throat and out, black blood flying wide to land upon the red-soaked straw.

As Jörn dragged the corpse away, Aulf threw up, losing the meager meal he had taken that day, heaving until nought but bile came forth.

They quenched the torch and once again stood in the moonlight shadows. And Jörn's voice came quietly through grim blackness. "Get used to it, boy. There's thirty-nine more of them out there."

* * *

Aulf dragged the next corpse away, and the third one as well, for it seemed that the maggot-folk could not resist the taste of mule, though rumor had it that they preferred the flesh of horse . . . or even that of Man. And one by one the sentries came, the third one saying something in Slûk, the language of the Spawn, as he entered the stables, as if speaking out to one of the warders who had entered before him, not knowing that they were now dead. Yet what he said is not known, for neither Jörn nor Aulf spoke the tongue of the Foul Folk. Even so, Jörn cut his throat as he had the other two, and Aulf dragged him away.

They waited a long while, yet the last sentry did not come. "Mayhap he's gone asleep upon a full belly," whispered Aulf, the lad now armed with a Rückish tulwar as well as his staff, the long, curved blade wicked and deadly, its edge coated with a black grume.

"Mayhap," agreed Jörn. "Regardless, we must make our move, for a Hlōk could awaken and wonder where the sentries have gone.

"Let us get on with the business of slaughter, my sister's son, for time passes, and north a beacon burns while this one does not.

"And remember, Aulf, Hlōks first, when you get the chance, for they lead the others. And if any of the maggot-folk snore, save them for last, for their sounds will cover the murder of their kith."

The quarter-Moon rode high in the sky when they stepped out from the stables, illuming the way to the cotes. And when they entered the first, pale beams shone through the wide cracks in the weatherworn shutters, shining down upon the ones sleeping within.

And the two of them stepped in among the helpless foe and began their grisly task, Aulf but barely containing his sickness at that which he did, yet doing it well, for Jörn's instructions had been thorough, and not a sound was made as throats were let and black blood spurted forth in silence. *Only Adon knows the cost done to our souls for the deeds we do this night.*

And the slaughter went on . . .

... and on ...
... and on ...
... in silence ...
... while tears ran down a young Man's face to fall away in the darkness.

Splattered with gore, arms wet to the elbows and slick with black blood, Aulf and Jörn were in the third cote when the torch-bearing sentry came through the door, and his shriek brought the surviving maggot-folk to their feet, tulwars, scimitars, and cudgels in hand.

Jörn cut down two ere they could get their bearings, but Aulf seemed frozen—whether in confusion, indecision, or fear, it is not known. Yet Jörn shouted, "The guard, Aulf, the guard!" and the lad leapt forward and slashed down the Rūck at the door, cleaving his head in twain, brain and bone flying wide, guttering torch falling to the ground outside, Aulf at last joining the fray.

As the youth turned to the battle within, Jörn sprang backward, evading a blow from the scimitar wielded by a tall Hlōk. "Out, boy! We'll hold them at the door!"

Aulf jumped for the door, bashing aside a Rūck who had leaped to block the way, yet taking a blow from the foul one's cudgel upon his left arm, the limb falling numb. Even so, Aulf skewered the foe and won free, as feeling returned to his hammered arm, pain squalling from left elbow to shoulder.

Coming after, Jörn yet engaged the Hlōk, and the Man stumbled and fell backward over the body of the slain Rücken sentry and crashed down across the door stoop, slamming to the earth. Laughing in wicked triumph, the Hlōk raised his scimitar to hack downward. Yet Aulf stepped forward and swung the captured tulwar with all his might, the driven edge cleaving, and the Hlōk's hand was shorn from his arm, his weapon falling, the dark, grasping fingers still clutching the grip as the wide blade clanged to the ground.

Kicking out at the shrieking Hlōk, Jörn regained his feet. "The fire, boy! The fire! I'll hold them here! You light the beacon!"

Catching up the dead sentry's fallen torch, Aulf ran for

the balefire mound, his breath harsh in his ears as he pounded up the hillside. Yet behind him came racing a Hlōk, the foe having smashed through the latched shutters of the cote window and jumped outward in pursuit. Heedless of the danger, Aulf ran onward.

The lad reached the crest of the hill only to find it barren. The Foul Folk had scattered the balefire mound! Even so, a glance through the pale moonlight showed that the pile of extra wood was yet stored under the pole-roof shelter. But as Aulf turned to race down and fire it, the Hlōk came upon him.

Chang! Shing! Blade engaged blade. Scimitar 'gainst tulwar, and the Hlōk was skilled and the lad was not. Perhaps the battle would have been more even had Aulf his quarterstave, yet Fate dictated otherwise and the youth defended with unfamiliar blade instead.

Jörn turned from the last fallen foe, the enemy within the cote all dead, for they had not been able to bring their meager numbers to bear upon him; he stood at the doorway and they could come at him but one at a time and none thought to leap out the window and come at his back, and the whole of the foul force was now slain. *Yet wait!* There came from the hillside above him the sounds of steel upon steel. *Aulf!* The Man turned from the house of slaughter and desperately ran upward. *The lad engages, and he has not the training!*

Dodging and darting among the ruins of squat buildings, the Man dashed upslope, his heart pounding in fear for his nephew. Suddenly the sounds of combat ceased, and in the following silence there was only the hammering of Jörn's heart and the thud of his footsteps and the rasping of his breath as he ran upward through the moonlight. And then there came the sound of shrieking from above.

Atop the hill the Hlōk plunged his scimitar over and again into Aulf's fallen body, stabbing downward with a reversed two-handed grip in such force that the cruel point repeatedly punched into the ground below, the Hlōk screaming in hatred as he stabbed the blade time and again through the corpse. Hence it was only at the last moment that he detected movement behind, and he was only partially turned toward it when Jörn's blade took off his head.

And far to the north a balefire faintly glimmered in the distance, woefully shouting out for all who could see that grim War had begun.

Jörn lit the fire on Beacontor just ere dawn ended that fearful night of slaughter. He stood back and wept, watching the flames whirl up into the paling sky. And he muttered a prayer under his breath, yet what he said is not known but for the last of it:

> The glory road, a gory road,
> Is not where heroes run,
> For heroes are but common Men
> Just doing what must be done.

Jörn gazed through tear-filled eyes as the fire raged, consuming Aulf's body, the lad laid to rest atop the pyre ere it was set aflame, the bodies and weapons of his foe laid at his feet, and the fire took them all.

Jörn looked upward in the fading night, as if willing his sight to see Aulf's spirit as it was lifted up by the flames. "You found your moment of glory, lad," he whispered, "yet was it worth the price paid?"

And southward, eastward, and westward the warcry of the balefire of Beacontor shrieked out through the darkness, and Men took up arms and armor and said farewell to loved ones.

Jörn took up his sword and girded himself for battle. Challerain Keep stood many days to the north, yet he, too, would answer the summons of the High King.

As the dawn broke over the land, there sounded a call from downslope. There on the road wending upward came a squad marching: it was the relief come at last, the force of Men who would stand sentry upon Beacontor, coming unto the wreckage atop the mount.

Jörn looked once more at the fire, the funeral pyre, the balefire, the warcry. "Aulf, once I told you that there are no good reasons to fight a War, only bad ones, *glory* being the worst of the lot. Yet I did not tell you the whole of it: aye, there *are* no good reasons to fight a War . . . except perhaps to gain revenge."

Accoutered in his worn armor, Jörn shrugged into his all-weather cloak. And bearing his knapsack with its meager provisions, he turned and started down the hillside.

And in the One-Eyed Crow, Feeny's words fell to silence, his tale told at last. And none inside said aught, their jewel-like eyes wide with unseen visions. Nought but the frigid wind outside spoke, its raging voice squalling in shrieking grief, a furious icy wailing that hammered upon clapboards and rattled windows and shook the very foundations of the tiny tavern, as if seeking vengeance for dark deeds long past.

The
Transformation
of Beau Darby

"Ooo, now, Feeny," whispered Nob Haywood, his voice quavering, his slight frame shivering as well, "I don't want to be going to my bed with *t-that* t-tale on my mind. Why, I'll be dreaming about R-Rūcks and such g-gettin' their throats cut all through the n-night."

Nodding in unspoken agreement, Warrows looked at one another in the deep shadows in the One-Eyed Crow, jewel-like eyes wide and glittering with reflected fire-light, their minds' eye conjuring up visions brought on by Feeny's tale of the slaughter atop Beacontor. And the wind moaned about the tiny inn, hurling snow against the ice-laden windows, the blizzard pounding as would lost souls hammer for entry. And a desperate pall seemed to settle upon the trapped Wee Folk.

As if to press back the dark mood, Will and Arla Brackleburr turned up the wicks on the low-burning lanterns, bringing warm yellow light to brighten the place. Even so, still the storm howled and boards creaked and groaned and windows rattled, and it seemed as if the Warrows would be trapped inside *forever,* or so thought several of them.

"I say, Gaffer," piped up Dilby Higgs, peering at the eld Warrow, "have you got any tales that might make our dreams a bit more pleasant?"

"Yar, Gaffer," agreed Bingo, "something that'll put a smile on faces 'stead o' these scowls I see all about."

The Gaffer cocked an eye at Will Brackleburr and raised his mug. Swiftly Will and Arla and their bucco, Alban, rushed about, refilling empty vessels with tea—or ale—as the patrons would have it. And when everyone was settled about the granther buccan, he cleared his throat and his gimlet eye swept across the faces before him.

"Well now, so ye want a change in thinking, eh? A transformation, so to speak . . . right?" At the eager nodding of his audience, the Gaffer spoke on. "Transformations, eh? . . . Transformations . . ."

Phoom! went the contents of Beau's bronze spoon as he held it over the open lamp flame, and a thick cloud of acrid yellow smoke blasted forth, billowing outward, whooshing upward. Hacking and coughing, snatching up his journal, the stripling Warrow fled, fumbling open the door of his experimentation shed, stumbling forth amid a roiling ocherous cloud, tears streaming down his cheeks as he blinked and squeezed his eyes shut against the stinging reek.

"Beau!" A voice called from the stone cottage. "Beau Darby, answer this minute!"

"Yes . . . *hck* . . . *hkk* . . . Aunt Rose," choked out Beau, getting clear of the yellow cloud.

A door opened, and a grey-haired eld damman stepped forth, concern mingled with exasperation in her face. Hastily, Beau hid the spoon behind his back. Too, he quickly felt his eyebrows. *Good. Still there. Not like the last time.*

"Beau, you'll be the death of me yet," said his aunt, wiping her hands on her blue apron, starting forward, pacing through the light covering of snow that lay on the ground. "Ever since you heard about those *Wizards,* well, it's just been one noisy bang after another; and if it isn't a rancid green cloud rolling out from that play shed of yours, then it's a . . . a . . . a smelly yellow one!" Her glittering sapphirine gaze had spied the jaundiced smoke leaking through the old goat-shed door and rising into the late winter sky to disappear upon the light breeze.

"That's just it, Aunt Rose." Beau's voice was filled

with fervor. "I'm going to be the first Warrow Wizard ever! And to do so, why, I've just *got* to experiment. You'll see, and be proud of me, too. Why, I'll be able to change lead to gold, and transform wicked persons into goats and frogs and things, and—"

"Oh, child," interrupted Aunt Rose, having reached the buccan, grasping him by the shoulders, peering deeply into his amber gaze, "you frighten me, half blowing yourself up and all, as you've done. Why, your eyebrows have just grown back, and . . . and . . ."—tears filled her eyes—". . . Oh, Beau, I just know that something awful is going to happen, what with all this talk of becoming a Wizard and these 'experiments' of yours. What if one of them were truly magic and changed *you* into a frog or a goat? And what for? What for?"

"Why, I just told you, Auntie," answered Beau, "so that I can do Wizardish things, like fly, and change shape, and—"

A look of disgust swept over Aunt Rose's face, stopping Beau cold, and she pushed the buccan back, holding him at arm's length.

Thinking that something terrible was happening, "What is it, Aunt Rose? What is it?" asked Beau, wildly looking about for whatever it might be that caused his aunt to behave so.

"You smell awful, that's what," replied the eld damman. Taking the stripling by the ear, she led him toward the cottage. "And I shouldn't wonder, what with all that yellow smoke reeking from your clothes. Why your grandsire ever had those jars and bottles filled with all sorts of strange things in the first place, I'll never know. And why he left them with your mother, *hmph;* why, if I didn't know better, I'd say he did it just so someone like you could make explosions and smelly gases, and whatever. It's a bath for you, my young bucco, and right now. And wash that brown hair of yours, too, for it's filled with the stench as well. And I want you to stop all this talk about transformations and flying and other such nonsense. Why, the only flying that's going to be done around here is that you are going to fly into the house, fly through a bath, and then fly out to the barn and feed and milk the cows and then fly through your other chores."

"But, Auntie Rose," protested Beau, "my experiment—"

"No buts, Beau." Rose's voice took on a resolute edge, and she let go of his ear and pointed an adamant finger toward the cottage. "Bath. Now."

As the stripling dejectedly trudged through the snow for the house, Aunt Rose followed after, her heart still aflutter over the detonation in the goat shed. Oh, she knew that some would say that she was just being a silly eld damman, but Beau was all she had . . . and in turn, she was all he had, his sire and dam having died of the plague when he was but a babe. And he seemed so *intense,* so *sober,* never laughing—perhaps if his parents had lived . . .

Watching him retreat into the cottage, she knew that she would never know what might have been had his parents lived—Rose's sister, Lily, and Lily's buccaran, Alvey. Still, Rose marvelled that she was able to do for Beau at all, for till he came along she'd never had a thing to do with a child, having never married. But even though she was nought but a flighty eld spinster, she *did* know that she was truly frightened by Beau's experiments, for the lad was concocting mixtures of the various types of the four elements, and heating them and cooling them, and setting them afire, freezing them with snow and ice in the winter, burning them with a Sun glass in the summer. Mixing earth with earth, fire with fire, water with water, and air with air. Mixing all together and mixing parts. Burning. Freezing. Melting. Stirring. Hammering. *Lawks!* Everybody knew that Wizards did such things and so it was *bound* to be dangerous, and who knows *what* he might conjure up? Perhaps one of his trials would result in an error that would do something physical to him, or worse yet, something *magical.* Her heart fluttered at the thought.

But though Aunt Rose was truly frightened, Beau was not. . . .

. . . And as the months passed and winter turned into spring and spring into summer and autumn neared, every day Beau would take one or more of the forms of the four elements—be it red powder or yellow, blue liquid or green, purple gas or white—and concoct some new amalgam, some admixture of water, earth, or air, and at some stage or other he would add fire or cold, heating, cooling, burning, or freezing, or combinations thereof, keeping a careful record of what he did in his experimentation journal. Sometimes the blend would produce foul smoke; at other times it would burn brightly. Often it would fizz or bubble or otherwise be active. Occasionally it would detonate. Yet most of the time it would form a turgid goo, and do nothing but appear grey, perhaps ooze a bit.

Yet always, no matter what else it did, it frightened Aunt Rose. But she hid her fear—she thought she was being silly and foolish, for she *had* been flighty all her life and she knew it. Besides, her few well-meaning friends whom she trusted implicitly had said, "Rose, give the stripling room to grow."

And she had.

And perhaps this was the best course; after all, Beau himself was becoming rather discouraged, for it seemed as if he spent most of his time chipping black char from his utensils or burying another unsuccessful immixture.

As of yet he had not changed his only lead ingot to gold, no matter what glop he poured over it.

Nor had he transformed any insect to another form, except dead.

And he certainly hadn't flown for any length to speak of, unless one counted the length from the shed roof to the ground.

Beau was thinking strongly of changing his career.

But then he heard the most wonderful news: a Wizard was coming to the Boskydells.

A Wizard!

A real Wizard!

It seems as if there was to be a celebration in Rood, some eighty or so miles west of Aunt Rose's farm, and one of the mysterious Wizards would be there to show magicks, to cast illusions, to provide fireworks, and who knows what all!

And he would be coming along the Crossland Road, and that was practically at Beau's front door.

This was Beau's chance!

At last, to talk with a true Wizard. Perhaps the Mage would share some secrets, or even better yet, take on an apprentice, take on Beau! The thought sent shivers of gleeful anticipation down the buccan's spine, and he attacked his experiments with renewed vigor.

And Aunt Rose's heart continued to flutter.

Days passed, and Beau kept an eye upon the Crossland Road. He would fly to its side whenever he espied a stranger or two, be they in waggons, on ponies or horses, or afoot, the stripling speaking with each. And though he met many people this way—Warrows, Dwarves, Men, and even an Elf—he had yet to meet the Wizard.

With renewed enthusiasm he flung himself at his grand art, determined to be a Wizard himself. And he clung to this determination right up to the day of the great explosion, the day Beau was transformed.

It happened this way:

"Beau! Oh, Beau!" called Aunt Rose from the back door, worried. She hadn't heard the young Warrow for more than an hour now, and it was nearing lunch time, when usually he was at her elbow. . . . *Hungry as a young goat,* she thought. *Waiting for the noon meal and telling me all about another one of his horrid experiments.*

She heard the clatter of his utensils.

"Beau Darby," she demanded, "stop that experimenting right now! It's time you cleaned up for lunch!"

Oh, that buccan! In his shed. Pouring some smelly goo into another, making a bubbling mess. Trying to change something into something else—

—WHOOM! came an earsplitting blast, and the door of the shed was blown ajar on its hinges and boards flew off the building sides, the roof jumping up and down. A boiling plume of green smoke gushed forth, and Aunt Rose's heart gave a great thump. She thought she was about to swoon, for her cheeks and forehead tingled just as if she might. Yet she did not faint and instead pulled her wits together, for she heard a crying, a bleating, coming from the shed.

"Oh, Lor!" she shrieked, dashing out and across the backyard, and through the billowing smoke and into the green-fumed shed. "Beau!"

Inside, groping through the ghastly cloud, "Beau! Beau!" she cried, tears streaming down her cheeks, tears caused by the bilious reek as well as by desperate fear. In the midst of the green fog she could see a shape. "Beau!"

But it was not a buccan she found; instead it was a little brown goat with amber eyes, sitting dazedly on its hindquarters.

"Beau!" called Aunt Rose, fanning smoke and peering about, looking for her stripling ward.

"Baa-aa-a!" bleated the kid.

"Beau!"

"Baa-aa-a!"

"Beau?"

"Ba-aaa-a!"

"Oh, Lor, child, what have you done to yourself?" Aunt Rose stooped down to the kid and lifted its chin, peering into its golden eyes.

"Baa-a-aaa!" bleated the little brown goat, and it gazed back deeply into her eyes, pleading for succor.

"Oh, Beau," Aunt Rose burst into tears, "I *knew* it would come to something like this. What are we going to do? Oh, what are we going to do?"

"Ba-aaa-aaaa?"

"Well, don't you worry, child," wept the damman spinster, "we'll think of something, we will.

"Here, let's get you into the house and see if you are hurt." And she stood and wiped away her tears with her apron. The kid, too, got shakily to his feet, and together they went into the house, Aunt Rose trying to soothe both her own fears and those of a frightened young billy.

Once inside, but for a small cut on his left ear, the grey-haired damman determined that the kid didn't seem to be injured, and she cleaned him as best she could, for as usual he didn't want the bath she deemed he needed.

In fact, Aunt Rose practically had to wrestle him into the tub, for he was bleating and jerking to keep out of the soapy water. "Beau, bucco, now you settle down," she commanded. "I know you don't especially like baths.

And as a goat, perhaps you can't help it if it's against your nature, newborn as it were. But, well, you've just got to have a bath. Whatever it was that transformed you into a four-footed creature, it had an awful smell to it, and the odor is all in your hair. Perhaps if we wash it out you'll be transformed back.

"And frankly, Beau, you also smell like the goat you've become, and that's that!"

And into the tub he went; bleating or not, he was going to get a scrubbing.

It was quite a struggle, and soap and water were splashed all over Rose and the kitchen, too, but eventually he was thoroughly scrubbed and dried and dressed in a clean pair of blue breeks and a yellow jerkin, though he did look rather silly got up so. And there was a bandage on his left ear, which he kept trying to flick off, but it stayed on and covered the shallow groove cut in it by a piece of flying glass during the explosion.

"Now, Beau," said Aunt Rose upon returning to the kitchen after cleaning herself and changing into dry clothes, "it's time for lunch. Time also to talk over just what we should do about your . . . *condition.*"

She set two places at the table and served up their lunch: peas, yellow beans, lettuce, cold beef, bread, and milk. As she took her chair, he jumped up on the other one and quickly ate everything but the beef.

"Beau, mind your manners!" she said sharply, then laughed. "Why, silly me. Of course you can't use a knife and fork. Go right ahead. Until we get you changed back, I suppose you'll just have to nuzzle and guzzle your food."

"Baaa-aa-a!" he answered, bobbing his head up and down.

During the remainder of the afternoon Aunt Rose just had a terrible time with him, for it seemed as if his goatish nature dictated that he get up atop the chairs and tables and cupboards and anything else of any height. And he didn't seem to be of any help in resolving the dilemma of how to transform himself into a Warrow, and poor

Aunt Rose was left to struggle with this thorny problem alone.

"Oh, Beau, if you just hadn't wanted to become a Wizard . . ."

"Naa-aaa-aa!"

"Well, what are we to do?"

"Na-a-a-aaa?"

"Off the counter, Beau! That's better. Surely there's a way to undo what's been done."

"Naa-a-aaa."

"Perhaps if we're fortunate it'll wear off after a time and you'll be your old self again. —Get down!"

"Naa-aaa-a."

And that was the way it went throughout the afternoon: Aunt Rose stewing over the problem and discussing it to no end and to no resolution, shooing the billy down from the furniture. The Sun sank toward the horizon and shadows lengthened, and it was very late on that September afternoon when Aunt Rose in her exasperation exclaimed, "By Adon, it would take a Wizard to straighten out this mess!"

As it dawned upon her what she had said, she grabbed the goatling by the jowls and cried, "Beau! That's it! That's just exactly what we'll do!"

Rose began rushing about, gathering up things. "They say there's a Wizard supposed to be passing through sometime today. He'll probably stay in Raffin tonight and go on to Willowdell tomorrow. Well, I'll just take you there and he'll straighten things out, right enough."

"Baa-aaa-a!" The kid leapt up to a chair and onto the table and back to the floor, appearing to express joyous approval.

"Well, let me just get a lantern and my bonnet and shawl, and, oh yes, a coat for you. The night will be chilly when we start back."

Chattering in excitement all the while, Aunt Rose rushed off to her bedroom to fetch the clothes, as the Sun set and dusk swept across the land. And as she returned along the hallway, she heard a bang, as if a door had burst open or something had fallen over . . . or as if a faint echo from a blast.

As she stepped forward, she heard the delighted laughter of her Beau.

She rushed to see, and there he stood, his normal self, laughing gleefully.

"Oh, Beau," she cried, tears springing to her eyes, "you're back."

Laughing with joy, Beau nodded.

"You've been transformed."

Again he bobbed his head up and down, laughing still.

She hugged him to her and laughed, and Beau laughed, too. Her voice was filled with relief. "Now we don't have to go see the Wizard."

With a quick squeeze Beau stepped back from her embrace, holding her at arm's length. "Auntie, I don't know how you could tell, but I am indeed transformed. And indeed I *don't* need to see the Wizard, for I already have.

"And he spoke with me and asked just what I'd been up to. I showed him my journal and explained to him my experiments. He questioned me closely, and I had to answer sharp. He was most impressed with my knowledge on the effects of mixing the various elements, hot or cold. He told me that I would make a natural healer, for with but a small amount of new knowledge, especially in herbs and simples, much of it here in this book he gave me, I can mix healing medicines and philters and physiks to cure the ill.

"Somehow he knew about my sire and dam dying of the plague, and he said I'd be much happier as a healer than as a Wizard's apprentice. He said he'd recommend me to a healer in Willowdell, and I am to study under him, said that he'd put in a word for me.

"And this wonderful book! It's all about medicinal herbs and curing elements and their mixing and treatment. He showed me how to read it, for there is a simple Wizard's secret to that.

"I talked with him all afternoon, and I didn't see that the time was slipping away. I didn't mean to stay away without your permission, but he was so nice. Gruff but nice.

"Oh, Auntie, this simply has been the *best* day of my life.

"And you are right: I am indeed *transformed!*"

Aunt Rose looked at him in astonishment. "Best day of your life? How can you say that, Beau? Why, it's been the worst day of mine, what with all this goat business and the transformation and everything.

"And what do you mean, you've been with the Wizard all afternoon?

"Why, now, I don't pretend to understand all this wizardry hocus pocus, but I do know that a person can't be in two places at once—"

Aunt Rose was interrupted by a sharp rapping on the door. It was the neighbor: Arlo Reedy.

" 'Scuse me, Miss Rose," called Arlo through the open door. "I know it's getting late and all, but have you seen a little spiker? Brown he is, and just a youngling. The nanny's lost him, and the little bleater's run off."

"Would it be a wee goatling dressed in a pair of blue pants and a yellow shirt?" asked Beau, giggling.

"Wh-what?" sputtered Arlo. "A kid got up in clothes?"

"Well, if he fits that description, then there he stands, and there he was when I got back from Raffin." Beau laughed in glee, pointing at the top of the cupboard, where stood proudly a little billy dressed in blue breeks and yellow jerkin, munching one of Aunt Rose's cut flowers, nought but a scrap remaining in the vase.

Aunt Rose looked from Beau to the wee goat and back again. And she thought of the bath and luncheon and the long, long one-sided conversation she'd had trying to solve a "thorny problem." And then she, too, broke out in giggles, which soon turned to the most infectious, side-splitting laughter ever heard in the Boskydells. Arlo stood in the doorway, a dumbfounded look on his face, watching Rose and Beau laughing as if they were entirely mad. But then he, too, was caught up in the howling glee, and they roared at the absurd sight of a tiny goat in yellow shirt and blue trousers. And the house shook with their whoops. Every time they would nearly come back to their senses, the he-goat kid would look seriously at them and flick his bandaged ear and say, "Naa-aaa-aa!" and gales of mirth would peal forth again.

It *was* one of the best days in Beau Darby's life, for it

indeed was the first day of his transformation, and it began with joy.

The One-Eyed Crow rang with laughter, tears running out from jewel-like Warrow eyes and down Warrow cheeks, Gaffer Tom cackling with high glee, hilarity all about. As the merriment ebbed, the joyous atmosphere falling toward sanity, the Gaffer would again bleat, "Naa-aaa-aa!" and gaiety would burst forth once more.

It took a longish time for the folks in the 'Crow to settle down, and even then chuckles would titter forth.

But at last Nob Haywood spoke up: "Hoy, Gaffer. That was a fine tale, but like as not, untrue. I mean, what with Wizards and all in it, it's not as if anyone knows where they've all got to. I mean, they haven't been about since ... since ..."

"Since the Ban War," interjected the Gaffer. "And Nob, the tale is true, or so I believe. For as has been passed down through the ages, lore has it that Beau Darby was one of the companions of Tipperton Thistledown."

A shocked look passed over the features of every Warrow in the 'Crow.

"You don't mean," spoke up Bingo Peacher, "that he was the same Beau what accompanied Tip on his last mission, now, do you?"

"Aye," replied the Gaffer softly. "The very same."

Outside the One-Eyed Crow, the wind slammed into the walls, rattling boards and shrieking down the chimney, raging at those within. While inside, respectful Warrows removed their hats.

The Dammsel

Y'know, Gaffer, speakin' o' healers like Beau Darby puts me in mind o' a tale I once heard concernin' a healer down by Thimble," announced Teddy Cloverhay.

Gaffer Tom turned from the ice-laden window and gazed through the lantern light toward the waggoneer, while outside, wind-driven snow flew like sling bullets, hammering upon field and forest and fen alike, hurling at dwellings, great drifts piling up against ridges and tree trunks and embankments and walls, piling against any upright surface or slant.

Using his cane, the granther Warrow stumped the few steps to his customary chair and sat, and after filling his briar with pipeweed and lighting it, he looked expectantly through the wreathing smoke at Teddy. "Well?"

Instantly all the other Warrows in the One-Eyed Crow gathered 'round, and Teddy cleared his throat.

"I was told that the events o' this tale occurred some hundred years agone, back in the winter o' 4E1917, or thereabout, down there in Thimble.

"Now Thimble is a wee town at the end o' a spur road off the Tineway, in Southdell, and to the north and south lie woods, but east and west the Land is open.

"And in this town lived a healer; they said his name was Fenmoss, Fenweed, or some such.

"In any event, one night, during a blizzard—somewhat

like the one blowing outside—there came a knock on his door. . . ."

The soft rapping could be but barely heard above the moaning of the wind, yet for some reason Arly Fenbrye was wakened. Even so, still he lay in his bed for some moments, his mouth tasting like iron, his eyes feeling gritty, trying to isolate what had brought him to. At last he heard the quiet tapping again, and he thought that it might be a tree branch ticking against his cottage, pressed by the gusting flaw, yet no tree grew close enough.

Groaning with fatigue, Arly swung his feet off the bed. He was yet dressed, for he had come home and had collapsed without disrobing. There was plague upon the land, and Arly had had no rest for several days running.

Shivering in the chill, dark cottage, Arly fumbled about and found his boots, slipping them onto his feet. Then he lit a candle.

The interior of the cottage looked preternaturally sharp in the pale, wavering light, all colors and edges somehow emboldened, yet at one and the same time soft and fuzzy and flickering. Muzzily he chalked it up to lack of sleep, rubbing his gritty eyes, yet the hues and shades and sides and angles remained as soft and bright and sharp and fuzzy as before.

Again came the soft tapping.

Bearing the candlestick holder, the healer made his way toward the door, the light a pale amber sphere about him, while outside the wind moaned and snow flew 'cross the 'scape, and it seemed as if a sobbing groaned down the chimney.

A frigid blast of air gusted inward as Arly opened the door, and his candle was nigh extinguished. Yet he cupped his hand about the flickering flame, and it grew to fullness once more. And the sight that met Arly Fenbrye's eyes caused him to cry out in concern. A wee damman stood without, not more than a chit, and she was dressed in nought but a nightgown. And the icy wind blew down upon her.

"Oh, lor, child!" Quickly, Arly scooped up the youngling and bore her inside, kicking the door to, closing out the wind. His heart pounding, Arly wrapped her in a blanket and set her on the edge of the bed and examined her hands and feet—*Oh, my poor child, your feet are bare.* Carefully he began briskly rubbing her wrists and ankles—*Lor, as cold as Death*—slowly working his way down to her fingers and toes. Even so, the chill clung adamantly unto her in spite of Arly's efforts.

He turned to his hearth and began laying in tinder and kindling, preparing to start a fire. And all the while he spoke to her, trying to keep her spirits up, or his own, he knew not which. "Adon, child, the night isn't fit for any to be out and about. Yet here you are, traipsing through the wind and across the snow and ice as if it were but a summer's eve. Whose dammsel are you? Who is your sire and dam? And how old are you? Not more than nine or ten, I'd judge. And how come you to be out on a night such as this? What brings you forth in the storm? Are you lost?"

But as he knelt upon the brick of the fireplace and placed another bit of tinder, a tug came at his elbow, and he turned to find her beside him, the blanket abandoned, her large sapphire-blue eyes level with his and pleading.

"What is it, little dammsel?"

Again she tugged on his sleeve, pulling him up and toward the door.

"You wish me to come with you, is that it?"

Once more she pulled at his sleeve.

Mayhap someone's fallen outside. "Ho, lass, but you're not going out dressed like that, in nought but a blue cotton nightgown embroidered with a pink rose bud. No ma'am, you're not, and that's that." Quickly, Arly pulled on his coat and gloves, and wrapped the youngling in the blanket once more, taking care to cover her hands and feet. Then he scooped her up—*Lor, she has little or no weight to her.* "Which way, tiny one?"

Pointing, the youngling led the healer through the wind and snow to his small byre out back, and there in the stalls she indicated that he was to harness pony to cart.

In spite of his doubts—*How far did you come, child?*—Arly hitched the winter-shagged horseling to the light two-wheeled covered carriage, placing the wee damman within. And out into the storm they fared, the pony struggling, hauling the rig across the snow-laden roads, Arly driving, the mute lass directing his route.

And, lo! they had gone no more than a mile when the wind began to abate, the storm to slacken, and within another mile the blizzard had passed. And still the blanket-wrapped child pointed forward, and across the 'scape they went.

In the airy dark, in spite of all, Arly found himself nodding asleep, then jerking awake, then nodding asleep once more; for he was exhausted beyond measure, having had no rest in four days, his time spent caring for others in the plague-beset village of Thimble.

It was the pony cart stopping that jerked Arly awake at last. The horseling stood still in front of a small cote. Overhead, a bright Moon shone down upon the snow. On the seat beside him lay the blanket, and the wee damman was just disappearing through the cottage door.

"Hoy, little dammsel, wait for me," he called, catching up his bag of herbs and simples and other supplies, swiftly stepping down from the cart and hurrying after, glancing about as he moved across the trackless snow. In the bright moonlight he recognized where he was: *Hoy! The Brinster place—Wait a moment, now, that's some twelve miles from my cote! How could that youngling have—?*

In that instant he reached the door, and a low moan interrupted his thoughts, and it came from within the cottage.

Inside, it was dark, but moonlight shone through a window, and Arly found a candle to light. In one of the bedrooms, he discovered Rory and Daisy Brinster, their foreheads burning, their skins aflame, their breathing harsh and labored, the Warrows fevered with the plague. The small damman stood at their bedside, gazing upon them.

Quickly, Arly stepped to the kitchen and built a fire and set water in a kettle above. He dug through his bag and haled out two kind of herbs, and ground them fine with his mortar and pestle, and carefully measured out the resulting powders and thoroughly mixed them together in the proper proportion, all the while cursing at the slowness of the fire, urging the watched pot to boil.

At last he held a hot liquid, steaming now with the odor of mint and spice from the herbs. Slowly and carefully he raised up the Brinsters, just enough to sip the drink, Daisy first, Rory after. And he eased them back down, each breathing quieter than before.

When they seemed to be resting more easily—*Perhaps I got to them in time*—the youngling turned away and silently retreated to another room.

Casting a glance at the patients, Arly followed after, stepping into the other room to see that the dammsel got some sleep.

There he found her, lying in her cold bed, dressed in a blue cotton nightgown embroidered with a pink rose bud. And at last he understood how she could have fetched him . . .

. . . And why she never spoke.

Taking her by the hand, Arly judged that her little heart had stopped some hours past, slain by the plague that gripped this house. Still her heart had been great enough to hold onto love even after passing into Death's domain.

And in that love, her tender soul had sought out one who could aid those she cherished.

Weeping, Arly closed her eyes and folded her hands upon her still breast. "Godspeed, bright spirit," he whispered, then stepped away to tend to those who were yet among the living.

In the One-Eyed Crow, Teddy's voice fell silent, his tale told, and not an eye was dry. Outside, the wind moaned past, sobbing down the chimney.

For
Want of a
Copper Coin

Grey morning had come, its wan light battered by the shattering blizzard that yet raged down upon the Bosky. For two days the elemental fury had ravened across the Land, trapping, freezing, destroying what it could, whelming upon any and all that stood in its way. And now began the third day of the icy blast. In hamlets and villages, in cottages and huts, in burrows and flets, and in stone field-houses and stilted fen-houses Warrows endured. And so, too, in the main did their flocks and herds, be they chicken or goose or duck, be they cow or pony or sheep, huddled as they were in barn and byre, in hutch or pen, in deep hollow or swale, or even inside their masters' dwellings.

In one of these places of durance, the One-Eyed Crow, another morning of blizzard imprisonment began with a hearty breakfast—of eggs and toast and strong hot tea, and of blueberry preserves put up last fall by Arla Brackleburr herself, the damman spooning out great indigo dollops upon the toast-brown bread.

As she scooped up a purplish spoonful for Nob Haywood's toast, Teddy, sitting next to him, looked up at the damman and queried, "Say, Arla, what be y'r own favorite tale?"

Arla paused in thought, the blue spoon full and hovering, Nob licking his lips and maneuvering his toast under, waiting . . . waiting. Suddenly she stepped to the next buccan at the table and ladled Nob's spoonful onto Teddy's toast, Nob lunging sideways to try to intercept the errant deposit, to no effect, his maneuver in vain.

"Wellanow, Teddy," replied Arla, her Weiunwood brogue giving away her place of upbringing. "I'd suppose 't'd be th' tale o' th' sevin apples and th' copper coin, 'twould."

Neddy, next in line, looked up, his large sapphirine eyes wide. "Seven apples? Copper coin?"

"Aye, Neddy," answered the damman, dabbing preserves upon his toast, stepping to the next in line, Nob Haywood now following her silently, his own dry toast outheld, as would a beggar hold forth a cup for alms. "Have ye niver heard th' tale?"

Spreading the blueberry jam across his toast, Neddy looked up and shook his head *No*.

Arla promptly handed the spoon and the jar of preserves to Bingo Peacher—who shoveled out a share onto his own browned bread and passed the preserves onward, Nob anxiously following the container about the table, wondering if there would be aught left for the naked toast he bore—while the damman got herself a cup of tea and sat down at a spare place.

"I don't know th' truth 'o what't'tis that I'm about t' tell ye, but this be th' tale as I heard it whin I was but a wee younglin' at me mither's knee.

"Naow, 't seems that there wance was a family o' Warrows a-livin' on th' edge o' th' 'Wood. A crofter, he was, was Rafferty Redleaf, and wily; and his woife a match t' be marveled at, and Coley was her name.

"Wan day, Rafferty noticed a harse standin' still nixt t' his fince at his archard, for 'twas apples he grew. And Rafferty wint doon t' invistigate jist why there'd be a harse runnin' loose nearabout, and all. For 't could be that th' harse's roider had fallin doon and was ainjured, y' see. And whin he got there . . ."

Rafferty Redleaf strode down the path toward the stone fence bordering the road passing by his croft. Autumn was in the air, yet this day, though crisp at dawn, was warming under the late morning Sun. All about Rafferty,

trees were laden with red apples, for it had been a marvelous growing season, with a goodly amount of rain and
sunshine, and a scarcity of pests. With such a crop there
would be plenty of cider and fresh fruit to bear to the
market at Stonehill. And what he didn't sell immediately,
he could turn into apple jelly and apple butter and apple
sauce and dried apples for sale at a later date, along with
more cider, naturally. And, of course, there would be apple pies and tarts, baked apples, apple dumplings, and
other assorted mouth-watering dishes that Coley, his
dammia, would make throughout the fall and winter. At
the thought of it all Rafferty reached up and plucked a
ripened red apple from an overhanging branch and took a
juicy bite. *Hoy, 'tis no wander that apples be m' fav'rit'
fruit.*

Near the gate, Rafferty could see the free-standing
horse. At the saddle, a bow and a quiver of arrows depended from leather straps affixed to the forecantle. Too,
there was a scabbarded saber, as well as a spear affixed to
the saddle on the far side. As he drew near, the horse
raised its head, and the buccan could see that it was
munching upon something. Yet still no rider did Rafferty
espy.

But when the Warrow came unto the low stone fence,
at last he saw the horse's owner. 'Twas a fair-haired Man,
twenty or thereabout. Richly dressed, or so it seemed to
Rafferty's eye. And he was up in one of Rafferty's trees.
At the main fork. Eating an apple. And the Man threw the
core down to the horse.

Standing on tiptoes, Rafferty peered over the fence. He
could see a number of apple cores lying on the far side.
Six in all.

"Heloo, stranjer," called up Rafferty.

The Man plucked another apple from the tree, then
looked down at the diminutive buccan, seeing a redheaded Warrow with green eyes gazing up at him.

"Hello, yourself, little Waldan," replied the Man, set-
tling back into the crotch of the tree, taking a bite from
the red fruit.

"I be Rafferty Redleaf," called up the buccan. "An'
them be me apples what't'tis y'r eatin', naow. An' I'd

take 't kindly if y'd pay me a copper f'r th' sevin what I c'n see y've eatin' already, and a copper f'r ev'ry sevin thereafter."

The Man laughed. "What? Me? Pay a copper for that which grows free on trees?"

"Free on some trees, I shouldn't wander," replied Rafferty, "but on these trees they'll be f'r costin' ye a copper f'r ev'ry sevin you and y'r harse eats, naow."

"My short friend," responded the Man, "'twas Adon who supplied the apples for the taking, and I'll not be paying you for that which Adon Himself provides."

Rafferty glared up at the Man. "Sure, an' it was Adon what made th' trees, and that I'll not deny. But it was me own great-great-granther what planted these trees here in this valley archard. An' it was his bucco what followed in his footsteps, and then his bucco in turn, and then his bucco and his bucco, me own sire, thereafter. And naow 'tis me what tends this place, that and me own.

"And so, me foin young Man, 'twill be a copper that y'll be payin'. F'r these apples are mine naow, me own crop, jist as they were me sire's and his sire's and his and his before him. And that's a fact that even Adon Himself would not deny."

"By the scales of Redclaw," said the Man, leaping down from the tree, "perhaps you have a point. Even so, I don't believe that I'll pay you outright for the apples, for Adon's bounty; yet I'll tell you what I will do: I'll contest you for them."

Hoy, naow, this foin young brigand would be f'r cheatin' me out o' me due, thought Rafferty. *Wellanow, we'll jist see about that.*

"What be it that ye have in mind, young sar?" asked the buccan. "Would 't be a riddlin' contest, naow? A contest of us matchin' our wits 'gainst wan anither?"

"Oh no, my short friend," replied the Man, stepping to his horse and taking down his elegant bow and quiver of fine-fletched arrows. "I propose a shooting match. You *do* use a bow, now, don't you? At least I've heard that you Waldans do, with some skill I might add, or so say the rumors."

"Aye, some Warrows use bows, me an' mine among

them. Y'r proposal, what be it y're thinkin' o'; what be th' terms o' th' contest?" asked Rafferty, his thoughts racing.

As the Man strung his bow, he set forth what he had in mind. "Let us say that we set up a target. And the one that puts the most arrows nearest its heart, well then, that one is the winner. Should you win, then I'll pay you a copper. Should I win, then the apples are free."

"Well, sar," responded Rafferty, "contest or no, ye owe me f'r th' apples. Yet I'm a sportin' soul, but f'r this kind o' contest me eyes ain't what they've been in th' past. Still, ye wouldn't have any objections t' me havin' a champion, naow, would ye? 'Tis only me bucco that'd be shootin' th' bow f'r me naow. Jist anither Warrow."

"None whatsoever," replied the Man, his voice filled with confidence, "for I've yet to be beaten in this skill."

Rafferty opened the gate and beckoned the Man inward. "Well, bring y'r harse up next t' th' house, f'r I've got an upwellin' spring there that he can get a drink from, and we'll set th' target up there by th' byre.

"Too, I'll get me bucco and his bow and arrows, and he'll be shootin' f'r me, he will."

After they reached the sparkling clear-water spring by the house, Rafferty stepped inside and was gone for a long while, and the Man was beginning to think that the Waldan was backing out of the agreement, despite the consequences of such a deed. For it was well known that Fortune Herself would look with disfavor on one who broke the compact of his word—especially when that word involved a contest, be it of arms or skill or wit. Likewise, Fortune favored the bold, and the cunning and talented and swift. And so the Man wondered if the Waldan would indeed risk ill fortune by refusing to go through with their agreement, with their game, for the small one was gone long. Yet the wee buccan finally appeared, and following him was another redheaded Waldan, this one younger.

"This be me bucco," announced Rafferty, "and he'll be doin' th' shootin' f'r th' Redleafs."

The elder buccan set two haycocks against the side of the byre, the barn to be a backdrop so that stray arrows would not be lost. Too, upon each he pinned a modest square of reed parchment, after showing the Man that they were identical in size, a hand span or so to a side, each parchment with a dark X inked dead center.

They stood next to the house, and through the several open windows the Man could hear a voice singing inside. It sounded like a female Waldan, a damman.

"Ye'll both take a rangin' shot or two," said Rafferty. "And remember, X marks th' spot, it bein' th' real target y'r aimin' at."

Both the Man and the young buccan toed a line and prepared to let fly with their first ranging shot, the Man drawing swiftly and loosing his arrow, striking parchment fair and square, the shaft but a small distance from the X. Yet still the buccan beside the Man had not loosed his arrow, and the Man turned about to watch.

The young Warrow fumbled with the arrow, as if uncertain how to set it 'gainst the string. Slowly he drew, back and back, till the bow was full bent. Yet he did not loose the shaft, but wavered the point about, as if seeking the target, as if seeking to remember how to aim. And he stood poised so long that the Man thought the Waldan would *never* release. And the young buccan's arms began to tremble with the strain of holding the bent bow and drawn arrow for that length of time. Yet at last he shot. *Thuun! Shsssh! Thunk!* the buccan's missile flying high and to the left, missing the haycock altogether and thunking into the wood of the barn.

Seeing the effort spent by the Waldan, the Man smiled unto himself. "I'll have you know that this won't be much of a contest," he declared.

A side door flew open, and a damman came scurrying out. She, too, had red hair but stood a half a head shorter than Rafferty's three feet five inches. "Oi, laddie me bucco," she called, rushing up to the young buccan, "ye f'rgot y'r fav'rit' headband."

As she reached up and tied the leather strap about the young buccan's head, "His dam," said Rafferty to the Man. Then added, "His mither . . . me woife . . . Coley."

When the headband was in place—"Thank ye, Mither," said the young buccan—the damman returned to the

172 Dennis L. McKiernan

house. The two archers readied for their second ranging shot. Yet this time, ere the Man could even bend his bow, swift as lightning the young buccan set shaft to string and drew and loosed, his arrow punching dead center in the X.

A moment later, the Man's shaft again struck the parchment, a bit high and right of center.

As they stepped forward to retrieve their ranging arrows, the Man casually glanced over at the Waldan's leather headband. Although it seemed to be an ordinary strap of deer hide, still, it was the only thing that might account for his incredible improvement ... though perhaps it was nought but good fortune that guided the Waldan's hand. The Man would wait and see.

"Alroight, naow," announced Rafferty as the twain returned from the haycocks, "them what gets closest t' his X with th' most arrows, well then, he be th' winner. But if there be a tie f'r closeness, wellanow, I'd be f'r thinkin' that him what finishes first would be th' overall winner, for that'd seem t' me t' be th' fairest tiebreaker o' all. What d'ye say, O Man?"

The man nodded *Yes,* for even though his confidence had fallen somewhat, still, those terms were common to archery contests.

"Sevin arrows, then," called Rafferty, stepping to a place where both bucco and Man could see him, out of the line of fire. Inside the house the singing stopped, and curtains on windows drew aside.

"Ready?" asked Rafferty, holding up his right hand, receiving a nod from the Man and a nod from the young buccan as well.

"Then *shoot!*" he commanded, his right hand flashing downward in signal.

Before the Man could even draw—*Ththththunn-thththunn! Shshshshhh-shshshhh! Thththththnk-thththnk!*—it sounded to him as if seven bows were fired simultaneously. And seven arrows hit the Warrow's target all in a cluster. Four arrows striking the X so close to dead center that it could not be told which had punctured the cross point and which had not, while three other arrows split the shafts of three that had struck slightly first.

The Man whirled about, and there stood the young buccan smiling up innocently, as if he had loosed nought but
a single shaft.

Inside the house, the singing resumed, coming from behind the windows now covered once more with curtains.

Clearing his throat, Rafferty spoke. "Wellanow, young
sar, would ye like t' have a go at it, or d'ye admit defeat
anow?"

Not ready to concede, the Man turned and loosed his
shaft, the arrow striking perilously near the heart of the
target. But when they took a close look, it was plain to
see that his shot had fallen outside the pattern needed to
win. Even so, still he cast the other six arrows, doing his
best, for he was honor-bound to do so.

And although he performed quite well, when he was
done, the young Man unstrung his bow, signifying defeat.

"Alroight, then," said Rafferty, "that'll be a copper y'r
owin' me f'r them sevin apples what you and y'r harse
ate."

A shrewd look came over the Man's countenance.
"Again I say, I'll not pay for that which grows free upon
trees, *but*"—he held up a palm, forestalling Rafferty's
protests—"*but* I'll pay you a silver for that headband
your son is wearing."

"A *silver*!" sputtered Rafferty. "A *silver*! Why, I'll
have you know that it's worth sevin times as—"

"Done!" cried the Man. "And don't try to back out of
our bargain. Seven silvers it is, and not a copper more!"

"Ar, me and me big mouth!" cried Rafferty. "Yet a bargain be a bargain, and there's no doubt o' that, and so
shall this bargain stand. Sevin silvers I said, and so sevin
silvers it'll be."

Quickly the Man opened his purse and counted out
seven silver pennies, handing them to the Waldan, receiving the leather headband in return, quickly stuffing it into
his purse alongside his coins.

"Wellanow," said Rafferty when the exchange had been
made, "don't be f'r puttin' that there purse away, f'r ye
still owe me a copper f'r them sevin apples what you and
y'r harse ate."

The Man seemed to sink into thought, his eyes following Rafferty's son as the young buccan trudged back into the house.

"Another contest?" queried the Man, pleased with himself for the gain of the headband, even though he had lost the previous match.

Rafferty seemed to consider long before answering. *Ho, tryin' t' cheat me again, eh? We'll jist see about that, now, won't we, me foin friend.* "Well, sar, contest or no, ye still owe me f'r th' apples. Yet I'm a sportin' soul, and since ye chose the last match, this time I have the roight t' choose.

"Naow, there be two trees what fell in th' last big blow hereabout, and I'm o' a mind t' cut 'em up, t' clear th' land. O' a like size they are, and that be a fact; and so I say that a fair contest would be choppin' them trees into cords o' wood. Whoever finishes first, wellanow, then he's th' winner. And if there be a tie, well, him what cuts th' most cords, then that wan be th' winner o' th' tiebreaker, and th' winner overall.

"Before ye object, I've got a good, sharp Man-sized axe f'r ye t' use; found it in th' road—no doubt fell from a waggon passin' by, I shouldn't wander.

"Anyhow, that be th' contest and them be th' terms. D'ye agree?"

The Man looked down at the wee buccan. "Hah! I accept on the conditions that the axe is to my liking, and that I get to choose which of the two trees I chop."

"Wellanow, I have a condition on me own part, too," responded Rafferty, "and it be this: F'r this kind o' contest, me arm ain't what it's been in th' past. Jist as we did with th' bow, ye wouldn't have any objections t' me havin' a champion, would ye? 'Tis only me bucco that'd be choppin' th' wood f'r me naow. Jist anither Warrow."

Again the Man looked long at the Waldan. "Agreed," he said at last.

"I'll jist get me bucco," said Rafferty, stepping into the house. Yet he was gone so long that the Man was beginning to think that, despite the consequences, the Waldan was backing out of the agreement. Yet the wee buccan finally appeared, and following him was a redheaded Waldan.

"This be me bucco," announced Rafferty, "and he'll be doin' th' choppin' f'r th' Redleafs."

They went to the barn and took up axes, the Man well pleased with the one offered by the Waldan for his use. Stepping to the edge of the farm, they came upon two felled trees, some sixty or seventy feet apart in the woods, separated by living trees and underbrush.

After the Man chose which of the two he wished to cut, Rafferty bade them each to test their blades upon a small sapling that had been overturned.

Thwack! With but one blow the Man's sharp axe sheared completely through the wrist-sized trunk, but the young buccan's blade took several hacking blows to achieve the same.

Seeing the effort spent by the Waldan, the Man smiled unto himself. "I'll have you know that this won't be much of a contest," he declared.

In that same moment the redheaded damman named Coley came hastily through the woods, bearing a small rusty axe.

"Oi, laddie me bucco," she called, rushing up to the young buccan, "ye f'rgot y'r fav'rit' axe."

"Thank ye, Mither," said the young buccan, taking the rusty blade; and the damman headed back toward the house, bearing the shiny axe away.

Lightning-fast swung the buccan's rusty axe at the downed sapling, this time—*Thwack!*—shearing through with one blow as well.

Gazing wide-eyed at the wee rusty axe, the Man was not as confident as before. Yet he looked at the largeness of the contest trees, and the smallness of the Waldan, and regained some of his former certainty.

Each contestant took up a position at his tree, and neither could see the other because of the intervening growth between. But Rafferty stood where both could see him. "Ready?" called Rafferty, holding up his right hand, receiving a nod from the Man and a nod from the young buccan as well.

"Then *chop*!" he commanded, his right hand flashing downward in signal.

Before the Man could swing even once—*Thwackk-*

whakkk-aakk-thak-whakk—a barrage of axe blows rack-
eted through the woods, and it sounded to him as if seven
axes were chopping simultaneously.

"You're cheating!" he shouted, running toward the
sound.

"Cheatin'?" shouted Rafferty, taking off his hat and
hurling it to the ground. "If any be th' cheat here, then it
be th' wan what won't pay th' copper f'r th' sevin apples
what he and his harse ate!"

When the man reached the other tree, the young buccan
stood there holding his rusty axe, wood chopped all
about, the wee one smiling innocently up at the Man, not
even perspiring, as if he'd chopped but a small amount.

And thick, green underbrush stood silently all about,
taller than the buccan, mute witness to what had occurred
hereat.

There was yet a goodly amount left to the buccan's
tree, and so the Man returned to his own, determined not
to be beaten by such a wee little one as was the tiny redheaded Waldan.

And Rafferty picked up his hat from the ground and set
it once more atop his head.

The Man set to work, chopping for all he was worth.
And again from the direction of the buccan's tree came
what sounded as seven axes furiously chopping.

The Man was no more than halfway finished when the
frantic hacking at the other tree fell silent and the young
buccan, bearing his rusty axe, walked forth from the undergrowth, signalling that he was through.

The Man went and looked, and the Waldan's tree was
thoroughly chopped, the cut wood neatly stacked in cords.
And even though the Man knew that he had lost, still he
completed chopping up his own tree and stacking the
cordwood, for he was honor-bound to do so.

And although he chopped quite well, when he was
done, the Man lay down his axe, signifying defeat.

"Alroight, then," said Rafferty, "that'll be a copper y'r
owin' me f'r them sevin apples what you and y'r harse
ate."

The Man looked down at the buccan. "Again I say, I'll
not pay for that which grows free upon trees, *but*"—he

held up a palm, forestalling Rafferty's protests—"*but* I'll pay you a silver for that rusty axe your son is bearing."

"A *silver*!" sputtered Rafferty. "A *silver*! Why, I'll have you know that it's worth sevin times as—"

"Done!" cried the Man. "And don't try to back out of our bargain. Seven silvers it is, and not a copper more!"

"Ar, me and me big mouth!" cried Rafferty. "Ye've trapped me ag'in! Yet a bargain be a bargain, and there's no doubt o' that, and so shall this bargain stand. Sevin silvers I said, and so sevin silvers it'll be."

Quickly the Man opened his purse and counted out seven silver pennies, handing them to the Waldan, receiving the rusty axe in return, and when they reached the house and his horse, he stuffed the axe into his saddlebags, all but the handle, which stuck out a bit.

"Wellanow," said Rafferty, when the axe was put away, "don't be f'r keepin' that there purse shut, f'r ye still owe me a copper f'r them sevin apples what you and y'r harse ate."

Again the Man seemed to pause in thought, his eyes following Rafferty's son as the young buccan trudged back into the house.

"Another contest?" queried the Man, pleased with himself for the gain of the axe along with the headband, even though he had lost both of the matches.

Once more Rafferty seemed to consider long before answering. *Ho, still tryin' t' cheat me, be he? We'll jist see about that wance more, me foin young friend.* "Well, sar, contest or no, ye still owe me f'r th' apples. Yet I'm a sportin' soul, and since I chose th' last match, this time ye have th' roight t' choose. And if I agree t' it, wellathen, we'll have anither go at a match, naow, won't we."

The Man took a sling and sling bullets from one of his saddlebags. "Let us say that we set up seven targets each. And the one that strikes all of his targets first, well then, that one is the winner. Should you win, then I'll pay you a copper. Should I win, then the apples are free."

"Well, sar," responded Rafferty, "again I say, contest or no, ye owe me f'r th' apples. Even so, if ye agree t' me terms, wellathen, I'll play. F'r this kind o' contest, me whirlin' hand ain't what it used t' be, but ye wouldn't have any objections t' me havin' a champion, would ye? 'Tis only me bucco that'd be slingin' th' bullets f'r me naow. Jist anither Warrow."

"None whatsoever," replied the Man, his voice filled with confidence, "for I've yet to be beaten in this skill."

"Well then, I'll get me bucco and his sling and sling bullets, for he'll be throwin' f'r me, he will."

Rafferty stepped inside and, as before, was gone for a long while. Yet the wee buccan finally appeared, and following him was a redheaded Waldan.

"This be me bucco," announced Rafferty, "and he'll be doin' th' hurlin' f'r th' Redleafs."

The elder buccan then spanned a loose fence rail upon the two haycocks next to the byre, explaining that the barn would act as a backdrop so that stray sling bullets would not go awry and strike an innocent farm animal. And then he placed fourteen pebbles atop a fence rail, seven along one end for the Man, seven along the other for the young buccan.

They stood next to the house, and through the several open windows again the Man could hear the damman's voice singing inside.

"Ye'll each take a rangin' shot or two," said Rafferty.

Both the Man and the young buccan prepared to let fly with their first ranging shot, the Man swiftly loading a bullet and whipping the sling about and loosing the missile. *Crack!* one of the Man's target pebbles was cleanly struck from the rail.

Yet still the buccan behind the Man had not loosed his own bullet, and the Man turned about to watch.

The young Warrow fumbled with the bullet, striving to place it in the leather sling pouch, as if uncertain how to set the ovoid in the sling pocket. Then he whirled and whirled and whirled the sling about his head, spinning it endlessly, it seemed, his free hand pointing and wavering awkwardly, as if striving to choose a target, as if seeking to remember how to aim. And he whirled so long that the Man thought the Waldan would *never* release the bullet. The young buccan's legs began to tremble with the strain of whirling the sling for that length of time. Yet at last he loosed the bullet. *Thunk!* the buccan's missile flying wide of any target, missing pebble, fence rail, haycock, and nearly missing the barn entire.

Seeing the effort spent by the Waldan, the Man smiled unto himself. "I'll have you know that this won't be much of a contest," he declared.

A side door flew open, and again Coley came scurrying out. "Oi, laddie me bucco," she called, rushing up to the young buccan, "ye f'rgot y'r fav'rit' sling."

Now the Man's heart sank, for once more the buccan had been given a "fav'rit' " item. Even so, he managed to acquire both of the previous "fav'rit' " things. *Magical, I deem.*

When the exchange of slings had taken place—"Thank ye, Mither," said the young buccan—the damman returned to the house.

The two slingsters readied for their second ranging shot. Yet this time, ere the Man could even spin his bullet, swift as lightning the young buccan set ovoid to pocket and whipped his arm about but once and loosed— *Crack!*—his bullet picking a pebble cleanly off the railing.

A moment later, the Man's own bullet plucked another pebble off.

As Rafferty stepped forward to replace the dislodged pebbles upon the railing, the Man casually glanced over at the Waldan's leather sling. Although it seemed to be an ordinary strap of deer hide, just as the headband had been, still, it was the only thing that had changed between the buccan's first shot and his second, the only thing that might account for his incredible improvement . . . though perhaps it was nought but good fortune that guided the Waldan's hand. The Man would wait and see.

"Alroight, naow," announced Rafferty as he returned from the railing, "them what first knocks off all his sevin pebbles, well then, he be th' winner. But if there be a tie f'r speed, wellanow, I'd be f'r thinkin' that him that uses th' least shots would be th' overall winner, for that'd seem t' me t' be th' fairest tiebreaker o' all. What d'ye say, O Man?"

The Man nodded *Yes,* for even though his confidence

had fallen to low depths, still, those terms were common to sling contests.

"Sevin pebbles, then," called Rafferty, stepping to a place where both bucco and Man could see him, out of the line of fire. And just as was for the bow-and-arrow contest, inside the house the singing stopped, and curtains on windows drew aside.

"Ready?" asked Rafferty, holding up his right hand, receiving a nod from the Man and a nod from the young buccan as well.

"Then *throw!*" he commanded, his right hand flashing downward in signal.

Before the Man could even hurl his first bullet—*Thththththak-thak-ththakk!*—the bucco's seven pebbles disappeared from the rail, snapped off by what sounded to him as seven sling bullets striking simultaneously.

The Man whirled about, and there stood the young buccan smiling up innocently, as if he had cast nought but a single bullet.

And inside the house the singing resumed, coming from behind windows now covered once more with curtains.

Defeated, the Man turned and methodically loosed his sling bullets, doing his best, for he was honor-bound to do so, managing to knock all pebbles off with but eight sling shots.

And although he threw quite well, when he was done, the Man rolled up his sling, signifying defeat.

"Alroight, then," said Rafferty, "that'll be a copper y'r owin' me f'r them sevin apples what you and y'r harse ate."

Once again the Man offered a different bargain. "I repeat, Waldan, I'll not pay for that which grows free upon trees, *but* I'll pay you a silver for that sling your son is holding."

"A *silver!*" cried Rafferty. "A *silver!* Why, I'll have you know that it's worth sevin times as—"

"Done!" cried the Man. "And don't try to back out of our bargain. Seven silvers it is, and not a copper more!"

"Ar, me and me big mouth! Will I niver learn?" Rafferty slammed clenched fist into open palm. "Yet a bargain be a bargain, and there's no doubt o' that, and so shall this bargain stand. Sevin silvers I said, and so sevin silvers it'll be."

Quickly the Man opened his purse and counted out seven silver pennies, handing them to the Waldan, receiving the plain sling in return, quickly stuffing it into his purse alongside his coins and headband.

"Wellanow," said Rafferty when the exchange had been made, "don't be f'r puttin' that there purse away, f'r ye still owe me a copper f'r them sevin apples what you and y'r harse ate."

This time the Man did not even wait for the son to reach the house before he asked, "Another contest?" He was greatly pleased with himself for the gain of the deerhide headband, and the rusty axe, and now the plain leather sling, even though his pride was stung at losing each of the matches.

By Adon, he's still tryin' t' cheat me out o' me copper. Well, we'll jist see th' which o' us comes out th' better. "Well, sar, contest or no, ye still owe me f'r th' apples. Yet I'm a sportin' soul, and since ye chose the last match, 'tis me turn ag'in.

"Naow, there be two fields o' late-summer oats what need harvestin', and I'm o' a mind t' do it t'day. O' a like size they are, and that be a fact; and so I say that a fair contest would be harvestin' th' oats and gatherin' them into bundled sheaves f'r carryin' to th' byre f'r thrashin' and winnowin'.

"Whoever finishes first, wellanow, then he's th' winner. And if there be a tie, well, him what cuts th' most sheaves, then that wan be th' winner o' th' tiebreaker, and the winner overall.

"Before ye object, I've got a good, sharp Man-sized scythe f'r ye t' use; found it in th' road alongside o' th' axe ye used earlier—no doubt they both fell from th' same waggon passin' by, I shouldn't wander.

"Anyhow, that be th' contest and them be th' terms. D'ye agree?"

The Man looked down at the wee buccan. "Hah! I accept on the condition that the scythe is to my liking and that I get to choose which of the two fields I harvest."

"Wellanow, I have a condition on me own part, too," responded Rafferty, "and it be this: F'r this kind o' contest, me back ain't what it's been in th' past. Jist as we did with th' bow and th' axe and th' sling, ye wouldn't have any objections t' me havin' a champion, naow, would ye? 'Tis only me bucco that'd be harvestin' th' field f'r me. Jist anither Warrow."

Again the Man looked long at the Waldan. "Agreed," he said at last.

"I'll jist get me bucco," said Rafferty, stepping into the house. Again he was gone a long while, yet finally reappeared, and following him was his redheaded buccan.

"This be me bucco," announced Rafferty, "and he'll be doin' th' cuttin' f'r th' Redleafs."

They went to the barn and took up a large scythe and a small sickle, the Man well pleased with the sweeping blade offered by the Waldan for his use, chortling in glee over the smallness of the young buccan's sickle. Striding toward the back of the farm, they came upon two fields of oats, a hundred or so feet apart, a thick hedge windbreak between the fields, concealing one from the other.

After the Man chose which of the two he wished to cut, Rafferty bade them each to test their blades upon a small strand of wild oats growing beside the road.

Shhhhk! With a wide sweep the Man's sharp blade sheared through an armful of oats, but the Warrow's blade took several cuts to achieve the same.

Seeing the effort spent by the Waldan, the Man smiled unto himself. "I'll have you know that this won't be much of a contest," he declared.

In that same moment the redheaded damman came hastily down the farm road, bearing a small rusty sickle. The Man's heart at one and the same time sank at the probability of losing another contest as well as leapt in joy over the prospect of gaining another powerful artifact.

"Oi, laddie me bucco," called Coley, rushing up to the young buccan, "ye f'rgot y'r fav'rit' sickle."

"Thank ye, Mither," said the young buccan, taking the rusty blade; and the damman headed toward the house, carrying the shiny sickle back.

Lightning-fast swung the buccan's rusty sickle at the

oats, this time—*Shhhk! Shhhk! Shhhk!*—shearing through the same amount with but three blows.

Each contestant took up a position at his field, and neither could see the other because of the intervening windbreak between. But Rafferty stood where both could see him. "Ready?" called Rafferty, holding up his right hand, receiving a nod from the Man and a nod from the young buccan as well.

"Then *cut!*" he commanded, his right hand flashing downward in signal.

Before the Man could swing even once—*Sshhkk-hhkkk-sshkk-shk-kk*—a hissing of cutting sickles sissed across the hedgerow, and it sounded to him as if seven sickles were slicing simultaneously.

"You're cheating!" he shouted, running toward the buccan's oat field.

"Cheating?" shouted Rafferty, taking off his hat and hurling it to the ground. "If any be th' cheat here, then it be th' wan what won't pay f'r th' apples he and his harse ate!"

When the Man reached the other side of the windbreak, still he could not see the buccan, for the oats were too tall. Even so, he ran until he came at last to where the bucco was, and the wee one stood there holding his rusty sickle, cut and sheaved oats all about, the young buccan smiling innocently up at the Man, not even perspiring, as if he'd harvested but a minor amount.

And the yellow oats stood silently surrounding, taller than the buccan, mute witness to what had occurred hereat.

There was yet a goodly amount left to the buccan's field, and so the Man returned to his own, determined not to be beaten by such a wee little one as was the tiny redheaded Waldan.

And Rafferty picked up his hat from the ground and set it once more atop his head.

The Man set to work, scything for all he was worth. And again, from the direction of the buccan's field came what sounded as seven sickles slicing furiously.

The Man was no more than three-quarters finished when the frantic *Shhhkking* in the other field fell silent, and the young buccan, bearing his rusty sickle, walked forth from behind the hedge, signalling that he was through.

The Man strode to the windbreak and peered through, seeing that the young buccan's field was cut clean, all oats silently standing in bundled sheaves. And even though the Man knew that he had lost, still he completed harvesting his own field and binding the sheaves, for he was honor-bound to do so.

Although he scythed quite well, when he was done, the Man lay down his blade, signifying defeat.

"Alroight, then," said Rafferty, "that'll be a copper y'r owin' me f'r them sevin apples what you and y'r harse ate."

"Again I say," repeated the Man, "I'll not pay for that which grows free upon trees, but I'll pay you a silver for that rusty sickle your son is bearing."

"A *silver*!" shouted Rafferty. "A *silver*! Why, I'll have you know that it's worth sevin times as—"

"Done!" cried the Man. "And don't try to back out of our bargain. Seven silvers it is, and not a copper more!"

"Ar, me and me big mouth!" cried Rafferty. "Yet a bargain be a bargain, and there's no doubt o' that, and so shall this bargain stand. Sevin silvers I said, and so sevin silvers it'll be."

Quickly the Man opened his purse and counted out seven silver pennies, handing them to the Waldan, receiving the rusty sickle in return, quickly stuffing it into his saddlebags next to the rusty axe, once they had returned to the house.

"Wellanow," said Rafferty, when the sickle was put away, "don't be f'r keepin' that there purse shut, f'r ye still owe me a copper f'r them sevin apples what you and y'r harse ate."

"Another contest?" queried the Man as the bucco trudged back into the house, the Man pleased with himself for the gain of the sickle along with the sling and the axe and the headband, even though he had lost all four of the matches.

Ho, still trying to cheat me, be he? We'll jist see who outwits who, me foin gullible. "Well, sar, contest or no, ye still owe me f'r th' apples. Yet I'm a sportin' soul, and since I chose th' last match, this time ye have th' roight t' choose. And if I agree t' it, wellathen, we'll have anither go at a match, naow, won't we?"

In the fifth contest, the Man chose to try Rafferty's skill at throwing daggers. And Rafferty asked if his bucco couldn't throw instead, since Rafferty's wrists weren't what they used to be. And this time, ere the Man could get off even one throw, seven daggers slammed into the bucco's target, virtually simultaneously. And for seven silver pennies, the Man purchased the bucco's fav'rit' wool wristlet.

In the sixth contest, Rafferty chose to pit his bucco against the Man in a match to see who could shear seven sheep the fastest, Rafferty's bucco of course acting as champion for his sire, since Rafferty pled that his clippin' grip wasn't what it used to be. And this time it sounded as if seven shearers were at work. And once again for only seven silver pennies the man purchased another of the bucco's fav'rit' items, a pair of rusty shears.

But it was the seventh and final contest that told all. This time it was again the Man's choice as to just what the contest would be.

"Well, my wee Waldan, I won't pay for what Adon grows free on trees, but I'll give you a copper if you beat me in a footrace."

"Footrace!" exclaimed Rafferty. "Lor, ye must think me daft, what with y'r long-leggedy stride and all. Why, Man, it'd be like ye racin' y'r harse 'gainst me little pony."

"Ha!" laughed the Man. "I knew that you would back out in the end."

Fire smoldered in Rafferty's eyes. *Thinkin' t' cheat me out o' me copper penny, is he. Wellanow, we'll jist see about that.* "Alroight, a footrace it'll be, but I get t' set th' course. And, oh, by th' bye, since me legs ain't what they used t' be, I want me bucco t' be me champion. He's jist a wee Warrow, y'know."

The Man agreed, certain that he could outrun any Waldan in a fair race.

And so, Rafferty went into his house to get his bucco and was gone for a long while, and the Man began to think that, despite the consequences, the Waldan was backing out of the agreement. Yet the wee buccan finally appeared, followed by his redheaded bucco.

"Wellanow," said Rafferty, "wouldn't ye like t' warm up y'r legs? How 'bout a shart dash from th' spring t' that big oak, there?"

Rafferty drew a line in the dust, and the Man and the young buccan stood behind it; at Rafferty's signal, off they sped, the Man outrunning the bucco by a good ten yards in forty.

As they came huffing and puffing back to the spring, the Man smiled unto himself. "I'll have you know that this won't be much of a contest," he declared.

In that moment, out rushed Coley. "Oi, laddie me bucco," she cried, "ye f'rgot y'r fav'rit' pair o' socks." And the ones she bore were quite tattered.

"Thank ye, Mither," said the young buccan, shucking off his boots and changing his socks, pulling on the raggedy pair: his toes stuck out through holes, and one of the heels was worn through, the other worn thin, and the tops of both were well frayed. The damman headed back into the house, carrying with her the fine pair that the bucco had removed. And now the young Man wasn't so confident as the bucco slipped back into his boots.

"Naow, this'll be th' which o' it," said Rafferty. "Th' race'll start and finish here at th' spring. Ye'll proceed down th' road"—Rafferty pointed out the route as he spoke—"past th' barley, then turnin' left at th' lane. There ye'll find a farm road, wan what runs entirely about a goodly part o' th' croft. It swings down there past th' big oak tree y'can see in th' distance yon, then further along it crosses th' bridge, then after a bit it goes 'round th' hillock, running along f'r a while till it comes past that large rock. Back it proceeds a fair bit toward th' house, turnin' thither by th' tall pine tree. Then it's back t' th' spring and th' finish line." Here, Rafferty took up a stick and scraped a new line deep in the dirt by the upwelling stream. "Ye'll start at this line and finish here, too, and th' first wan across after runnin' th' circuit'll be th' winner."

"Hoy now," complained the Man. "That's quite a long race. Why, it must be a mile or more, full 'round."

"Aye," agreed Rafferty, "that 't 'tis. Are y' thinkin' about conceding already? If so, then give me th' copper what y' owe f'r th' apples ye an' y'r harse ate."

In response, the Man stepped up to the mark and said, "Let's get on with it."

Rafferty looked at his bucco, and the young buccan lined up beside the Man.

Standing out to the side where both could see him, "Be ye ready?" asked Rafferty, raising his hand.

Receiving a nod from each, "Then *go!*" he cried, slashing his hand down through the air.

Immediately the Man began pulling away from the young buccan, his longer legs eating up the distance. Glancing aback, he could see the Waldan straining, yet losing ground. "Ha!" he yelled. "Fav'rit' socks, indeed!"

As he passed the corner of the barley field and entered the lane, he thought that he saw the exhausted Waldan stumble and fall into the grain. And he laughed.

But when he next glanced aback, here came the buccan, running faster than ever.

Exerting himself, once again the Man pulled away from the Waldan. And once again he could see the buccan straining to keep up the pace, the wee one running as hard as he could go, fatigue beginning to cause a stagger in his steps on the rough farm road.

Finally the Man saw the Waldan fall behind the large oak tree. But in a flash, it seemed, up he sprang again, running faster than ever.

And now the Man began to feel the strain, tiring as he was, for the young buccan was actually keeping pace with him. Even so, the Man knew that in this long race he himself could not keep up such a fast pace, yet he deemed the wee one would wear out ere he did. And so he pressed onward, racing for all he was worth.

Crossing the bridge above the meandering stream, the

road swung leftward, circling to come back around toward the now distant farm house.

Risking another glance, again the Man saw the buccan begin to lag, falling back once more. And in that moment the wee one missed the bridge, rolling down the embankment and out of sight.

But the Man's yelp of victory turned to a cry of dismay, for up out of the creek came the redheaded buccan, running faster than ever before.

And now the bucco began to gain on the Man, his hasty, quick strides starting to overhaul those of the larger runner. Gasping with the effort, sweating profusely, the Man pushed himself to his limit. Even so, still the buccan gained ground. Yet as he passed 'round the hillock, the Man saw that the Waldan was gasping, too, ere he was lost to sight past the curve.

But when the bucco came 'round the bend, he was running faster than ever, the Warrow making up yards and yards of ground on the now weary Man, swiftly closing the gap between them.

Lungs heaving, a stitch growing in his side, groaning with the effort, even though he was nearing exhaustion the Man gritted his teeth and ran as he'd never run before.

But still the bucco gained ground, and was now but some twenty strides behind. And the Man could hear his following footsteps pattering against the earthen farm road.

As he passed the great rock, the Man glanced aback and saw the terrible effort put forth by the Waldan. Here the road wended a bit, and so the Man concentrated on keeping his footing upon the treacherous way. And when next he looked hindward, he moaned in surprise for here came the bucco, running even faster than before, gaining ground with his quick feet.

"You'll not pass me!" groaned the Man, and he reached deep down inside himself and ran to his utter limit. Yet the Waldan slowly made up ground, his footsteps sounding at the Man's very back.

Gasping, heaving, not getting enough air, still the Man held off the bucco as he flashed past the great pine tree and turned on the final leg. Ahead he could see Rafferty jumping up and down, yelling out something, but the Man's breath was so harsh that he could not hear what Rafferty's words were.

And in that moment the young buccan passed him, running even faster than ever.

Shouting in fury—*"Yaahhhh!"*—the Man found energy he knew not that he possessed. And, lungs pumping like bellows, worn legs hammering up and down, feet slamming 'gainst the hard-packed earth, he managed to draw even with the Waldan.

Side by side they raced, the finish line just yards ahead, fire burning in the Man's lungs, the muscles in his legs feeling as if they were torn, shredded, his arms lead weights, his shoulders wet clay, his heart nigh to bursting, a hammer in his chest.

And the bucco glanced sideways at him . . . *and smiled!*

It was too much for the Man, and of a sudden he stumbled, crashing to the ground as would fall a bag of grain, loose, whelming, sprawling, his arms outstretched but too weak to fend. He skidded through the dirt, the side of his face scraping against the barnyard, his slack mouth filling with earth, grit grinding into his eyes.

He slid some eleven feet, then stopped, his fingers falling inches short of the finish line.

Lungs heaving, gasping in pain, nigh sick to his stomach, black spots swimming before his eyes, blinking frantically and spitting out mud, he glanced up with dirt-filled eyes to see the bucco standing on the far side of the victory line, still grinning.

The Man purchased the bucco's fav'rit' socks, holes and all, for seven silver pennies, stuffing them into his now nearly empty purse alongside the other artifacts: the deerskin headband, the leather sling, and the wool wristlet. And forget not, in the Man's saddlebags were a rusty axe, a rusty sickle, and a rusty pair of shears, each purchased for seven pennies as well.

When the deal was done, "Wellanow," said Rafferty stubbornly, handing the Man a gourd dipper of water to slake what had to be a terrible thirst, "don't be f'r puttin' that there purse away, f'r ye still owe me a copper f'r them sevin apples what you and y'r harse ate."

Before the Man could reply, Rafferty held up a hand, forestalling any protests or disclaimers. "Look, me foin young sar, there be this about wan what tries t' cheat anither, and it be jist this: 'tis fair t' cheat a cheater, f'r then he gets his due.

"And if ye don't get th' gist of that which I be tellin' ye, then p'rhaps ye'll find th' answer in th' words o' th' followin' riddle:

> *"O' th' many times th' crofter plowed,*
> *Though not th' ground, y'see,*
> *Sevin good seeds were planted there,*
> *Yet no green plants were these.*
>
> *"Sevin blessin's grew from them,*
> *Sevin gifts from his woife,*
> *Tell me th' crop th' crofter raised,*
> *For it be a secret o' loife."*

As the Man gulped down the dipper of water, again Rafferty spoke. "This be th' last o' th' contests, foin sar, f'r I'll not be aplayin' no more with ye. Yet within that puzzle, y'll discover jist why it be ye lost."

Still huffing and puffing and sweating, the Man yet sat upon the ground by the spring and tried to fathom the meaning of the riddle. Perhaps his mind was mazed by the effort of the long, long race, but he could make no sense of the rhyme. He looked up at Rafferty, shrugging his shoulders, admitting defeat.

A smile came over Rafferty's features. "Wellanow, this be th' way I see it. Ye tried t' cheat me out o' me copper f'r the apples what ye and y'r harse ate, but instead 'twere ye what got cheated, and I'll tell ye why.

"Thinkin' ye were gettin' somethin' *special*, outwittin' me as ye were, ye paid sevin times sevin what th' headband was worth, and sevin times sevin th' price o' th' axe. And sevin times sevin th' worth o' th' sling, and sevin times sevin f'r th' sickle. Ye paid sevin times sevin th' price o' th' wristlet, and sevin times sevin f'r th' shears. And here at th' end ye paid sevin times sevin th' worth o' th' socks, for like all th' others, they were not *special* at all, except in th' mind o' th' wan who would cheat anither.

"Sevin times ye lost, and each time it cost ye sevin silvers. So sevin times sevin silvers ye paid, all t' save but a single copper.

"But 'twere not only th' silvers ye lost, f'r ye chopped me wood, harvested me oats, and sheared me sheep. And all f'r wan copper penny. Naow, that be what I call a bargain.

"It seems t' me, me foin young sar, that y've more than paid f'r y'r folly. F'r sevin times sevin years ye'll remember this lesson ye've learned, if ye live that long, that is.

"So think not t' cheat a Weiunwood farmer, or any other, f'r that matter, for niver will ye know whin ye'll run up against somewan cleverer than ye be, perhaps sevin times sevin as wise.

"And naow I see th' puzzlement in y'r eyes, wanderin' jist how 'twere done.

"Well, look behind ye, me foin young sar, and ye'll see th' answer t' th' riddle, th' answer t' jist how I arranged y'r downfall."

The Man looked behind, and there stood Rafferty's seven sons, seven redheaded buccos, alike as peas in a pod. Each bore a bow and arrows; each wore a brace of throwing daggers and a sling and bag of bullets depended from each one's belt; each had hands that were calloused, made so by the work of the croft, in which each was skilled. And each breathed somewhat heavily, and their shirts were stained with sweat, as if they'd just finished running a relay race afoot.

Long the Man looked, then whirled about and peered at the placement of the windows along one side of the house, and observed how they overlooked where the arrow and sling and dagger targets had sat; and he thought how simple it would be for experts to cast shafts or bullets or blades from within the dwelling, striking targets next to the barn.

Back at the seven buccos the Man stared, these peas-in-a-pod brothers, and thought how easily these wee folk could hide in thick forest undergrowth, or among oats in a field, or in a dark barn with sheep shearing stalls, and how if one of them was running a race and dropped out and another secretly took his place and continued running, a Man couldn't tell one from the other and so he'd never know the difference.

And he thought of the seven times Rafferty had gone into his house to "get me bucco," and of how on each occasion Rafferty had been gone a long, long while, the time no doubt spent with Coley and the buccos plotting just how to "cheat a cheater," how to give him his Just Due, in each case devising a clever trick to fool the one who still owed Rafferty "a copper f'r them sevin apples what you and y'r harse ate."

And then the Man burst out in laughter, rolling about upon the ground in glee. Long he laughed, and heartily.

Rafferty, seeing the young Man's reaction, signed his sons that there was no danger, and so they unstrung their bows and seated well the throwing knives back into the scabbards. For the Warrows had not known just how the Man might behave, once he was told of their ruse.

Seeing the Man's good nature, whooping in glee and rolling on the ground as he was, Rafferty offered to give the Man's silver back to him in trade for the things he'd bought. But this just caused the Man to howl all the more, and he waved the buccan away, laughing till tears streamed down, begging the Waldan to say no more, for his ribs hurt from all the joy.

And Rafferty Redleaf began to smile, and so too did his buccos. Coley came out from the house, and she was giggling. Then all the Warrows broke out in laughter, and soon were slapping their knees and holding their sides, joining the Man in gaiety. And for his part, the Man held onto his stomach and rolled on the ground, having the greatest belly laugh of all.

There they were in Rafferty's barnyard: one rolling in the dirt, others fallen to their knees, some holding onto a fence, others holding onto one another, Rafferty with his arms about Coley; and the valley fair shook with their laughter, fair shook with the joy of buccos and buccan and damman and Man. And if any stranger had passed by in that moment, well, he would have thought them gone completely mad.

And so, they became the best of friends, did the Man and the Redleafs. From that day forward, the Man was most scrupulously fair in all his dealings, even the minor ones, for he'd learned a lesson he'd remember forever . . . or for seven times seven years. And each time he would think of it, he would laugh at the memory.

Yet there was this as well: "Hoy, little Waldan," chortled the Man, fishing about in his purse, "you've taught me a lesson, and that's a fact, and I would not let it go unheeded." At last he found what he sought after—"Here," he said, and held forth a copper coin.

Long did Rafferty stare at the outheld copper, then finally he said, "You keep it."

Long, too, did the Warrows laugh when Arla's tale had come to the end, there in the One-Eyed Crow. Especially Gaffer Tom, for he, like other Warrows, delighted in tales where the Wee Folk outwitted Big Men, or Giants, or other *Outsiders*.

At last the glee died down, and a stillness fell across the Warrows within. And yet the wind howled outside, raging as if in fury, battering at any and all in its path, unaffected by the humor inside the 'Crow.

Finally, amid sporadic chuckles bursting forth now and again, Teddy spoke up, breaking into the amused thoughts of those yet reflecting upon the tale. "Hoy now, Arla, y' never did tell us the name o' the Man."

Arla looked at Teddy in surprise. "Oi naow, Teddy, I'd've thought ye'd've guessed by naow. That were th' tale o' how Rafferty Redleaf met Bram, th' King o' Jord."

Wide-eyed, Warrows looked at one another, their faces once more breaking into glorious smiles.

When Iron
Bells Ring

Argh!" interrupted Nob. "That ain't what's important here. Why the Rūcks and such ran, where they got to—it's all beside the point! The important thing is Stoke! Was he dead? Did they get him? Did Tomlin's silver bullet do him in? Was he burned up. What, Gaffer, what?"

Again all eyes turned to the Gaffer.

Slowly he filled his black pipe carved in the shape of an owl's head, none saying aught in the silence, Neddy quietly getting a burning taper to light Gaffer Tom's briar. After a couple of puffs, the granther buccan's eyes swept across the expectant faces of the waiting Warrows.

"Well, Nob, let me say this about that. . . ."

Outside, the blizzard shrieked and yawled, and darkness descended upon the hammered land as icy day slipped into frigid night, though no one in the 'Crow took note of it.

"Down from Daemon's Crag they came, down from burnt Dreadholt, Urus bearing Riatha, for she had a broken arm and leg, Tomlin in the lead, scouting, Petal trailing after, guarding their rear. And they made their way down to Sagra, that frightened village at the base of the slope, there at the end of the Grimwalls in Vancha.

"And the people of Sagra were overjoyed to hear of Stoke's demise, or flight, for none of the four knew which had occurred. Yet the villagers cared not, for the evil was gone once more, and they were safe again.

"Urus, it seemed, had the hands of a healer, for Riatha prospered under his care, her bones knitting straight and true, and at last she was ready to travel.

"Back from Vancha they came, making their way unto their holts to rest awhile ere renewing pursuit of Stoke once more, had he survived. For they knew that if he yet lived, the evil Baron would go to ground a lengthy time ere taking up residence in some distant Land to once again wreak horror.

"And so they headed for their homesteads, faring together for a while, until their ways would separate, Riatha aiming for Arden Vale; Urus, the Greatwood; and Tomlin and Petal, the Weiunwood dear.

"When they came unto Stonehill, Urus and Riatha bade the Warrows farewell and set out easterly, for their own holts lay yonder that way. But ere they pressed onward, once again they renewed their pledge to one another, vowing that if he had somehow escaped the fire, they would pursue Stoke until he or they were dead.

"And they moved back into their Weiunwood steading, did Petal and Tomlin, for King's messenger Arnor had kept his promise and had returned the horses unto Banlo and his dad at the Stonehill stables, redeeming the holt of the Warrows.

"Three years passed, and Petal was delivered of a wee buccan, their first child, and they named him Small Urus in honor of their Baeran friend.

"Another year passed, and lo! a messenger came from Riatha, and he bore with him two silver knives, Dwarven made. They were the original knives that Petal had traded to Captain Solini for passage to Vancha. Riatha had managed to trace the blades, to discover their whereabouts and recover them, and now sent them to Petal.

"Another thirteen years went by, and Tomlin and Petal were delivered of three more wee ones, two of which were dammsels, and the last child another bucco. And they named them respectively Little Riatha, Silvereyes, and Bear.

"All told, seventeen years had passed since last they had seen Riatha and Urus, and their oldest youngling was fourteen and the youngest, eight.

"In that seventeenth year, upon Mid-Year's Day, the family had gone down to Stonehill, or rather to its edge, for it was the time of the Weiunwood Fair, celebrated by the folks of the 'Hill as well as those of the 'Wood.

"And in the midst of the gaiety, in the midst of the fair, during the great picnic, during the games—where Tomlin's buccos competed in the sling-throwing tournament, and lo! Petal's dammsels engaged in the knife-throwing meet—a Man taller than the other Men, so tall and dressed in forest green leathers, came in among the celebrants, and he was seeking a pair of Waldana. . . ."

Oi! went up the shout of the crowd as Little Riatha's blade *thunked!* into the heart of the target.

Ah! they shouted once more as—*thnk!*—Silvereyes' knife sped after, ticking her older sister's steel, it was so close.

These two were the last in the contest, each having survived several matches to come to the championship go. Along the way they had defeated Big Men and older buccen as well, some of them three or four times the dammen's ages, along with one younger. Only twelve and eleven summers did these two wee maidens hold, both of nearly like size, two feet seven inches and two feet eight, respectively; yet they threw knives as would an expert, for Petal had begun training each as soon as they could grasp a blade. And now they cast 'gainst one another, did Tomlin's and Petal's two dammsels, and there was not whit to separate them on this day.

Along the sidelines stood their proud parents, Tomlin with his hands gently down upon Bear's shoulders, the youngling buccan standing before his sire, beside his dam, watching his sisters, waiting for his go with the slingsters, when he along with Small Urus would try their hand at winning as well.

As the judges walked up to the target, the wee youngling's eyes strayed, and he saw a giant of a Man moving among the crowd at the far edge, the tall one wearing green.

Oi! went the crowd again as the judges held a hand over each damman, signifying another tie. For the third time they moved the targets back five paces. One more cast would each maiden get, the final one of the match, then it would be over, win, lose, or draw.

Then it will be my *turn*, thought Bear, his eyes again following the Man in green as the tall Human bent down and spoke to a buccan there on the opposite side. Bear watched as the Warrow's eyes searched the crowd, finally alighting upon Tomlin and Petal and Bear, and much to Bear's surprise, the buccan pointed straight at them.

Hooray! shouted the crowd, and Bear looked to see what had happened. There in target center quivered two knives, his sisters' last throws. And who had won, he couldn't determine.

As the judges walked up to the target, along with Little Riatha and Silvereyes, Bear again turned his gaze unto the crowd, seeking the Man in green. *Gone!*

He looked up and back to say something to his sire, and lo! there was the tall Man directly behind, tapping Bear's father upon the shoulder, who at the touch turned about.

"Be ye Pebble, little one?" asked the Man in green, his voice a deep rumble.

At Tomlin's nod, "Then name the one who bears the starsilver sword," said the Man, "and I will name the one who sends word to Tomlin and Petal."

Yay! shouted the crowd, drowning out Tomlin's answer.

"Riatha," repeated the Warrow, his voice now raised above the babble of noise.

Mistaking Tommy's answer as a naming of which dammsel had won the contest, Petal turned around, beaming. "Nay, by a whisker 'twas Silvereyes for the first time—" she began, but when she saw that Tomlin was looking up at a huge Man, a Baeran from the size of him, her heart clenched and her voice jerked to a halt, for she knew that some dire word was at hand.

The Man nodded at Tomlin's answer, and he produced a wax-sealed letter, giving it over to the buccan. "Aye, Riatha is the name I sought. And Urus is the name I give in return.

"I am Ruar. I come from the Greatwood and am bound for Challerain Keep. Ere I set forth, Urus called me aside and bade me to bear a message unto Riatha in Arden Vale, and to you here in the Weiunwood."

Tomlin's own heart hammered as he took the parchment, and he stared at the brown wax seal, pressed with the likeness of a bear, and he turned it over and again in his hands. Then he looked down at his youngest bucco, the wee lad not yet two foot tall. "Find your brother, Bear, and remind him that it is time for the slingsters to throw. We will be there shortly."

As Bear scurried away to locate Small Urus, Little Riatha and Silvereyes came through the crowd, smiling broadly. "Wellanow," said Little Riatha to dam and sire, "I do believe that we showed them, we two: the Big Men, the buccans, everyone. Silvereyes especially, though I deem Lady Fortune smiled down on her today. Else 'twould be me bearing the winner's ribbon."

As Silvereyes beamed, her pale blue gemlike eyes atwinkle, Little Riatha hugged her sister, and Tomlin and Petal hugged them both.

With a final squeeze, Petal stepped back. "Run along now to the slingster field. Your brothers get set to go against their elders, and it would cheer them to see your faces in the crowd.

"Your sire and I will be there directly."

Holding hands, the two maiden dammen set out for the sling field, while Tomlin and Petal and Ruar made their way to the shade of a large oak tree.

With hands slightly atremble, glancing at Petal, Tomlin at last opened the missive.

Tomlin, Petal:
   There are fragmentary tales of some evil eastward in the Grimwall. Though scant, these stories hint at Wrg and Vulgs and disappearances, hence, Stoke may have survived the fire at Daemon's Crag. I am sending word by Ruar to let you as well as Riatha know that I plan to set forth on Autumnsday to seek the source of these rumors, after Prince Aurion completes his training and sets forth for Caer Pendwyr.
   You need feel no obligation to join me, for these

*are but unfounded tales. Yet should you not hear
from me by the Autumnsday after, gather Riatha and
come seeking. I will leave a record of these rumors
and my plans with my kindred.*

Urus

Without speaking, Tomlin handed the missive to Petal,
watching her face drain of blood as she read it.

When she looked up from the parchment, Ruar cleared
his throat and handed Tomlin another wax-sealed letter.
"From Riatha the Elfess," the Baeran rumbled. "She in-
structed me to give it over to you after you had read the
Chieftain's letter."

Again Tomlin's hands trembled as he broke the seal
and opened this second message.

My dear Waerlinga:
*I plan on setting forth from Arden Vale a Moon
before Autumnsday, to travel to the Greatwood,
there below Darda Erynian, to join Urus in his
search for the truth.*
*I repeat Urus's admonition: ye need feel no obli-
gation to join us, for these are but unfounded tales.
Yet should ye not hear from one or the other of us by
the Autumnsday after, gather aid and come seeking.*

Riatha

Again, Tomlin handed the missive to Petal. This time
her face held its color, for she had accepted the worst.

Though his heart was pounding with the news that
Stoke might yet live, as if to distract himself Tomlin
looked up at Ruar. "You named Urus 'Chieftain.' Does he
again lead the Baeron?"

"Nay," replied the Man. "Our Chieftain he was, in the
past. But after what Stoke did, Urus claimed he wasn't fit
to lead and stepped down, though none held him at fault
... except for Urus himself. Even so, still we call him
Chieftain, though he no longer holds the post. Gaer is
Chieftain now."

After the Baeran fell silent, Tomlin asked a second
question, to occupy his mind, to keep from dwelling on

the possibilities, to keep from dwelling on what these rumors of an evil in the Grimwall might mean to his buccos and dammsels, and to Petal, and last of all, to himself. "Urus mentions Prince Aurion and training."

"Aye," responded Ruar, "the Prince is with us, the Baeron, and Urus shows him the core of our heart. Learning the ways of the woods, he is. Tracking, foraging, hunting, fishing, more: the Chieftain fosters in him a respect for the forest and the dwellers within, nurturing those skills that will stand him in good stead for all the rest of his days. Just as he did the High King before, when Galvane was but a lad."

Tomlin cocked his head to one side. "Urus taught King Galvane?"

Ruar nodded. "As a child. Briand, too."

The buccan's eyed widened. *Just how old is Urus? Briand was slain back in '53, some seventeen years past. And if Urus taught him woodcraft when he was a child, that'd be some forty-two or—*

Ruar's deep voice broke into Tomlin's speculations. "For nearly as long as there have been High Kings and Baeron, each of the Kings has sent unto us his male offspring in their tenth summer, to learn how to listen to the Land and to hearken unto its voice, to learn its ways and foster its well-being.

"It is said that in elden times, my people came upon an injured child wandering naked and lost in the wilderness. He knew not his name, nor those of his parents, for the injury was to his head. We took him in and nurtured him as one of our own.

"A season passed, a summer, and in the early fall a Baeron patrol discovered the hidden remains of a slaughtered escort, and concealed with them was a standard, bearing the colors of Pellar. When the patrol bore the tattered flag into the village, at the sight of golden griffin upon scarlet field, of a sudden the lad remembered all.

"He was Prince Alon, son of High King Galor; and his escort had been slain by the Wrg and stripped, and he himself had been left for dead.

"And to veil their crime, the Foul Folk dragged all into

the forest and covered them over with cut brush, not knowing that such would act as a beacon unto the Baeron.

"We returned young Alon unto his dam and sire.

"And King Galor avenged himself mightily upon the Foul Folk.

"But ever since, the Baeron have trained the sons of the High Kings—in the love of the Land, in its ways, in its nurturing.

"And we do this when they are but ten, as was Prince Alon, for as the sapling is bent, so grows the tree.

"And *that* is why Prince Aurion is in the Greatwood, for he is ten. And Urus is his mentor."

At that instant Bear came downcast back unto Tomlin and Petal. "I lost," he said, his face chapfallen.

Mustering a smile, crackling parchment still in hand, Petal knelt down and hugged him. "Another time, Bear, and you'll perhaps win one."

"Oh, I won three," replied Bear, "but then a Man beat me."

"Three!" exclaimed Tomlin, clapping Bear on the shoulder. "Wellanow, that's quite good. After all, you are only eight. Plenty of time to sharpen your skills in all the tomorrows yet to come."

At the mention of "tomorrow," Petal stood and folded the letters from Urus and Riatha and stuffed them in her wide pocket. "Come, Tommy. We will deal with these later. But now is the time of the celebration, and if he's yet in the hunt, let us cheer Small Urus on."

Much to Bear's delight, Ruar hoisted the wee lad up to his shoulder, and Baeran, buccan, damman, and youngling made their way unto the slingster field.

The following morning, Ruar spoke his farewells and then continued on his journey to Challerain Keep. Why he went there is not recorded.

The next weeks were difficult ones for Tomlin and Petal, and more than once the buccan found his dammia weeping, and more than once did he weep as well. It was a time of hard decision, for they had a family to consider, beloved buccos and dammsels. And yet they were pledged to aid Riatha and Urus, to run Stoke to earth and slay him. Too, their own hearts called out for vengeance against this monster, for each had lost loved ones to his hideous pleasure: Tomlin his dam and sire; Petal her sire as well. Even so, that Stoke was mayhap alive, perhaps even found, tore their hearts asunder, for they could not bear to leave their children, but would not take them along on a mission fraught with peril. Yet they could not leave their children untended, to raise themselves, as it were. But both sire and dam knew that they *must* go, knew that they *must* leave their children behind, that they *must* join Riatha and Urus, for they *could not* allow such a creature as Stoke to stride the face of Mithgar.

Hence, many were the days and nights filled with agonized discussions, filled with tears and tearing hearts, for few were the choices at their beck. And they examined the options that lay before them, and explained these alternatives to the children, who clamored to go but were denied, whose faces went ashen at what was to be, at the thought of their parents leaving them, at the thought of their parents facing off once more against Stoke. And after all was said and done, in the end, they journeyed to Budgens, there in the Boskydells. And they met with one of Tomlin's distant cousins, Dorry Breed and her buccaran, Argo, who had two buccos and a dammsel of their own.

When they had told their tale—of Stoke and his madness, of the murder of their kindred, of their pursuit of this fiend, and of their pledge to Urus and Riatha—Dorry and Argo opened their arms wide and gathered in the children, whispering to them that their sire and dam had to go, and that here they would be loved as if they were their very own.

And so it was settled: the children would stay with their kindred; Tomlin and Petal would go with Riatha and Urus.

On the morning that they left, Tomlin took his children to one side to speak his farewells. "If we do not return, hone your skills to the uttermost, and if you are of a mind, then when you come to your young buccan years, to your young damman years, go after Stoke, not only to avenge us, but also to forever rid Mithgar of this monster. Silver weaponry, remember—as your dam and sire bear— silver missiles, silver blades, for little else will do him harm. Wait for Bear to reach this age, twelve years hence, and then seek aid from the Lian, and from the Baeron."

He hugged each of them and kissed them, and Petal came and hugged and kissed each as well. Yet she said nought, for her heart was breaking, and all were weeping, and she could not get words past her tears. And yet her embrace and kiss spoke eloquently for her.

As the morning Sun rose past the dawn, Tomlin and Petal mounted up on their ponies and rode away, down the Byroad Lane toward the great Crossland Road beyond.

Over the next weeks, slowly the Warrows made their way eastward: through the Boskydells to the great Thornwall and beyond; past Edgewood and thence once more unto Stonehill; and onward by the Bogland Bottoms and past Beacontor and the Wilderness Hills; into Drearwood, the place dark and dismal and gloomy, its hoary trees yet foreboding though the great Purging had taken place some twenty-two years past, back in '48, when the Lian Elves and Wildermen at last drove the dreadful creatures from these environs; and finally they came unto Arden Vale, there in the north of Rell, known as Lianion unto the Elves.

They were stopped by two Lian Guardians, there at the entrance unto the Vale, there at Arden Falls, where the water roared in cataract and swirling mist rose up between the close-set canyon walls to hide what lay beyond.

After hearing their tale and seeing Riatha's letter, the warders led the two Waerlinga behind the falls, a road passing under, churning vapor all about them, and they came up into a narrow gorge.

Nigh this entrance they passed by the bole of a gigantic tree, towering high above. Like a pine it appeared, yet leaves it had and not needles. Dusky they were, as if holding luminous twilight, Elven in its glow even in the Sun. Yet this tree was alone of its kind, here in the Hidden Vale, for as they rode onward, no more did they see;

'twas evergreen forest thenceward on into the narrow gorge.

In a twoday they came unto the mainmost Elvenholt, and there they were greeted by fair Riatha, who knew that they would come in spite of the release she had given them, in spite of the release granted by Urus as well.

That eve they were escorted unto the Elven Court, shining and bright and filled with gay music and silver laughter, where Talarin and Rael reigned over all, here in the Northern Reaches of Rell. They supped among the company of noble Elves, the twain but tiny Wee Folk. Nonetheless the two were revered and honored, for they were Waerlinga, and that explained all, at least unto the Lian.

At their table sat Gildor and Vanidor Goldbranch, tall and fair, and the eye could not tell them apart, for they were twin to one another, these sons of Talarin and golden Rael. To their right sat Faeon, small and graceful and as beautiful as her mother, and sister to the twins, she here on a journey from Darda Galion, the fabled Eldwood to the south, where she was consort to Coron Eiron, leader of all the Elves upon Mithgar. Too, there was Riatha and her cousins, Alors Inarion and Valarel; tall and straight-limbed were these two, and with hair as black as the wings of a raven.

And Petal did not know that such wonder and grace and beauty existed in all of Mithgar, nor did Tomlin, here among the Elvenkind. Yet the two of them would have cast all aside—the bright music and silver laughter, the vivid tapestries and fine silks and satins, the graceful dancing and singing voices, the sumptuous banquet, piquant and delicious—could they but see their buccos and dammsels one more time.

Out from Arden Vale rode the trio, Riatha on a fine grey gelding, Petal and Tomlin upon their stolid ponies. East they went some days and upward, up into the Crestan Pass there across the Grimwall. Then down again and across the plains, now on the Overland Road, aiming toward a forest afar, called by some the Great Greenhall, known as Darda Erynian by others, past the mighty Argon

River. More days it took for this travel, yet this was not their next goal, for it lay southeastward many miles. The Greatwood was where they fared, there where Baeron dwelled. South and east, beyond the River Rissanin.

By ways known unto Riatha, through the forest and vale they wended, fording clear streams as well as sparkling rivers, at times escorted on their way by the Dylvana, the green-clad woodland Elves of Darda Erynian, singing in the twilight.

As they forded the River Rissanin to come into the Greatwood, the nature of their escort changed: shadows moved among the boles of the trees, Wolves, it seemed, or mayhap Bears or even great, huge Men, there at the edge of vision.

At times the trees themselves seemed to move, bringing eld legends welling up from childhood hearthtales.

Accompanied by this strange escort as they travelled southerly, of Elves and Wolves, and Bears and Men, and perhaps the trees as well, Tomlin and Petal were grateful to be with Riatha, for the forest dwellers knew her as a friend and warded well their journey.

Too, the Greatwood was a vast, vast timberland, some seven hundred miles long and two hundred and fifty wide. Yet the Elfess rode straightly toward where they were bound, and at last, together, they came unto a woodland village, hidden among foliage green at the edge of a great treeless space in the midst of the forest, the gigantic glade known simply as the Clearing, so broad that the woods beyond could not be seen, some thirty miles distant.

And in this village they found Urus.

It was a week ere Autumnsday.

With Urus was a slender manchild, ten summers old. Aurion was his name, a Prince of the Realm, the eldest of High King Galvane. Tall he was for his age, with hair dark brown and a ready smile. Sharp was his gaze out of eyes piercing blue, yet humor twinkled deep within each; for at this time and place he still had two eyes—in but another decade he would lose one of them venturing 'gainst the Rovers of Kistan, and then would don a scarlet eyepatch and thereafter be known as Aurion Redeye, and as Good King Redeye when he ascended to the throne. But that was yet to be, and for the nonce he was simply Aurion, for he would suffer none to call him by his rank.

That night they sat in council: Urus, Riatha, Tomlin, and Petal. Too, Aurion was there, for Urus would have the lad gain experience in matters such as these. Mentor and pupil were these two for a single week more; then would Aurion fare unto Caer Pendwyr, there to meet his sire returning from the summer Court, held in Challerain Keep. But on this night the five of them considered but one thing: the whereabouts of a monster: Baron Stoke.

"East it is," rumbled Urus, "in the Grimwall, or so the rumors say, that something dark and deadly preys upon the mountain dwellers in the night."

Tomlin glanced up from the fire. "Near Vulfcwmb, where he was before?"

Urus shook his head. "Nay, little one. Farther east. Nigh the ruins Dragonslair, there where the earth shakes and trembles."

An elusive thought tugged at the edge of Tomlin's mind. *Dragonslair? Now, what—?*

Aurion's exclamation broke through Tomlin's shell of concentration. "Dragonslair? That's where Black Kalgalath was slain!"

He's right. Elyn and Thork and the quest of Black Mountain. It ended there at Dragonslair ... or so they say.

"Aye, lad," responded Urus, smiling at the Prince. "And the earth yet quakes from the time of the Dragon's doom."

"I heard them sing of it at the Gathering," said Aurion.

Petal raised an eyebrow. "The Gathering?"

"Aye," answered Aurion, pointing outward toward that great treeless space. "In the Clearing on Year's Long Day.

"Urus says that each Midyear, all Baeron who are able gather in its center, where tales of great deeds are told, especially those of Baeron heroes and heroines, though others are recounted as well."

Urus cleared his throat. "It is the greatest of honors to

have tales told and songs sung of your deeds there at the Gathering. One day, mayhap . . ."

Urus's voice fell silent, and after a while Tomlin spoke up. "Among Warrows tales are told year 'round of things that folk do, great and small. Even so, it'd be nice to have someone sing of my own deeds—mayhap at my graveside."

A stricken look came over Petal's face, and she clutched her buccaran's hand. "Oh, Tommy, say not such things, for they might come true."

Tomlin laughed. "Fear not, my dammia, for I plan on living to a ripe old age. Besides, the chances of me doing a deed worth a song, well . . ."

Again a silence fell upon them. But after a moment Riatha brought them back to the subject of the council. "Urus, about these rumors . . ."

And long into the night they spoke, of Vulgs and such and Baron Stoke, and of victims dragged into his lair.

The following day, a small force of warriors, armed and armored, clad in scarlet and gold, came riding across the Clearing and into the village. It was Aurion's escort, come to accompany him back unto Caer Pendwyr. And five days after, they rode out again, the Prince in their midst.

Yet ere he went, he came unto Tomlin and Petal, pledging his aid should they call for it. And though he was but ten, every inch a Prince he was, and the Warrows knew that aid would come if they but asked.

And now Baeron and Waldana and Elfess watched as Aurion rode away, southerly, out across the wide Clearing, the Princeling mounted on a dappled grey, midst chestnuts and bays and blacks all about, spear-borne pennons snapping in the breeze, rampant golden griffin on scarlet field.

And when they could see the future King no more, when the last standard passed beyond the horizon, they turned and strode back into the forest, where awaited mounts of their own.

East and north fared the foursome, for Riamon and Garia and Khal and beyond, unto and through the northwesternmost corner of Aralan, striking for a section of the great Grimwall, that cold stone spine of Mithgar, to pass into those mountains dire where lay the ruins of Dragonslair.

And as they slowly made their way 'cross the Land, slowly, too, did the seasons creep across Mithgar: the trees gradually shifting from green to yellow to gold to brown, the leaves falling and swirling down in the occasional wind and rain, until at last nought but barren branches clawed upward in the now chill air. And the edges of winter could now be felt pressing down upon the Land.

It was some sixty days after Autumnsday when the four rode into the village of Inge, there in the far northwest reaches of Aralan. Northward they could see the sullen mountains of the dark Grimwall looming into the bleak November sky.

And now and again here in this region the earth would tremble, shivering in memory of a cataclysm some twenty-four centuries past.

The hamlet of Inge had but one inn, the Ram's Horn, where room and board could be purchased, and local news came free. Into this inn stepped the foursome, welcoming the chance to sleep in beds for a change, and to take hot baths, and to eat heartily cooked meals, and to stable their mounts and give them a rest as well; for all were weary of the road: buccan and damman, Elfess and Baeran, and horse and pony, too.

That evening, the Ram's Horn was swelled nigh to bursting with locals, come to see the Wee Ones, they did, and the Elfess, and the huge Man. Too, they would hear of events from faraway places and exchange a word or so, should the visitors desire.

"Nowt!" exclaimed the elder. "No Baron Stoke what I've heard of. But about these disappearances, well, that be another thing altogether.

"Stoneford, now. They all disappeared. Left wreckage behind, too. The trackers said they was taken north, into the Grimwalls, where none but the foolish go."

"Har!" exclaimed another elder. "Leastwise they didn't go into the Mire, now did they?"

Sensing a pointless argument was about to begin, as to which was the more dangerous, the Grimwall or the Khalian Mire, Riatha spoke up. "This Stoneford, where might it be? And how many disappeared, and when?"

Several voices broke out at once, but the elder quickly took command. When quiet reigned: "Seven months back it was, or nearabout, for none can rightly say, three families as lived at the ford, helping waggons across in the spring waters, for a fee, they was the ones what disappeared, Men, Women, children. Fourteen people all told.

"The rivers, you see, come down from the Grimwalls, both east and west of here, and they flow south into the Khalian Mire.

"Stoneford lies to the east, a few miles along the tradeway."

Urus looked up from the stick he was whittling on. "And the tracks led north, you say."

"Aye, north," replied several voices.

"What kind of tracks?"

This time it was a young Man who spoke up: "They was some what said as they was the spoor of the Foul Folk. But them tracks was old, and none could tell for sure."

"Up to Dragonslair, I shouldn't wonder," said another.

Others shook their heads, *No,* and one said, "No, not Dragonslair, what with it belching out melted rock and fire and blasting great stones up into the sky. Besides, it's all ruined, its wall blowed down, or nearabout. And the fumes, well, I hear they are poison. What would a Rutch or Drōk or Ogru or Guul want with such, anyway?"

Urus again spoke up. "I'd like to talk to the one who saw the tracks."

"Ar," responded the elder, "he's long gone. 'Twas a blader, he was, all set to pay for help getting his waggon across the river, coming as he were from beyond that way, bringing his knives and whetstones and such for trade. But they wasn't a body at the ford to help him, and no trace of any, or so he said, even though he searched. But he did find tracks and wreckage, as if they'd been a fight.

And he came on here 'cause he was scared to stay there, though he had a devil of a time crossing alone."

At that moment again the ground shuddered, and the building jolted and rocked, and crockery rattled.

And none of the Inge residents seemed to take notice, for the juddering of the earth was a commonplace part of their lives.

The next month or so, Urus, Riatha, Petal, and Tomlin travelled along the margins of the Grimwall, searching for evidence of Stoke. Small hamlets they sought out, and villages, and dwellings, farms, campsites, and sometimes nought but a lean-to, or a slow-moving waggon on the winter road. They spoke with merchants, trappers, crofters, woodsmen, and others, seeking some word of Stoke. Yet they found nothing to tell them that he was in this part of Mithgar, though the wrecked dwellings at Stoneford spoke silently of a dark deed done.

At last winter struck in all of its brumal fury, and the foursome returned to Inge to await the loosing of its icy grip. Four weeks they remained, then six, seven, and they had begun to speak of returning to their homes, to their loved ones, for nought of Stoke did they hear, neither fancy nor fact, neither rumor nor truth.

Mid February had come, and once again grey winter day found them studying the map that Petal had made of this part of Mithgar. Much of it she had drawn by speaking to locals, sketching as the person spoke with her; too, the damman had shown her evolving sketch to each, asking their opinions as to its accuracy, corroborating where possible the distances and directions and numbers given to her by others, verifying her chart. Trappers and travelling merchants and hunters were especially helpful, or any others who ranged widely as a matter of course. And she had redrawn the map several times as more accurate information came her way.

As the four studied Petal's most recent sketch, Obart Hensley, the innkeeper, came bearing a tray with hot mugs of tea, setting it down at the edge of the table, handing each a cup. He, too, peered at the sketch. After a moment: "Wellanow, y' dona have the monastery marked up there on the north slope."

All eyes looked up at Obart, Petal's glittering amber. "Monastery . . . ?" she asked, taking a quill from the holder, uncapping her tiny inkhorn. "Where?"

Wiping his hands upon his apron till they were thoroughly dry, Obart's thick finger lightly touched the map parchment. "Here . . . or nearabout," he said. "North and east of Dragonslair. Atop a crag. A rock mountain. Above the great north glacier." Obart's finger traced a route through the Grimwalls, starting at Inge, following the river valley north and west, then turning northeasterly to pass by Dragonslair, continuing until the north slope of the Grimwalls was reached. "Mayhap one hundred ten, one hundred twenty miles threading through the mountains, though less, could you fly like a bird."

Petal touched the map. "Here?"

"Or nearabout," replied Obart.

The damman placed a small dot at the point indicated, then made a notation: *Monastery, here or nearabout.*

Riatha indicated to Obart that he was to take a seat. "Tell us about this monastery, friend."

The innkeeper stepped back to the counter and poured himself a mug of tea as well. Then he sat at the table with the four. "Wellanow, there be nowt too much to tell. The monastery has been there since elden times. Built in the days before the Ban, or so they say. Had something to do with the glacier, or the Untended Lands to the north, or the Barrens beyond, they tell . . . though what that may be, it's a puzzle, all right. Abandoned for the most part, the tales would have it, though tended now and again."

Urus took a short sip from his mug. "Be there any dwellers at this monastery now?"

"Oh, aye," replied the 'keep. "Some years back they came, the monks. Been there ever since. Prayin' for the Land to settle, I hear. Prayin' to stop all this shuddering and shaking, though Adon knows when that might be."

As if listening to Obart's words, a quiver ran through the earth.

Cocking a significant eye at the foursome, Obart said,

"Damn near broke Mithgar in two did Kalgalath when he died, or so I hear.

"They say as the sound alone nigh destroyed Inge. And whole forests were blown down 'tween here and there and roundabout. And powdered stone sifted down from the sky, like snow. And it rained black rain. And lightning could be seen stroking deep within the Grimwalls, over by Dragonslair, or what was left of it.

"And some say that Thork hisself was brought to Inge, by Giants, no less, for he needed healing, fighting with the Dragon like he did. . . ."

Obart paused, and long moments passed while legends of old tumbled through the minds of each. But at last he said, "And *that's* why the Land trembles, for there 'twas on Springday that Black Kalgalath met his doom, there at Dragonslair.

"And them monks, well, they live in the monastery and pray for the world to settle, though it's shook so for nigh onto twenty-four centuries, back when Dragons were last awake."

Riatha looked up from her tea. "This monastery, hast thou been there?"

At Obart's shake of the head, Riatha asked, "What dost thou know of it, then? Its shape and size, the number of its dwellers, its buildings, and whatever else thou can say."

"All I know is nought but rumor, Lady," responded Obart. "They say it is made of stone. A tower, I think the tales tell. And as to the monks, some ten or twelve dwell therein, mayhap more, I wouldn't know but shouldn't wonder."

Little more did they learn from the innkeeper. And none else in Inge could add much to what they had heard, although a visit by Riatha and Urus to the town's store-keeper did confirm that ten or twelve seemed right as concerned the number of monks, the merchant imparting some tidings as well—"Sold 'em flour, I did, and it was enough for that number, ten or twelve. Down here every summer or two, one comes, leading a train of mules, pur-chasing a winter's stores, though this year none came."

At this last Riatha glanced at Urus. The Baeran nodded

slightly, indicating that he understood her unspoken comment. They would have to go to the monastery to check on the well-being of the monks, to warn them in the least, and to gather news concerning the disappearances, should they have any news, and if Fortune so favored, to gather word of Stoke's whereabouts.

And so, as the weather ameliorated, the season marching toward spring, the foursome set forth, aiming first for Dragonslair, and then turning toward the Great North Glacier beyond, seeking an eld monastery, following a trail of speculation, as they had done all along.

Even though spring stepped toward Mithgar, the icy grip of winter yet clutched the Grimwalls, and snow lay deep upon the land. The wind blew frigid and cut through their clothes, and they grew chill while riding. And so at times they would take to foot, slogging through the drifts, for the effort of walking warmed them. Even so, it tired them as well, and their progress was slow.

Yet not a week passed ere they came within sight of Dragonslair, the great, ruined firemountain belching smoke, now and then blasting huge rocks into the sky, the air thundering, and here and there rivers of molten lava ran red up out of its bowels and down its stubby flanks. Of brimstone and sulphur smelled the wind when it blew their way, and at night an eerie blue fire could be seen flaring in the crater—Kalgalath's ghost-fire, Riatha named it. "They say that every Springday, Kalgalath's ghost rises up from the fire and flies beyond seeing up into the sky, only to come plummeting at last down the very throat of the firemountain, whelming the Kammerling into the world, blasting Dragonslair to ruin, all but that eastern slope yon."

Like a maimed hand, the middle slope of the eastern slant yet stood, rearing into the air, a wall that somehow had survived the ruin of Kalgalath. For here it was that the mighty Dragon had met his doom, here at the hands of Elyn and Thork, the great Fire-drake plummeting down to destroy the very mountain in which he lived.

And still the land juddered and shook, here along the Grimwalls, e'en though the firemountain had detonated

nigh two thousand four hundred years agone. Here was
the epicenter, here at the ruins of Dragonslair, for as
Riatha put it: "Yet unto this day the earth remembers that
destruction, that mighty whelming, as a bell remembers
its ring."

That the land had shuddered off and on for such a long
while was a mystery in and of itself, or so Riatha said, re-
marking, "The Loremasters say that the Utruni—the
Stone Giants—were here at Kalgalath's doom, centuries
past, and remain. And yet it was at this time of destruction the land became unstable, and it has shaken for lo
these many years; and that is a riddle: For Utruni work to
shape the land, to raise its mountains and carve the river
valleys. And in this work they strive to gentle the earth,
to ease the quaking of the world, quelling it. And yet here
the Utruni have let *this* land continue to judder, even
though nearly twenty-four hundred summers have passed.
"It is as if they are waiting for something to happen. . . ."

Across this jolting realm the foursome plodded, past
the fire and brimstone and molten lava, past the rocks
blasted upward and the boiling reek, past the maimed ruin
of Dragonslair, past the place sung of in many a bard's
songs. A week or more did the shattered firemountain
dominate the 'scape, first before them, then to their left,
then fading into the mountains rearward. And slowly they
swung northeastward, aiming now for the great glacier,
there along the north slope of the Grimwalls, where they
were told that nearby stood a solitary monastery, an isolated place where prayerful monks dwelled within.

A late winter blizzard swooped down upon them as would
a wild, clawing beast. And they stumbled upon a refuge of
a sort, a low overhang scooped out of stone in the side
of a mountain, and nearby stood a winter coppice. Within
but an hour the temperature plunged down into icy depths,
and had they not found shelter and kindled fire, they would
have perished. Even so, they were miserable, especially in
the frigid night, and their steeds fared no better.

A week they subsisted, and still the wind hurled ice
and snow across the mountains, dragging their spirits

down. But at last the weather improved, though the skies were yet grey, and they set forth once more, north and east, across the shaking Land.

Just after dawn on Springday morn, leading their steeds up a rocky slope, they came on foot to an overlook, and gazed down upon the vast glacier. A great, wide frozen river of ice, down from the mountain crests it sinuously twisted past them and far beyond, to a high north face of the Grimwall. The Land immediately below the distant precipice they could not see, for the massif plummeted steeply hundreds of fathoms, and the glacier fell unseen unto the frozen plains of the Untended Lands. Way beyond lay empty, snow-laden barrens, stretching unto the northern horizon, as far as the eye could see. Yet the eye did not dwell upon these featureless, distant barrens but instead was drawn unto the vast, twisting, sinuous shape below. And though this glacial river was made of ice, and seemed frozen in place, Riatha assured the Waerlinga that it did indeed flow, though so slowly as to be unnoticeable to all but those who could take the time to observe its creep—and Elves were among those who had the time to note the gradual motion.

"There," rumbled Urus, pointing, and yon where his outstretched arm indicated, some miles away, on a rocky slope above the glacier, there stood a tower and several large buildings and some small, walled about, all made of stone.

It could be nought but the monastery.

It took much of the morning to find a way down unto the glacier, and when they reached its surface, they found it was raddled with wide cracks and deep crevices, belying the smoothness seen from afar. Like monstrous boulders, great, jagged chunks of ice lay on the surface of this frozen river, where the juddering Grimwalls had fractured the glacier, scattering the shatter about. Too, there were blocky pinnacles, tall and steep and strangely shaped, sculpted so by the wind. White it was and snow-covered, yet here and there the glacier was clear ice, like cold glass, and light plunged deeply into the bluish depths below. And through this fractured, tumbled 'scape, past huge boulders of ice and wind-carven tors, wended the foursome afoot, Urus probing the path they took, seeking firm footing, now and again backtracking to make their way about some blockage—a crevasse wide or an abutment steep or snow too deep to broach.

It was late afternoon when they reached the stony plateau where lay the ancient monastery. They mounted up and rode the last furlong across the windswept, barren rock, steel-shod hooves aclatter as they came unto the wall and through the open gate.

And horse and pony alike shied and skitted at every shadow and swirl of wind.

No sign of life did they see as they rode into an open yard ringed about by grey stone buildings, most storage sheds, though some were dwellings. Directly ahead was the main tower, backed against the wall. Forty or fifty feet high it was, and round, some eighteen feet across and made of stone as well; it was capped with a steep-canted slate roof. The tower itself jutted up centrally from a large squarish building, a building perhaps eighty feet wide and twice as many deep, and two or three storeys high, itself with a slanted slate roof all way 'round. Window slits there were, shuttered over, along the high stone walls. The tower, too, bore window slits, shuttered as well, winding up and about, as if following a spiral stair—except nigh the very top, where wide archways ringed darkly 'round.

Before them, up a step or two, stood two great wooden doors.

Closed.

And no one came forth to greet them.

" 'Ware," warned Riatha, her voice low. "Though it seems abandoned, still I deem this a likely place that Stoke would seek out."

A tremble juddered through the earth.

Tomlin glanced at the wan Sun, low in the sky to the west, near setting. "Why is it," he growled, "that we always seem to come upon places such as this when night is about to fall?"

Urus dismounted and led his skittish steed unto a tethering post. "There is yet an hour or so of daylight left. Too, we will need shelter when the darktide comes, for should the wind rise off the glacier, it will be frigid at these heights."

Petal dismounted too, tethering her pony next to Urus's black. "I don't like the way the ponies and horses are acting. It's as if they sense something."

"Aye, little one," agreed Riatha, tying her grey to the pole. "Something unpleasant."

"Or evil," added Tomlin, coming last.

Again the earth trembled.

"Let's go," said Petal, slipping a knife from its sheath. "Even now the Moon rises."

To the east a yellow gibbous Moon, waxing nigh fullness, cleared the horizon, while the red Sun yet fell toward the western rim.

"Which way?" asked Tomlin.

"The tower," growled Urus, moving toward the steps.

And so they went: Urus first, morning star in hand; Petal, then Tomlin after, knife and sling ready; Riatha last, starsilver blade, sparkles within aglint.

They stopped before the door, and Tomlin lit a small lantern, for they knew not what lay inside, dark or light, or who if any dwelt within.

At a nod from the buccan, Urus tried the door, swinging the leftmost panel inward upon creaking hinges.

A vestibule they entered, the hallway short, and before them stood another set of closed doors. These, too, Urus tried, and once more found them unlocked, though these swung outward.

They stepped into a great, open chamber with a high-vaulted ceiling, unlighted but for the daylight seeping inward and Tomlin's feeble lantern pressing back the gloom. Off to the sides in the shadows loomed pillared posts buttressing overhead galleries to left and right hugging the walls, narrow enclosed stairs pitching upward immediately at hand, to either side, east and west, leading to those balconies. Across the chamber, near the far wall, stood an altar with Adon's glyph carven thereupon. And farther on, at the back wall, off to left and right, again enclosed stairs led upward unto the galleries.

"A hall of worship," breathed Petal as they stepped across the stone floor, her voice resounding in the great, hollow space even though she but whispered ... while behind, the portals they had entered slowly swung to, hinged as they were to close without an aiding hand, deepening the darkness within, shutting with a soft echoing *doom ... oom ... oom.*

Now only the light of the hand-held lantern pressed against the swaying shadows.

A tremor thrummed through the floor as the earth shivered again.

Riatha looked about. "Here the monks gathered—Adonites, it would seem—to lift their voices in prayer, asking that this land settle, if Innkeeper Obart be right."

Forward they started across the stone floor, their footsteps ringing hollowly in the wide gloom.

Now they came unto the altar.

" 'Ware," growled Urus, pointing.

Adon's glyph had been defaced.

Behind the altar, lying on the floor was an aspergillum, a small hand-held device for the ceremonial sprinkling of blessed water. Ivory and silver it seemed: a hollow ivory cylinder affixed unto an ivory handle, sparsely decorated 'round with heavy silver wire crisscrossing in an open geometric pattern. A silver chain was attached to the tip of the handle, forming a wrist loop. Urus picked it up. The top of the cylinder had tiny holes in it for dispensing contained liquid, though Urus's quick glance saw no manner by which it could be filled. "A priestly instrument. Not likely to have been abandoned even in haste. Something dire has happened here to cause it to be left behind." The Baeran hung the dispenser by its chain unto his belt. "Mayhap we'll find the owner."

If Foul Folk were about, speculated Tomlin, *surely they would have taken such as a treasure ... unless they left it behind for a reason: perhaps they cannot abide the*

touch of silver; perhaps because it is holy; perhaps . . .
perhaps . . .

Breaking the buccan's train of thought, Riatha started
up one of the narrow stairways, toward the west gallery,
Petal in tow. Quickly, Urus and Tomlin followed, single
file, for the steps would permit no other mode.

The gallery was empty, though a wide canvas cloth
covered part of the wall. Lifting the cloth away from the
wall, behind they found a large stained-glass window de-
picting Adon and Elwydd and the making of Mithgar. The
red Sun outside threw horizontal light through the hued
glass, transforming the ruddy rays into myriad rainbow
colors.

Along the gallery and to the distant end down the con-
fining steps they fared, and across the chamber and then
up again, onto the balcony opposite. Yet no sooner had
they gone half its length, finding nought, than from below, muffled, they heard marching feet and cursing . . .

. . . And out from behind the altar, through a concealed
door now swung wide, fetching up against the wall—
boom! . . . oom . . . oom—came tramping Rūcks and
Hlōks, thirty or so, their harsh voices and marching feet
now echoing hollowly.

And in their midst came slinking five slavering Vulgs.

And these beasts lifted their muzzles and snuffled the
air and yawled, their howls rebounding throughout the invaded sanctuary.

Shouting some Slûkish command that reverberated
from the stone walls, the force below them spread wide,
searching, the Vulgs racing, noses to the floor. Up the
steps to the other balcony they ran, and down again, heading for the gallery opposite, following the scent.

"Swift!" shouted Riatha, her voice ringing through the
chamber as well. "Fend the stairs for they are strait and
will confine the foe to come against us but one at a time."

But Urus had already anticipated her, and choosing,
sprinted for one enclosed stairwell, while she ran for the
other, weapons at the ready.

Vulgs raced up the steps where stood Urus, while Rūcks and Hlōks came at Riatha.

Chnk! crashed morning star. *Shhkk!* slashed silveron sword. And howls and screams rent the air as foe fell injured or slain.

Tomlin's sling bullets and Petal's knives *sissed* into the enemy as well, felling where they struck. And though neither Warrow could hurl at the foe within the enclosed stairs, still Rūcks and Hlōks milled about on the floor below, queueing up to mount the steps.

"Tommy," shouted Petal, "there are too many! What will we do?"

"Fight on, love! Fight on!" replied Tomlin, hurling another bullet. "And if any get past Riatha or Urus, they're the ones to strike!"

As if his words were prophetic, Riatha was hurled back, and several Foul Folk leapt toward her.

Zzzzzak! a bullet brained one of them. *Thkkk!* a knife seemed to spring full-blown in another's throat. *Shhkk!* Riatha's blade took a third one down, and once again she pressed the foe hindward, though now red blood, not black, stained the Elfess's tunic.

Tomlin now moved closer to wounded Riatha, cursing that he knew not how to handle a sword, for his sling, though deadly, would not hold back the charge the Foul Folk were certain to mount. And with Riatha blocking the way, he could not at this time bring his sling up to bear upon the stair-encased foe.

Behind, Petal loosened a small grappling hook and silken cord she always carried upon her belt, praying that she was not too late.

Whirling the grapnel about her head, she let fly, the iron claw hurtling across the open space to the other balcony, where it lashed about the top rail and *clang!* caught.

In that moment Vulgs slammed into Urus, knocking him hindward, and two of the great black beasts stepped forth onto the gallery. While at the other end, again Riatha was pressed back.

Hauling the line taut, Petal tied a knot that haled it tighter still, the cord thrumming with tension. "O

Adon"—she cast her words unto the heavens—"keep the land steady and, please, let me remember my training!"

And while combat raged on the balcony, the damman mounted the bannister and stepped upon the rope and outward, her arms wide for balance, and started for the other side, treading a narrow cord high above a hard stone floor.

Below, two Rūcks glanced up and yelled, and raced for the stairs opposite, running to come upon the balcony where Petal would alight.

RRRAAAAWWWW! A great brown Bear now raged against the Vulgs, savage beyond understanding, claws rending, teeth shredding. Yet the black beasts were all over the creature Urus had become, fangs slashing, blood flying wide.

Tomlin's sling *hummed* as the buccan hurled bullets into the Rūckish foe surrounding Riatha, while her blade took others down. Yet it was clear that the battle was lost, for they were too many, and they had breached the stairwell. Slowly the two fell back, back toward Urus, the Bear now down with swarming, snarling Vulgs atop him.

Petal, balanced upon a narrow cord high above an unyielding stone floor, saw that she would have to run upon the rope if she were to outrace the Rūcks coming to intercept her.

She had not done so for nearly twenty years, back when she had entertained crowds in her father's travelling show.

And even if she ran, she did not know if she would be in time.

Yet to do otherwise would result in certain death.

And so, ignoring the sounds of blade on blade and snarling beasts and yawling voices and the screams of the dying behind her, the wee damman gritted her teeth and ran . . . *on a narrow cord . . . above a stone floor . . . for the other side.*

And sprinting along the balcony toward her came two Rūcks, cudgels upraised, shouting in victory, for they knew that they could slay one so small, they knew that they could bludgeon her to death.

Running along the rope, Petal reached the balcony rail

but a step or two before the Rūcks came upon her, and she leaped toward the wall—"O Adon, let me not be too late!"—crashing into the canvas, rending it down as the stained glass behind shattered, the damman falling to the floor with a thud at the very feet of the Rūcks, cloth tumbling down all about her.

And the horizontal rays of the setting Sun streamed into the monastery.

And on this balcony as well as that, the Rūcks fell dead, as did the Hlōks, withering into ashes.

And so, too, perished the Vulgs.

The last of the Sun's rays burned the Vulg poison from Urus's veins, though there is some question as to whether any poison but that from another werecreature could permanently do a werebear in, though now he wore the shape of a Man. And his slashes and tears and other hurts were painful, yet he could manage.

Riatha had taken several cuts, one deep, and she had been battered by cudgel. Yet after treatment and binding, the bleeding stopped, or seeped but slowly once bound.

Petal had nought but a bruised elbow, where it had struck the floor. And Tomlin was completely unscathed.

And as Urus with his hands of healing treated Riatha's injuries, on the opposite balcony Tomlin held onto Petal, whispering just how much she meant to him, for he fully realized that he could have lost her, to Rūcks or Hlōks or other such, or to a cold stone floor.

As to Petal, she could not stop giggling and weeping at one and the same time, and she was giddy with relief, knowing what a close thing it had been. For she hadn't trod a rope for nigh two decades, and she knew that Fortune had turned a smiling face down on her; either that or Adon had turned His own face her way. She had survived a deed beyond desperation.

And she had saved them all.

After Tomlin had held her and stroked her hair and whispered unto her, tears running down his own face, she at last kissed him, for everything was all right once more. Even though they were thousands of miles from their buccos and dammsels and home, and found themselves in a region where the very earth shuddered and quaked, in the Grimwall Mountains, in an isolated monastery, at night, and pursued a madman if Man he was, and their comrades were wounded, still, everything was all right, for dammia and buccaran had each other.

The Warrows retrieved Petal's hook and rope as well as her knives, and rejoined Urus and Riatha.

"I deem Stoke must be here," said the Elfess once all hurts were attended to. "Yet we may have not eliminated completely his minions."

Urus nodded, then added, "When last we met him, he had no more Wrg than we faced here today, except mayhap for Vulgs."

Tomlin sucked his breath in between his teeth and glanced up at the now dark window. "There is no more Sun to bring down Adon's Ban upon them."

"Thou art right, Wee One," responded Riatha, "and the danger is grave if there be more *Rûpt*. Yet *Spaunen* or not, we must search out Stoke, if he is here, and slay him if we can."

"Behind the altar," rumbled Urus. "The Wrg came from there, and there he is likely to be."

Glancing around, Urus saw all nod in agreement. "Then let us trap this viper in his pit."

As all stood to go, again a trembling of the unstable earth juddered through the mountains.

Behind the altar was a sacristy, but all the robes and vestments had been torn and trampled, and excrement was smeared thereupon. A door led out one side, and beyond was a hallway with rooms left and right.

In some of the rooms were signs of slaughter, for blood had splashed upon the walls, and the floors were stained with dark grume.

But it was in the rooms below where they found the corpses, long dead, flayed, their abdomens bursted from the inside outward, as if they had been impaled by some horrid instrument.

And Elfess and Baeran and Warrows were ashen-faced, and they trembled in rage to once again see such violation.

And while Tomlin and Petal kept pace in the hallway, standing watch on the corridor, Riatha and Urus searched the rooms, the Elfess those on the left, the Baeran those to the right.

In one room Riatha found his vile implements, tools and devices and appliances and instruments, all to torture and maim and slay. These she smashed in fury, especially one, which she utterly destroyed.

In yet another room, a bedroom, in a closet, she discovered the flayed skins, and she knew then that this was Stoke's lair. She threw the skins upon the coverlet, and over all poured lamp oil from the wall lanterns and set the bloody sheets afire, all the while weeping, for she knew Stoke's hideous purpose and would burn his evil down unto the very stone floor.

And rampaging through the halls and slamming in and out of other rooms, of other quarters, was Urus, rending open doors, ripping aside curtains, upending furniture, beds, likewise searching for a fiend. Yet what he found is not noted, for he stalked through the chambers, his lips clamped thin in grim silence.

The Warrows stood ward in the hallways, keeping track of the Elfess and the Baeran and of one another, for should Stoke be flushed from hiding, then they would sound the alarm.

And flushed he was, though they nearly missed him, for only a footscrape did they hear and a blackness in shadow did they see flitting at the dark distant end of the ebon-clad hall as the monster fled across and upward, running for his life.

"Hoy!" yelled Tomlin.

"Stoke!" screamed Petal.

After him they raced still yelling, Riatha and Urus coming in their wake.

Up they ran and up. Up from the rooms below. Up from the foul one's lair. Up through the monastery and past the sanctuary, and into the tower above, the steps spiraling upward 'round and 'round great thick ropes dangling down.

And now Urus passed the Warrows, the Baeran's legs

longer as he leapt up the stairs. Too, Riatha passed the
Wee Folk, her stride longer as well.

High above they could hear Stoke running, fleeing upward in panic.

And even as they ran, a silver bullet nestled in
Tomlin's sling, while an argent knife filled Petal's hand.

As they neared the top, they heard Urus roaring in fury
and Riatha weeping.

Tomlin, then Petal came up through a trapdoor and into
a chamber where massive wooden yokes held great iron
bells now silent. All around, archways opened into the
night, and framed in one were Riatha and Urus, she weeping in frustration and staring outward, he raging at something beyond; northward in the bright moonlight they
could see a great, dark, winged shape flapping—Stoke
was getting away.

"Tommy," screamed Petal, but there was no need, for
his sling was already whirling as he ran forward.

And the loosed bullet glittered as it hurtled through the
air . . .

 . . . arcing . . .
 . . . arcing . . .
 . . . *and struck!*

With a horrid *Skraww!* down spun the creature, one
wing injured, the left, unable to bear the monster upward.
Down it spun and down, landing at last upon the white
glacier below.

"He's not dead!" growled Urus, and leapt for the stairwell, Riatha after, the Warrows coming last.

When they reached the courtyard, they found the
horses and ponies gone. "Damn!" raged Urus.

Riatha looked about. "Slipped their tethers and bolted
when the Vulgs howled, I ween. Yet mayhap—" She
whistled shrilly, and they heard steel-shod hooves upon
cobbles. The Elfess pointed and between two of the stone
buildings moved her grey, coming forward, and behind
came Urus's black and one pony, Tomlin's; of the other
pony there was no sign. Even though answering unto
Riatha's call, still the steeds skitted and shied, yet af-

frighted by the memory of Vulg howls. "Walk slowly," warned Riatha, "for I would not send them scattering."

As they stepped forward, cooing softly, Petal noted that Riatha's bandages seeped scarlet, her wounds having re-opened in the chase up the tower. "Riatha, you bleed."

Riatha's voice fell grim. "Later," she responded. "After dealing with Stoke. This time he, too, is wounded, and we've got to get him before he goes to ground; before we lose him."

They reached the steeds and took hold. Tomlin caught up the dangling reins of his pony. "You two go on. Petal and I will ride double."

A shudder passed through the earth, the unstable land jolting.

Urus and Riatha mounted up and galloped out beyond the stone wall, Tomlin and Petal upon the pony coming after. As the Warrows rode forth from the monastery, the gibbous Moon was nigh zenith and the air crisp and crystal clear; and here above the white glacier, the night seemed nearly as bright as if it were full daylight. Almost immediately they spotted their other pony wandering free out upon the wind-scoured mountainside stone. Riding to it, Petal leapt down and caught up her steed, and the two Warrows galloped after their now distant comrades.

Down below, downslope in the bright moonlight, Tomlin and Petal could see Riatha and Urus now upon the glacier, riding toward where they judged Stoke had fallen.

The Warrows guided their ponies down from the wind-swept granite until they, too, were upon the glacial pack, the Moon casting silvery blue glints from the surface unto their eyes. Again the earth shuddered, and the two heard the ice groan and break. And once more they realized how unstable was the land, and how the great shards and boulders of ice came to be hove up and out from the shatter to lie about on the surface.

In the distance before them, now and again the buccan and damman could see Riatha and Urus moving among the pinnacles and broken slabs, and after them they rode as fast as the shattered 'scape would allow. They came upon a hillock of ice, and away they saw the Elfess and Baeran stop and confer, the black and the grey sidle-stepping beside one another. The Elfess dismounted and clambered down over a rim to disappear, while Urus rode onward a distance and dismounted as well. When the Warrows reached the grey they could see why the steeds had been abandoned, for at their feet an ice bluff fell rough-faced some twenty feet or so, the barrier running easterly for mayhap a mile and westerly for as far as the eye could see. To the west they could see Urus's black standing. But of either Baeran or Elfess there was no sign in the broken field of ice ahead.

Petal looked at her buccaran. "Tommy, they will need missile weapons beside them. You find Urus. I will go after Riatha." And so saying, she dismounted and started down the bluff.

Though Tomlin didn't like this separating one from the other, still he turned his pony and rode unto the black.

A time passed and still the world shuddered as Tomlin made his way through the jagged ice. Of sign of Urus there was none.

And then he heard a scream.

Riatha slowly stepped among the shattered blocks of ice strewn across the pack, searching behind pinnacles and ice boulders. Of Stoke she found nought. Her wounds bled afresh, and she knew that she was weakened. Yet what she had said was true: they needed to find the monster before he could go to ground, before he could get beyond their reach yet again.

And so the Elfess pressed onward in spite of her wounds, in spite of the dizziness lurking at the edges of her mind.

She stepped past a huge ice boulder, her eyes peering through the bright 'scape for Stoke. And there came a distant scream—*"Riatha, 'ware 'hind you!"*—and heard a grunt of pain behind her, and whirled about just as Baron Stoke, his left hand broken by sling bullet, slammed a great jagged chunk of ice crashing upon her head.

And she spun down into a world of black.

* * *

Petal stepped softly among the gigantic shards, searching for the Elfess. The air blew chill across the ice, the damman grateful for her winter attire. The bright Moon shone down from above, saying nought to any. Of a sudden, in the distance, she saw movement.

Riatha!

Petal started forward, her heart glad, for at last here was the one she sought.

But then more movement caught her eye. Behind the Elfess. Arms upraised and stepping forward came Stoke!

"Riatha, 'ware 'hind you!" screamed Petal, now running forward, dagger silver in her hand. In horror she watched as Stoke crashed ice down upon the Elfess, and Riatha crumpled unto the ground.

Shouting wordlessly, the damman dashed across the glacier, her heart pounding. She saw Stoke bend over and take up Riatha's dark-silveron sword, grasping the shimmering weapon by its inlaid hilt, taking care not to touch the starsilver itself, handling it as if the blade would burn flesh. In horror, Petal saw him raise up the weapon laughing, preparing to behead the Elfess with her own midnight blade.

And the earth began to tremble.

Tomlin whirled at the scream, seeking its source. Suddenly he saw Petal at a distance, running, shouting. And then he, too, saw Stoke over Riatha's fallen form, raising up a scintillating weapon.

Tomlin began running after Petal, sling in hand, silver bullet loaded.

A shudder ran through the ice.

Petal screamed in fury, "Stoke, you bastard, no!" and the damman stopped and planted and threw, the silver blade whirling end over end through the air, a sparkling tumble in the moonlight.

And just as the sword began arching downward, Petal's knife flashed into Stoke's left arm, striking high, burying itself in muscle, blood welling darkly.

Stoke yawled and dropped the sword and clutched at

his arm. Yet he could not bear to touch the silver, his shrieks of pain ringing through the night.

Petal ran forward to get closer, for she was yet beyond her deadly reach, her second blade at the ready. In several running strides she was within her sure killing range, and she knew that with this throw she would slay him. But as she planted to hurl, the world jolted, and with a great CRACK! a vast fissure opened at her feet, rending the glacier in twain.

Petal slipped and fell, her dagger lost to her grasp as the ice juddered and yawned below her. She clutched at the surface, finding nought to grasp, and slid backwards over the edge and plunged into the gaping maw.

And in the distance, from the monastery, there came the sound of bells, the quake so strong as to set the tower to ringing.

As Tomlin saw Petal stop and plant and throw, he prayed that her aim would be true, for even now Stoke began the downstroke to behead Riatha with her own sword.

The Buccan's heart leapt with elation as he heard Stoke shriek and saw him drop Riatha's blade.

The sling felt hot in Tomlin's hand as he dashed forward. At last he came within his deadly reach and had a clear shot; and swearing vengeance for Riatha, for his father and mother, for Petal's father, and for all the other victims that Stoke had taken, Tomlin stopped and planted. Yet at that very moment the land jolted again, knocking Tomlin from his feet; and with a mighty sound of cleaving, the glacier split, a narrow, deep crevasse opening up. And as Tomlin lost his footing and fell, he saw Petal fall, too.

Then his dammia slid into the crevasse, plunging downward into the darkness!

"Petal! Petal!" Tomlin managed to get to his feet, and across the shuddering glacier he ran. Toward the crevasse. Toward the place he had last seen his dammia.

He thought he heard the sound of distant bells.

Of Stoke he gave not a thought.

Still the world jolted as the buccan came unto the edge of the great fissure, now some forty or fifty feet wide, the walls juddering about as of some wounded beast. Tomlin flopped on his stomach and peered over the edge.

And there to the right, clinging to a finger ledge some six or seven feet down, was Petal! His dammia!

Yet her grip was slipping upon the ice.

And a freezing chill oozed up from the icy depths, as if the glacier were a great breathing monster that held her in its frigid maw.

"Petal!" he shouted above the sound of rumbling world and of grinding and of splitting ice. And he crawled to come to a place directly above. "Petal!"

She was beyond his reach.

"Tommy!" Her eyes were wide and wild. Yet she called again. "Stoke! Kill Stoke!"

Tomlin glanced up. Past Riatha's felled body he could see a shimmering, a wavering, an indistinct form. Stoke was shape-changing into something else. What it was, Tomlin could not say. Yet a silver dagger protruded from the shape, glittering in the moonlight.

The buccan glanced at his sling, then looked again, this time seeing the length of leather for what it was. *My sling! If it is only strong enough!*

Again the earth jolted, and the walls of the crevasse moved closer to one another. Petal's fingers slipped again, and now she but barely clung to the ice, while below the grinding abyss fell sheer into ebon darkness.

Without further thought Tomlin extended his arm down to her, letting one end of his sling cascade while holding tightly to the other, the silver bullet falling from the pocket, plummeting down into the unplumbed depths far, far below, striking nought as it disappeared into the freezing black. Leaning, stretching as far as he could, down the leather dangled, and Petal reached up for it, touching, grasping, clutching, just as the world juddered again and she lost her grip on the ice.

But the sling held her.

Tomlin strained up and back, hauling her slowly upward, using his sling to hoist her, praying to Adon that it would not snap, sweat popping out upon his forehead with the strain, in spite of the dreadful cold rushing up from the bottomless pit below.

As he drew her upward, the juddering intensified, and to his horror, he saw the far wall begin to slide this way.

The crevasse was closing.

A glance at Stoke showed that his transformation was complete, and a great slavering Vulg stood where he once had been. A Vulg with a silver knife embedded high in its left foreleg, nigh its shoulder; left forepaw broken as well, shattered by a silver sling bullet when Stoke had been a flying thing.

Limping, the Vulg backed away and readied to run at the crevasse.

Even though wounded, still his hindquarters were as good as ever, and though he would be running upon three legs, nevertheless a creature such as this should be able to clear the width with ease.

Stoke was going to leap to the far side and escape!

Seeking purchase, Tomlin backed upon the slippery surface and pulled, and Petal's hands appeared over the side, then her face. He reached out and grasped her wrist, then took hold of the other.

Still the Land shuddered, ice heaving and groaning, the opposite wall of the crevasse sliding nearer.

Tomlin heard running feet pounding past him, behind, toward Stoke.

It was Urus! Come at last! The Man racing to intercept Stoke, racing to keep this monster from escaping once again, racing for blood and vengeance, racing to destroy this killer of hundreds, perhaps of thousands, this slayer of Riatha.

The Vulg's muscles bunched, and it took three running strides and sprang for the far side, now some twenty-five feet away, leaping to freedom, sailing through the air.

But at the very moment that Stoke leapt, Urus leapt, too, from a different angle, on an intercept course, *catching the Vulg in midflight*!

And together they fell into the crevasse as the world quaked and juddered, Stoke howling in fear, Urus snarling in rage, the Baeran's hands locked about the Vulg.

Snarling and clawing, down into the crevasse they

plummeted, into the blackness. Down they fell and down, Man and Vulg and silver knife, Tomlin and Petal listening in horror to the yawls and growls fading in the distance.

And just as Tomlin pulled Petal up and out, the earth gave a final jolt, and with a great *WHOOM!* and a blast of unbearable cold, the crevasse slammed shut!

And in the moonlit quiet that followed, nought was heard but the susurration of glacial air, and the sound of Warrows softly weeping, and the distant dirge of iron bells tolling: *doon! . . . doon! . . . doom!*

Petal's foot had been caught as the ice whelmed together, breaking bones as Tomlin pulled her up and out just in the nick of time. Supported by her Tommy, and retrieving her sole remaining silver knife, the damman hobbled to Riatha's fallen form as iron bells rang from afar, for they would take her corpse up off this glacier. And when they came to the Elfess, they wept to see her bloody features, and her bandages soaked with scarlet; but lo! she moaned, and they could see Riatha yet breathed.

After doing what little he could to stop the seeping, and making both as comfortable as he had the means, Tomlin left his dammia and the Elfess behind on the ice 'neath a gibbous Moon, and made his way back to the ponies and horses and thence unto the monastery; after a while he came again across the glacier, circling wide to the east, a travois behind each horse. He bore Petal and Riatha back once more unto the monastery, where they stayed until the twain were healed enough to travel. And it was a close thing with Riatha, for she had lost much blood, and the blow to the head had fractured her skull—a bit harder and she would not have lived. As for Petal's foot, it mended, but she would limp for the rest of her days.

Spring came, and with it the snowmelt, for it was on the night of Springday that Urus had fallen, bearing Stoke down into the crevasse; and perhaps that explained the severe quake, for it was also upon a Springday that Black Kalgalath had met his doom, making the Land unstable to this very day. But spring came, and from a stone monastery

the three of them watched as winter loosened its grip upon
the dark Grimwalls. Although it took some time for Riatha
and Petal to heal, still at last there came a day they set
forth from this fastness. But ere they left the high grey
monastery, they built a great funeral pyre upon which they
placed the remains of the slain monks. Thrusting in torches
here and there, they watched as the wood caught fire, perhaps saying a prayer or two, asking Adon to accept these
spirits winging upward on the whirling flames, asking as
well that Adon take care to watch o'er the soul of lost
Urus. Then they rode away, while behind the fire burned
brightly and white smoke rose up into the high blue sky.

They managed to get back to the Clearing on Mid-Year's
Day, to tell and sing of Urus's deed there at the Baeron
Gathering, Tomlin's voice strong telling the tale as tears
ran down his face, Riatha's own voice clear as she sang
of it, though she wept as well, playing a silver harp, the
notes cascading forth in silvery glissando, except at
song's end, where the harp strings knelled as would iron
bells ring. And all who heard of the deed that day shed
tears, for Urus was well loved.

By the end of summer, Tomlin and Petal came unto the
Boskydells, unto Budgens, unto Small Urus and Little
Riatha and Silvereyes and Bear, everyone a year older now.
    And once again they were a family.

Eyes were not dry as Gaffer Tom came to the end of his
tale, the granther Warrow's voice choked with emotion.
None said aught for a while, as outside the blizzard yet
hammered the vale, its voice yawling in torment.
    As if the howl of the storm reminded him of some dire
monster, at last Neddy cleared his throat and asked what
many there had wondered. "Ooo, Gaffer, was he dead?
Stoke, I mean, him being the kind of creature that he was
and all. Well, it seems to me that he might still be alive
and down in that icy tomb, him and Urus, frozen, locked
forever in one another's grips, battling endlessly, until the
world itself comes to an end."
    The Gaffer shivered, as if from some memory, and for

a long while they thought he wouldn't answer Neddy's question. But at last he said, "I can't comment on that, Neddy, for it would be a terrible thing indeed to be forever strugglin' in the grasp of your worst enemy, down there in the ice.

"You know, o' course, that Urus was a werecreature, too, turning into a Bear and all. Oh, not that he was any kind of a vile monster as was Stoke, for Urus was just the opposite; even so, if Stoke hisself ain't dead, wellanaow, then neither is Urus, I shouldn't wonder.

"As to whether or not they are still alive, that I cannot say.

"There is this, though: Some years later, Riatha went back to the glacier to mourn the passing of Urus. And deep within the ice, far, far below, she saw a faint golden glow, as of a light burning, there where Stoke and Urus had been carried to their doom. There was nought she could do about it, to discover its source, so deep was it buried down within the frozen glacier. And so she left the mystery of it behind, and came back unto her beloved Arden Vale to rest and to reflect upon all that had happened. Yet the memory of that light tugged always thereafter at her heart."

Before any others could ask any more questions, the Gaffer sighed and looked at Will Brackleburr. "Looks as if I'll be stayin' another night, Will. So if you'd help me up the steps . . ."

Aided by the innkeeper, again the Gaffer started up the stairs to his room. And as he trudged slowly upward, he could hear Bingo Peacher's voice behind:

"Hoy naow, they say as glaciers are just rivers of ice, creeping along inch by inch over the years; if that be true, then let me ask you, what happens if and when, hundreds or even a thousand years from naow, Stoke and Urus come to the end of that frozen river? And what happens if the glacier ever melts, eh? And if the glacier ever melts, wellanow, who's to say what might happen . . . ?"

At the top of the stairs, as the Gaffer and Will turned a corner, Bingo's voice faded away, lost in the yawl of the storm, and the granther buccan heard no more, though he nodded in understanding for what he had always known.

Epilogues

Sometime during the dead of night, the blizzard of 4E2017 finally blew itself out. The next morning dawned to peace and quiet and clear blue skies. In the One-Eyed Crow, Will and Arla Brackleburr served those who had been trapped a final breakfast ere they would return unto their homes.

In the middle of this last meal of the blizzard, Gaffer Tom's dammia came to get him, the wee granther damman walking with a slight limp. And a single thought flashed through all of their minds as she came to her Tommy, and it was an echoing of Gaffer Tom's words in the last tale he had told, words about a damman whose foot had been broken by a glacier: *She would limp for the rest of her days.*

"Well, Tommy," she said, her golden eyes aglitter, "I'm glad that I knew where you were. Else I might have been worried these past three days."

"Hush, Petal, my dammia," he responded, playing with a silver bob at his vest, "no cause for concern. Will and Arla took fine care of me. Now sit and have a bite, then we'll go home."

And so she sat and "had a bite," and afterward they went home, accompanied by Dilby, should they need help.

Feeny Proudhand prepared to depart as well, to get back to Budgens to his own dammia and buccos and dammsels. But he did not leave for two hours or more, for when the Gaffer and Petal had gone, those remaining behind began arguing as to whether or not Gaffer Tom was telling his own story, as well as that of Petal, his dammia; and Feeny got caught up in the controversy, arguing both sides of the question. And even after the Budgens wheelwright left, still the argument raged.

Regarding the glow deep in the glacier, there where Urus fell: It is said that because of that dim golden light, Tomlin and Petal asked that at least the firstborn buccan and the firstborn damman of all of their descendants thereafter be taught the sling and knife. Tomlin's sling and silver bullets and Petal's steel knives and the one of silver were handed down as heirlooms unto the firstling buccos and dammsels of every generation thereafter. And a small journal went with each, telling the tale of Baron Stoke, with instructions that should Stoke's evil again be suspected, to seek out the Elfess Riatha of Arden Vale, or if not her, to seek aid from the Lian Guardians and from the Baeron of the Greatwood. And if none of these were found, to travel unto the Court of the High King and invoke at last the pledge of Aurion, Prince of the Realm, made when he was but a manchild ten years old, there in the Greatwood, promising aid should they call for it, a pledge that would be redeemed by the sitting High King, whoever he might be.

Some would have it that the blizzard which raged over the Boskydells in 4E2017 was the work of Modru, a year prior to the beginning of the Winter War. Many are the claims that Modru was master of the cold, having the power to call down blizzards upon the Land. Not only is this claim alluded to in the tale of Agron's Army, but it is also claimed in the legend of Elyn and Thork and the Quest of Black Mountain. As to why this might be, that he, Modru, would visit a killer blizzard down upon the Boskydells, it is said that he would be avenged upon the Wee Folk, for it is told that one of them, a certain Tipperton Thistledown, precipitated the Evil One's downfall in the Great War, the War of the Ban. Whether or not this rumor is true—that Modru caused the blizzard of '17—it *is* a fact that he did send one of his Hordes to fall upon the Bosky during the Winter War—for revenge, or so it is claimed.

It was in the year after the blizzard of '17 that winter came early to the Bosky, even before the apple harvest, and many a crop and harvest were lost to the cold. And wild Wolves came down from the north and invaded the Seven Dells. Other things came as well, more deadly than any Wolf. But that tale is told elsewhere and will not be retold here.

Of the Warrows in the One-Eyed Crow, the Gaffer and Neddy and Teddy and Nob and Bingo and Will and Arla and all the others, many fought against the Horde and most survived the Winter War, the Gaffer and Petal among them.

Concerning the granther buccan, Gaffer Tom passed away on a soft spring night in 5E38, thirty-eight years after the Winter War. He was 129 years old. It is said that some weeks after his death, a beautiful golden-haired Elfess rode into the Boskydells. Who she was is not told, though it is said that a glitter-dark sword was girted upon her waist. Her path took her unto Gaffer Tom's graveside and then beyond. Yet it is also told that she sang there beside the Gaffer's grave and strummed a silver harp, but what she sang is not remembered, the words of the song long lost. Too, when the Elfess left, Petal was never again seen alive in the Boskydells, and some said that she went away with the golden-haired Lady, to Arden Vale, they said, though others claimed that she had gone to the Weiunwood to live with her children and grandchildren. Some seven years after, another grave was found beside Gaffer Tom's, and a stone carven with Elven writing stood at the site. It is said that several buccen and dammen placed it there, descendants of the twain, though what was written thereupon is not now known.

As to the One-Eyed Crow, it is claimed that some of the finest Boskydell ale is yet served therein, and that on warm summer nights as well as in the dead cold of winter, Warrows still gather inside over mug and pipe and meal to talk about the state of things and to speak of other places and other times ... and, oh yes, to mystically spin their glowing hearthtales full upon one another.

Know, too, my child,
that when iron bells ring
we will laugh or weep on the morrow

Afterword

It is interesting to note that much of Warrow tradition is oral. Oh, not to say that most Warrows aren't educated to read and write and do their sums—oh no, not at all. Many of the Wee Folk can do these things well before their second age-name change—much pride being taken by the winner of an arithmetic contest, a spelldown, or a display of calligraphy. Yet just as much pride is taken in one who can recite from memory the twigs, branches, limbs, trunk, and taproot of their family tree, or in one who can name the names of all the local heroes, such as naming those who long past went off to the War of the Ban. Oh, it isn't that these latter things are not recorded in books, for Warrows do indeed record many things to be studied by those who come after. Instead, it is the display of *remembered* knowledge, of *remembered* facts, that garners as much respect as does the display of cleverness and logic.

Hence, although in general Warrows are educated, many of the Wee Folk much prefer their gardens and fields and fens and woods, and would rather be in their vegetable patch or down at the One-Eyed Crow or Blue Bull or Thirsty Horse or any of the other Bosky taverns with a pipe and a mug of dark beer than to be tucked away somewhere with a dusty tome. And even when they do read books, they prefer those filled with things they already know about—such as the familiar hearthtales containing numerous stories of Warrow cleverness at outwitting Giants, Dragons, Big Folk, and other *Outsiders.*

Still, just like you and me, there are those Warrows who prefer to be curled up with a good book on a rainy day, or who stay up late at night, candles flickering or lamps alit, unable to stop reading.

In any case, though books are to be found in the Seven Dells, still on any day there can also be found gatherings of the Wee Folk in common meeting places—such as the One-Eyed Crow or at the hearth of some dwelling— where they speak of the news and mull over the way things were, the way they are, and the way they are likely to become. Yet most often they will be gathered about a granther or grandam, listening enthralled to a tale well told, a tale whose roots may extend centuries or even millennia into the past.

Thus, much of Warrow tradition is oral, and even though they have books, still they pass knowledge from generation to generation by elders telling youngers tales of interest, and perhaps this is why the elders are so revered, for they are precious stores of lore.

Mayhap in this reverence of elders, we *Outsiders* would do well to learn from the Wee Ones.

Final Note

The tale of the pursuit of Baron Stoke does not end with these pages. Some ten years after the events told in *When Iron Bells Ring*, in Arden Vale a prophecy was spoken to Riatha by the Elven seeress Rael:

> *When Spring comes upon the land,*
> *Yet Winter grips with icy hand,*
> *And the Eye of the Hunter stalks night skies,*
> *Bane and blessing alike will rise.*
> *Lastborn Firstborns of those who were there,*
> *Stand at thy side in the light of the Bear.*
> *Hunter and hunted, who can say*
> *Which is which on a given day?*

And a thousand years passed ...

Now the comet known as the Eye of the Hunter again rides Mithgar's skies, and the creatures of darkness ravage the lands anew, heralding the imminent return of their dread master, Baron Stoke. And so five brave souls answer the call of prophecy: Riatha and the Elf called Aravan; Gwylly and Faeril, last in a long line of Firstborn Warrow descendants of Tomlin and Petal; and one other, one restored from death's chill grasp. ...

This tale is told in full in Dennis L. McKiernan's novel *The Eye of the Hunter*, the gripping story of the final pursuit of the evil Baron Stoke.

Please turn the page for a special preview of
Dennis L. McKiernan's

ONCE UPON A SUMMER DAY

Available in hardcover from Roc

There is a place in Faery where eternal summer lies upon the land; it is a region of forests and fields, of vales and clearings, of streams and rivers and other such 'scapes, where soft summer breezes flow across the weald, though occasionally towering thunderstorms fill the afternoon skies and rain sweeps o'er all. How such a place can be—endless summer—is quiet mysterious; nevertheless it is so.

Separated from this magical realm by a great wall of twilight is another equally enigmatic domain, a region graced by eternal autumn, and here it is that crops afield remain ever for the reaping, and vines are overburdened with their largesse, and trees bear an abundance ripe for the plucking, and the ground holds rootstock and tubers for the taking. Yet no matter how often a harvest is gathered, when one isn't looking the bounty somehow replaces itself.

Likewise, lying past this realm, beyond another great wall of halflight, there stands a land of eternal winter, where snow ever lies on the ground and ice clads the sleeping trees and covers the still meres or, in thin sheets, encroaches upon the edges of swift-running streams, and the stars at night glimmer in crystalline skies.

And farther on and past yet another twilight border lies a place of eternal springtime, where everlasting meltwater trickles across the 'scape, and trees are abud and blossoms abloom, where birds call for mates and beetles crawl through decaying leaves and mushrooms push up through soft loam, and where other such signs of a world coming awake manifest themselves in the gentle, cool breezes and delicate rains.

These four provinces are the Summerwood and Autumnwood and Winterwood and Springwood, magical regions in the twilit world of Faery. They by no means make up the whole of that mystical realm. Oh, no, for it is an endless place, with uncounted domains all separated from one another by looming walls of shadowlight, and with Faery itself separated from the common world by twilight as well.

But as to the four regions, a prince or a princess rules each—Alain, Liaze, Borel, and Céleste—brothers and sisters, Alain and Borel respectively having reign o'er the Summer- and Winterwoods; Liaze and Céleste, the Autumn- and Springwoods.

They got along well, these siblings, and seldom did trouble come their way. Oh, there was that difficulty with the disappearance of Lord Valeray and Lady Saissa, and the two curses leveled upon Prince Alain, but Camille had come along to resolve those problems, and everything had then seemed well in order, at least for a while, though there yet was a portent of darker days to come. But at that time joy lay upon the land, with Camille and Alain betrothed, the banns posted, and preparations for the wedding under way.

Yes, all was well in these four realms, or so it seemed. But then . . .

. . . Once upon a summer day . . .

Out in the gazebo upon the wide lawn of Summerwood Manor, Borel sat and watched four black swans majestically gliding upon the wide, slow-running stream, the graceful birds keeping a wary eye upon the Wolves lying asleep upon the sward, all but the one who kept watch and eyed the swans just as warily, though a predatory gleam seemed to glint in the eye of the grey hunter. A balmy breeze stirred the silver of Borel's shoulder-length locks as he leaned back in the wickerwork chair, his long legs stretched out, his soft-booted feet resting upon a padded footstool. From somewhere nearby came the hum of bees buzzing among garden blooms, and lazy clouds towered aloft in the cerulean sky and cast their quiet shadows down.

How peaceful it was on this gentle day, and Borel closed his ice blue eyes, just for the nonce, his mind drifting along with the building clouds. How long he remained thus, he could not say, yet there came a muted sound of . . . he knew not what.

Borel frowned and opened his eyes, and then sat bolt upright, for the gazebo was changing, the floor turning to flag, the open sides to stone walls, even as he looked on in amaze. And beyond the windows of the now-stone chamber a seemingly endless number of free-floating daggers filled the air and blocked the light and cast a gloom o'er all. Opposite from him in the dimness stood a slim young lady, as if in meditation or prayer. Her head was bowed and her long golden hair fell down across the white bodice of her flowing dress. Her delicate hands were clasped together just below her waist. Across her eyes lay a gauzy black cloth or mayhap a band of shadow, as of a dark blindfold, or so it appeared.

And the lady quietly wept.

Borel stood and stepped closer. "Demoiselle, why do you weep?"

"*Aidez-moi,*" she said, her voice but a whisper. "*Aidez-moi.*"

Borel jerked awake and found he was on his feet, and the wind blew hard and moaned through the filigree, the late-afternoon sky dark with the oncoming storm. Then the summer rain came thundering down, and Borel's Wolves took shelter within. And while black swans sought refuge in the overhang of a streamside willow, Borel looked about, seeking . . . seeking, but not finding, even though it seemed there came to his ears an ephemeral echo of a desperate whisper flying past on the weeping air: "*Aidez-moi.*"

"I tell you, Alain, it seemed quite real."

Alain sighed. "A stone chamber surrounded by daggers and a blindfolded, golden-haired damsel within?"

Borel nodded. "And she needs help."

They sat in the game room at a small table on which lay an échiquier, the pieces arrayed before them, the brothers only a few moves into the match, for, after Borel had unnecessarily lost one of his heirophants, Alain had asked what it was that distracted him, and Borel had told of the vision.

From somewhere outside came the rumble of distant thunder as the remains of the storm moved away.

"And you think it was a visitation and not a common dream?" asked Alain.

"It seemed totally real at the time."

"And your Wolves . . . ?"

"They were outside the gazebo and sensed nought, or so I deem, for they were not agitated."

"Hmm . . ." mused Alain, running his fingers through his dark hair. "One thing is certain: the gazebo did not remain stone, and perhaps never was. I think if there was a visitation, it was you going to her rather than the other way 'round."

Borel nodded and a silence fell upon the two of them, and once more distant thunder rumbled. Finally Borel said, "If it was but a dream . . . ?"

"Then, Frère, there is nothing to worry about."

"Yet if she is real and in peril . . . ?"

"Then I know not how you can help, for there is not enough to guide you."

Again they fell into silence, but then Alain said, "Let us consult Camille and see what she has to—"

Chirping, a black-throated sparrow flew into the room, and three slender demoiselles followed: auburn-haired, amber-eyed Liaze in the lead; golden-haired, blue-eyed Camille next; pale-blond, green-eyed Céleste coming last.

Even as Borel and Alain stood, and the wee bird settled on Alain's shoulder, "Aha!" said Liaze. "We thought we might find you two hiding here. But sit! Sit! We've come to ask about— Why, Borel, you look positively morose on this gloomy day."

Camille gave Alain a light kiss on the cheek, and then looked at Borel and asked, "Why so glum, Brother-to-be?"

"I've had a vision," said Borel.

"Or a dream," said Alain.

Borel nodded. "Or a dream."

"Oh, my, Frère, said Céleste, her face growing somber. She pointed at the large round game table with chairs all about the taroc cards strewn on its surface. "Let us sit, and then do tell us of this dream or vision of yours."

As soon as all had settled, Borel related his vision to them, and when he had come to the end, he once again stated that it might have just been a dream.

Liaze shook her head. "Oh, no, Borel. I think it must have been a visitation, for if it were a mere *rêve* or *songe,* then it would not bother you so."

"She spoke in the Old Tongue?" asked Céleste.

Borel nodded. " '*Aidez-moi,*' she said—'Help me'— and no more. Yet how can I do so when I know not where she is?"

In that moment the sparrow chirped and flew down to the table and pecked at one of the cards.

"Mayhap Scruff has the right of it," said Camille, pointing at the bird.

"What do you mean?" asked Borel, as Céleste reached out and began drawing all the taroc cards to her, and Scruff flew across the room to the échecs table, where he had first found the two men.

"Just this," said Camille. "Could we read the taroc, perhaps it has a clue as to what to do."

"Ah, but we are not seers, hence cannot read the cards," said Céleste, as she gathered the last of the deck and began shuffling.

Camille frowned and said, "Lisane can."

"Ah," said Borel. "The Lady of the Bower. Even so, aren't her messages rather vague, hard to interpret until after the fact?"

Camille nodded. "It was only in hindsight that I understood."

"Then," said Borel, "I think she cannot help, for if it is a true vision, then the lady in the stone tower needs help now."

"Perhaps so, Borel," said Liaze. "Yet there is nought you can do until you know more."

"Are you telling me to go about my business and forget the vision?" asked Borel.

Liaze shook her head. "Borel, I think you must follow your heart. Even so, I deem that until you have more knowledge, there is little you can do . . . unless you happen upon someone who knows of a blindfolded lady in a stone tower surrounded by daggers."

A quietness fell in the chamber, and only Scruff across the room and scrabbling among the échecs pieces interrupted the still. Finally Camille said, "Perhaps she'll send you another vision."

As Borel nodded glumly, somewhere in the distance a bell rang.

"Dinner," said Alain, standing.

Céleste set the deck aside and stood as well, as did they all, and started out. Borel paused a moment and cut the cards and looked at the one turned up. It was the Tower, lightning striking the top, men plummeting down among the shattered and plunging stone. Borel sighed and shook his head and replaced the card and then joined the others.

Camille took Alain's arm, and Liaze and Céleste, one on each side, took Borel's, and they all trooped out, and none noticed the board on which the wee sparrow had been scratching and pecking away at the pieces: nearly all were gathered in the center and lying on their sides: spearmen, warriors, heirophants, kings and one queen. On the other hand, the four towers yet set upright in their corners. And in the midst of all the downed échecsmen, the white queen stood surrounded.

Tales of Mithgar as told by Dennis L. McKiernan

THE EYE OF THE HUNTER
0-451-45268-2

The comet known as the Eye of the Hunter is riding
through Mithgar's skies again, bringing with it
destruction and the much dreaded master, Baron Stoke.
Only a small band of worthies, united in their quest
can save Mithgar in its hour of need.

VOYAGE OF THE FOX RIDER
0-451-45411-1

An unexpected visitor, troubled by a mysterious
vanishing, and a prescient nightmare, enlists the help of
Mage Alamar. In a quest for her missing beloved, Mage
and Foxrider, Man, Elf, and Dwarf oppose a master of
evil bent on opening a path through which a
terrifying, dark power might come to the world
of Mithgar.

THE DRAGONSTONE
0-451-45456-1

A terrifying conflagration is coming to engulf
Mithgar—unless Arin can solve a mysterious riddle
which instructs her to seek the cat, the one eye, the
peacock, the ferret, and the keeper, for they alone will
aid her in her quest for the fearsome Dragonstone.

R417

Three novels in one volume!

Dennis L. McKiernan's

THE IRON TOWER
0-451-45810-9

The diabolical Modru is sending forth his
sorceress Shadowlight to cloak the lands
in darkness. Against ravaging hoards,
men, elves, and dwarves must stand united to withstand the baleful influence of
the Shadowlight. This omnibus contains
the first three *Mithgar* novels:

The Dark Tide
Shadows of Doom
The Darkest Day

R406